THE DIVORCE LAWYER

BOOKS BY ELLIE MONAGO

The Divorce Series

The Custody Battle

ELLIE MONAGO

THE DIVORCE LAWYER

bookouture

Published by Bookouture in 2024

An imprint of Storyfire Ltd.
Carmelite House
50 Victoria Embankment
London EC4Y 0DZ

www.bookouture.com

ISBN: 978-1-83790-815-8
eBook ISBN: 978-1-83790-814-1

ONE

"This isn't your usual day," Stylist says.

That's how she's listed in Esther's phone. It's not out of any disrespect toward her personally. It's not personal at all, that's exactly the point, and Esther always tips 25 percent for her twice-weekly blowouts. The issue is one of bandwidth. Esther knows too many people, and has no use for small talk.

She meets Stylist's eyes in the mirror. "No," she says, "not my usual day." Her eyes lower to her open laptop. As always, there's work to do.

"Is it a special day, then?" Stylist asks as she combs through Esther's wet hair. "I mean, would you like an updo or a chignon? We could even do extensions."

"Absolutely not," Esther says.

Esther is fifty-one years old. This is not her senior prom. She refuses to let Peter Tramboni turn her into some—

Who's she kidding? He's already turned her into someone she never thought she'd be.

But at the party tonight she will look defiantly like herself, in her black power suit with her jet-black hair in its signature bob, albeit freshly blown out. She'll make sure her makeup is impeccable, with a nighttime red lip to replace the daytime nude, and that's all he's getting. She has to show up, he's made that clear, but she doesn't have to pander. He's not the boss of her, not anymore.

Ordinarily, Esther aims for an appearance that's above reproach, just as she advises her clients. Appearance isn't power, really; beauty and sex appeal only offer the illusion of power. (Just ask Peter's most recent ex-wife, Bianca.) But how a woman looks can certainly *diminish* her power, and Esther won't relinquish any tactical advantage, nor allow her clients to do so in their contentious divorce proceedings.

Tonight, though, Esther will look perfect. That way, she can show Peter Tramboni he hasn't broken her.

It's possible that it's the wrong strategy as it rests on ego, when, typically, Esther prides herself on not being prideful and, therefore, she nearly always finds the right strategy. With Peter, the quickest path to freedom might be to look broken since that could very well be what he wants. He likes his women either dependent on him or broken and alone. He relishes doing the breaking. (Again, just ask Bianca.)

Right now, Bianca Tramboni is probably home, licking her wounds and grieving her loss. In the morning she'll deliver her four-year-old son, Stride, to Peter, who's been granted primary custody. Bianca will now only see her little boy one weekend per month. The rest of the time, he'll be in Peter's clutches.

Esther tries to comfort herself with the thought that the child will really be raised by nannies. Peter doesn't want all that time with his son. What he wanted was to make sure that Bianca didn't get it.

It mortifies and horrifies Esther that she's brought about such an injustice. After an entire career dedicated to preventing bad men from having access to their children, she's now abetted the opposite situation.

She had no choice, though. She has to remember that.

No, remembering her powerlessness doesn't help at all. She truly has no idea what will. Since yesterday's verdict, she's been in continuous torment. She feels as if she not only betrayed Peter's son but her long-standing mission to protect women and children from men like Peter. She betrayed herself.

Stylist lifts the blow dryer and, mercifully, the small-talk portion of their program is over. Esther indulges herself for just a second, closing her eyes, letting the white noise of the dryer envelop her. But only a minute later, she's rudely interrupted. The dryer has shut off. Her eyes open and she sees that Stylist is holding her phone.

"I'm sorry," Stylist says. "I just have to handle something super-quick."

On the screen, Esther glimpses that familiar logo, the one that now produces visceral disgust and dread. "That's the worst of them all."

"Excuse me?" Stylist looks up in surprise. Esther never engages her in random conversation.

But for once, Esther can't help herself. "Avoid Nimbus. Even Google is better."

"Google doesn't do everything Nimbus does."

It's reminiscent of Peter's tagline for Nimbus: *It's your everything*. Social media and search engine in one, it was designed as Google meets Facebook meets Twitter meets ChatGPT meets Reddit meets Pinterest meets...

But really, it's a tool for surveillance, counterintelligence, and misinformation. It's a threat to democracy. It's the ultimate consolidation of power in the hands of a megalomaniacal billionaire. Peter Tramboni wants nothing less than omnipotence. Esther's seen that firsthand.

"He's collecting all your data," Esther says.

"They all do that." Stylist is texting.

Esther doesn't know how she does it so fast with nails that long. It's just one of those millennial mysteries.

"Nimbus is different." Esther can't believe she's persisting, almost as if it's an intervention. "Peter Tramboni is."

"Doesn't he give more money to charity than any of those guys?"

Is that really what the average person thinks when they hear his name? In Silicon Valley there have been rumblings for years, and some profiles have hinted at the truth. He wants everyone thinking he's a disruptive genius who nurtures young talent as well as being a generous philanthropist (the Tramboni Center altered the San Francisco skyline forever), when he's actually a vengeful tyrant, sexual harasser, and sue-happy sociopath. Rumor is that he stole the initial technology for Nimbus, though he successfully defended himself in that lawsuit, while filing about a hundred more himself since. He's gag-ordered half the tech industry.

What on earth is Esther doing? She shouldn't be talking. Peter could be listening through the Stylist's app, or through Esther's phone. Unlikely, yes; impossible, no. With the finish line so close and Peter's victory party tonight, this is not the time to get sloppy. Normally, there's no one more careful and meticulous than Esther.

Sometimes it almost feels like Peter has hacked her.

"Everything and everyone is fucked." Stylist's smile is basically a shrug. "What am I going to do, crawl under a rock? They'll get you one way or another, right?"

"They won't get me."

By the end of the night, Esther Kahn will be free.

TWO

Esther is trapped inside Peter's absurdly lavish home, surrounded by the 1 percent. Who throws a victory party to celebrate winning a custody battle? It's a disgusting act by a disgusting actor, but Esther had to RSVP yes since Peter said she was the guest of honor. Then, in classic Peter fashion, he's ignored her all night; even in his toast, he never mentioned her by name, merely referencing a "brilliant lawyer" who had "done her part." Usually, he employs large firms with massive teams to oversee his many, many lawsuits. He's obsessed with the notion that people are stealing from him or otherwise wronging him, in much the way a cheater is obsessed with being cuckolded.

Esther has to hope that he'll keep on ignoring her and soon she'll be able to slip out, unscathed. This should be the last time she has to see him, or this horrid mansion.

Peter's compound is in an unincorporated part of Silicon Valley, for the fewest zoning restrictions and the maximum amount of land. Rumor is that he spent $100 million before he even broke ground. There's a Gothic iron fence and a long driveway to reach the house, which has an imposing stone façade, reminiscent of a European cathedral. Peter had a lake dug for his exclusive use, with a dock and multiple boats to choose from, though his superyacht is moored elsewhere. There's a twenty-car garage and a helipad. The party is being held inside a ballroom with a domed ceiling that's been hand-painted, *à la* the Sistine Chapel. The house has many chapel-like elements throughout, with stained glass and arches and tracery (a term Esther had never heard, but that Peter proudly explained meant the decorative interlacing ribs carved into stone). She's sure Peter intended it to feel to guests that they're coming into a house of worship, where the deity is Peter.

Then there's the technology: AI-powered sensors in every appliance and device that respond to commands, but also anticipate needs; voice control for temperature, lighting, and music (again, responding only to Peter's voice); smart locks (controlled only by Peter); advanced presence detection ("like motion sensors, but better," Peter said); walls that transform into television screens; walls that are actually medical diagnostic systems, monitoring all of Peter's vital signs continuously; walls that close in (not really, that's just how it feels to Esther). The walls of the ballroom have been subtly and incrementally changing color throughout the party so that the pale lilac from an hour ago has now morphed into a woodsy green. This reminds Esther of what else is undoubtedly living in those walls, with Peter most assuredly recording every conversation for playback later.

The architect was Greg Stanton, who also designed the Tramboni Center. Esther rues the day she met Greg—well, she met his wife Madeline first—and represented Madeline in their divorce. The ensuing custody battle put Esther on Peter's radar.

At least there's no shortage of bathrooms for Esther to enter for a brief respite. Peter's house has thirty, in a house with ten bedrooms. Peter allegedly wanted to make sure he had more bathrooms than Bill Gates does in his Lake Washington home.

Esther shakes her head as yet another robot proffers her a canapé. She hasn't been able to hold down any food today.

Because of her fear of Peter's surveillance, paranoia, and overall vengeful nature, she's been keeping her mouth shut and her wits about her for the past hour. She figures another thirty minutes and she can leave. She approaches no one and speaks only when spoken to. She makes sure to say nothing of interest. As a result, all conversations have been mercifully brief.

Her eyes flick involuntarily and persistently to Peter. She needs to know where he is at all times; she doesn't want any surprises tonight. She doesn't like surprises, period. Never has. That's the secret to her success in high-conflict custody battles: She's always the most prepared, and prepared to do more than any opponent, to go as far as necessary within the bounds of the law. Her genius is in knowing how elastic the law truly is.

But she can never know more than Peter, whose resources are limitless. Forget Mark Zuckerberg and every other Silicon Valley scion. Peter Tramboni is the ultimate disruptor. He moves the fastest and breaks the most (systems, hearts, wills). From what she's observed, money is just the means to chaos for everyone else and control for him. She's seen him up close and way too personal, as his divorce attorney.

His *former* attorney, since the case has settled.

This really should be a celebration for her. It's her emancipation. Bianca Tramboni's defeat was so complete it's hard to imagine she'll be coming back for more. That means Esther should be free.

But somehow, she can't quite believe that. It just seems too easy.

Any half-decent divorce attorney could have destroyed Bianca Tramboni, given all the dirt Peter had on her, having painstakingly collected it from the moment they started dating. And any number of divorce attorneys would have relished the opportunity to work for Peter. So why had Peter chosen and then forced someone to represent him who didn't want to? Of all the lawyers in the world—all the women in the world—why Esther?

Is that something Bianca Tramboni wonders as well, what had turned her into Peter's mark?

There's a large age difference between Peter and Bianca, his fifty-two to her thirty-two, and an even bigger chasm in terms of physical appearance. Peter is homely, squat, and bald with thick, untamed eyebrows. He has foreshortened limbs braided with muscle because he works out ferociously, multiple times a day, determined to cheat death. Bianca is gorgeous, like all his wives have been. They're not all gorgeous in the same way, though. Wife #1 was blonde and Amazonian; Wife #2 was a skinny redhead and a supermodel; Wife #3 was a dead ringer for Salma Hayek; and Bianca is a petite Snow White, alabaster skin and hair as black as Esther's.

None of the ex-wives are in attendance at the party, though Peter purports to be on good terms with all of them. The three wives that came before Bianca had one child each with him before their own splits. For Peter's most recent custody battle, they all dutifully provided testimony about what a good father he's been to the children they share, and while Esther didn't believe it for an instant, they played their parts convincingly. Like their lives (or their children's lives) depended on it.

That's the feeling Esther has as she moves through the party, observing Peter and his "friends": that everyone's just playing their role, trying not to get on his bad side. Peter is revoltingly jovial, dancing on the grave of his ex, laughing the loudest at his jokes. Esther remains on the outskirts, essentially trolling him for her own protection. When she sees him take even a step in her direction, she turns and heads the other way.

The guest whose presence surprises her most is Avery Brengle. During her prep sessions with Peter (when he was really prepping Esther), he talked frequently about Avery. She was someone he held in high regard because he thought she could do damage to him—that she might have the guts to actually try to land a blow. She could have shown up on Bianca's witness list for trial, if it had come to that. But of course, Peter (and Esther) made sure it never did. The point is, he hated, admired, and was attracted to Avery Brengle in equal measure. She might be the one who got away, the woman he loves the most.

God help her.

Yet Avery is here, mingling like she doesn't have a care in the world, as if Peter hasn't buried her in litigation for the past three years for intellectual property violations and stealing trade secrets. Peter had mentored Avery at Nimbus, which by his own admission involved sexual harassment, a brief affair, and stalking. But he said it had been the most vibrant collaboration of his life and that he'd "made" Avery, in the same way he claimed to have made Greg Stanton and a host of other people. He'd expected Avery to remain in his debt forever and, instead, she'd gone on to become a billionaire in her own right before the age of thirty, shutting him out of her venture completely. Hence, his sense of betrayal. Hence, the unceasing litigation.

How can Avery stand to be here? How can she stand to share the occasional laugh with Peter at his ex-wife's expense?

Esther will never understand Silicon Valley. She doesn't want to. But she has to admit, Avery is compelling, both online and in person. Like the rest of the room, even Esther's having a hard time keeping her eyes off the woman.

Avery made her mark and her fortune with the app Sleight —as in sleight of hand, the slogan being "Now you see it, now you don't." Text messages disappear totally, without a trace, and can be anonymous, if the user prefers. It lets you text people whose phone numbers you don't know; there's an incredibly comprehensive search function that allows you to find people by name and general location.

Since its inception, Sleight's been highly popular and highly controversial. Law enforcement and parent groups have called for it to be banned or at least severely restricted. They say it's a breeding ground for bullies, stalkers, and all manner of criminality. But despite all the criticism, it seems that nothing can stop Sleight, and nothing can stop Avery Brengle, the girl wonder/founder/developer/coding genius who just happens to be six feet tall and gangly beautiful. She's telegenic and social mediagenic, incisive, clever, and captivating, able to turn any adversity to her advantage.

While Avery is the second most notorious person in the room after Peter, Esther recognizes plenty of other faces. These are the Silicon Valley power brokers, running tech companies and venture capital firms. They decide what projects get greenlit and which ideas receive funding; the bets they place now will affect the future of the world. And watching the dynamics between them and their largely ignored wives, Esther knows she should be networking. There are clearly more divorces to come. Only she doesn't want their money. She doesn't want to swim in this pond.

Esther is ultra-competitive; she can't deny that. But she's always felt like being on the right side meant she was in the right. Yet what she did for Peter was dead wrong. Not that she had a choice in defending him, with zeal. If she'd crossed him, she has no doubt he would have exposed her secrets, gleefully, just as he threatened.

Esther has always taken on clients about whom she has a positive gut feeling and, perhaps more importantly, where she has a negative gut feeling about the husbands they're divorcing. She wants to go up against a bad guy and bring him down. And while she's never really had a positive impression of Bianca Tramboni, all her righteous indignation toward Bianca had to be manufactured; it didn't come organically as it did with, say, Greg Stanton. Or toward Peter himself.

As Esther circumnavigates the party, tracing Peter's movements, she's full of anger and disgust, but she's pretty sure no one can tell. For one thing, she's got an excellent poker face and for another, no one gives a shit about her. She's worthless to them.

Which is why she's astonished when Avery comes toward her with an enormous toothy grin. Esther actually has to look around to make sure that it is, indeed, aimed at her.

"Esther!" Avery says. "The woman of the hour!"

Esther dips her head in what might look like mock humility, but is actually shame. "It's nice to meet you, Avery," she says with her usual polite remove, while inside she's shocked to find a butterfly or two. Esther isn't prone to being starstruck, but Avery's magnetism is unparalleled.

Avery gestures for Esther to follow her and they move into a corner. Esther is conscious of how close she is to the wall, which means anything they say will later be heard by Peter.

Avery pulls out a lipstick and applies it, smacking her lips loudly. Then she doesn't put the lipstick away or even cap it, instead waving it around as she next speaks. "Noise cancellation," she says.

"Excuse me?"

Avery brandishes the lipstick. "There's noise-cancelling tech in here, which means that we can't be heard. This conversation will be just between us."

Is Avery for real? It seems absurd to imagine she would spend her precious time toying with Esther but it's equally absurd to imagine she has anything so important to say to Esther that it would require the cloak-and-dagger routine.

"You don't know what to make of me," Avery says matter-of-factly. "I get it."

All night, Peter's guests have had to lead off their conversations with Esther by asking, "How do you know Peter?" to ascertain her level of prestige. Once they learned she was just an attorney, they exited the conversation hastily. But Avery had made a beeline for Esther, and her feet are planted.

"I'm not like these people." Avery gives Esther a meaningful look. "I'm definitely not like Peter."

Esther stares at the lipstick-that's-not-really-a-lipstick (except that it also is—Avery had applied it to her gorgeous bee-stung lips) and debates what to say next. She's seldom at a loss for words, but it feels as if she's being subtly baited. She pauses to study Avery. Too many people are afraid of silence and speak too quickly. Esther won't make that mistake.

Avery is breathtaking up close, even with her long auburn hair pulled back in a tight bun and what appears to be no makeup except for the coral lipstick. She's wearing a light-brown cashmere poncho that hits mid-thigh with ripped jeans and Doc Martens. What if Peter put Avery up to this, and the entire conversation is a booby trap? Could he be testing Esther's loyalty, seeing what she'll say about him to a beguiling third party?

"You're probably wondering why I'm here tonight," Avery says. "Our lawyers wouldn't recommend that Peter and I socialize, would they?"

"I don't handle civil litigation."

"Short answer: I keep my enemies closer. But I can always use a new friend."

"There are a lot of people here who'd love to be your friend." Esther glances at her watch—she's the only attendee wearing one that's not smart—and adds, "Excuse me. I really should get home."

"I like you already." Avery smiles with what looks like genuine warmth.

Esther senses that Avery is good at establishing intimacy quickly, but Esther is skilled at avoiding it. It's not clear which of them will prevail.

"Excuse me," Esther repeats. Strangely, she finds she's not moving, as if she's waiting for Avery's permission. Or maybe she wants Avery to stop her? Esther doesn't know anymore. She's been under an awful, distorting haze ever since Peter steam-rolled his way into her life.

"I do my homework," Avery continues, as if she hasn't heard Esther at all. "I notice patterns. I notice exceptions to patterns. Peter chose you when usually he has reams and teams of lawyers. He zeroed in on you."

"Solo practitioners have certain advantages. You'd have to ask him for his precise reasoning." It's a careful answer. Another dull answer.

But Avery is undeterred. "Why did he let you stand alone?"

"He must have had confidence in me." Esther is measuring her words. Should Peter hear this later, he'll know she said nothing untoward.

"I've studied up on you, and I don't think you worked for Peter of your own free will."

Esther says nothing, though her eyes widen in surprise.

"I don't think you did it for the money or for the contacts. You're a woman of principle."

Esther doesn't confirm or deny. She's slightly flattered at Avery's attention and also rattled that Avery is sniffing around. It seems to support Esther's fear that her association with Peter won't end just because the case has.

"I think Peter did to you what he's done to so many others, and as I said, I can always use a new ally." Avery's smile is conspiratorial. "You'd make a brilliant confederate, Esther."

Esther's heartbeat quickens at the compliment as well as the insinuation that there's a war to be fought. Esther has no desire to enlist, given the ammunition Peter could use against her.

"Unfortunately," she says, "I have a full caseload right now. I can't add anything to my plate."

"You've seen how Peter operates. He doesn't surround himself with weak women. He surrounds himself with strong ones he can subjugate. That's what happened with Bianca. When she and Peter met, she was an up-and-coming fashion designer. Then, after they got married, she mysteriously lost her will to create. But you know all about that, don't you?"

Esther's nod is nearly imperceptible.

"Not that I'm a fan of Bianca's. She's kind of a bitch. But I do think she had talent. And spirit. He was drawn to that. He wanted to crush it."

It's jarring, hearing Esther's own theory put into words by a woman she barely knows, yet a woman she's seen everywhere: on the news, social media, government hearings, the Met Ball. Then there are the gossip rags (the general ones for celebrities, and the industry-specific ones for tech) where Avery's been linked for a minute to everyone from Brad Pitt and Miley Cyrus to climate activists to politicians to tech scions. The only time Avery commented publicly on her love life was to make it clear she would never, ever be with Elon Musk. "I value democracy," she said. "I'd die for freedom."

Meanwhile, Esther has never felt this hamstrung. There's nothing she wants more than to destroy Peter Tramboni, but she has to run away for her own protection. He really has weakened her. Subjugated her.

Also, she doesn't know Avery. This might not be a real offer anyway; it could just be a trick of Peter's.

"I need to go now," Esther says, her voice faltering just slightly.

Avery sticks out her hand and Esther stares at it uncomprehendingly for a second. Then she realizes Avery wants her phone. As if hypnotized, Esther complies by unlocking the screen and handing it over. Avery puts her number into Esther's WhatsApp.

"I could learn from you," Avery says, returning the phone. "I'm always down to learn."

"Thank you." In a state of disorientation, Esther slips away, the whole interaction already feeling more like a dream.

Time will tell if it was a nightmare.

THREE

Esther's had it. She's going home. If she never meets another billionaire, it'll be too soon.

Normally, she would say good night to the host before leaving a party, but this isn't just any party or any host. Peter hasn't demonstrated any further need for her services, and she has to hope that his apathy will hold up until she can make her getaway.

As she approaches the front foyer, a journalist waylays her, asking for a few quotes. Esther says things so banal that no one could possibly read into any of them, nothing that smacks of the cryptic. Nothing that could smell to Peter like betrayal.

The second she steps into the foyer, Peter seems to appear out of nowhere, almost as if he's been lying in wait, or had someone watching her this whole time to alert him. He takes home court advantage to a whole new level. She hated working here but he insisted she make the trek at least twice a week. Insisted on summoning her.

Her eyelids droop with exhaustion. Peter looks energized and buoyant as he blocks the door with his short but hulking body. She doesn't know if it's his signature move with everyone, but it is with her. He forces her to either wait until he's ready to move or to ask him to move—essentially, she has to beg to be let out of the cage. The humiliation of either choice is abject.

He's holding a glass of champagne. "Going so soon?" he asks. If eyebrows can smirk, his do.

"It was a great party," she says. "Thank you for having me. But I'm feeling quite tired."

He barks out a laugh. "Don't you dare talk to me like that, Esther. So formal. Don't feed me bullshit, not after all we've been through together."

"I'd like to go home," she says. No bullshit there.

"You've been trying to run away from me for our entire relationship, and I don't know why. I handed you a hot case. I was an exemplary client. I mean, how much more data could I have given you on my ex?"

Because to be loved by Peter Tramboni is to be surveilled. "You're right," she says. "You're the reason we won." She doesn't want any credit for this.

He tips an imaginary hat. "You did good, Esther. Like I knew you would. Hey, I'm a poet!"

Just because he's drunk and jaunty doesn't mean he's any less dangerous. "Thank you for everything." She hopes the faux gratitude will operate like an "open sesame" and he'll step out of the way.

No such luck.

"Why are you racing off? That room is full of people you ought to meet. Come on back. I'll introduce you. I'll tell everyone what a diabolical genius you are. They know that's my highest compliment."

It's how he thinks of himself. Revolting.

His face hardens. He can always catch a micro-expression. "You smell something rank, Esther?"

"No. Like I said, I'm just tired."

"I like when you let down your guard. Let down your hair."

He reaches out and touches the strands that lie against her cheek. She's trained herself not to flinch because if she does, it'll only go on longer. "Tell me the truth. Why are you so eager to run away?"

"These aren't my people. I'd stay if you needed me, but you don't. And you didn't mention me in the toast, so they don't know who I am—"

He laughs and points at her. "I always knew you had a huge ego! You pretend it's all about the children but really, you want to be recognized."

"No, this is your night."

"I wish you'd brought a date like I told you to. I would have loved to see how you are with a man. Or a woman. What's Esther Kahn like when it's pleasure, not business?" He leans in and whispers, "I bet you're a tiger in the sack."

Do not flinch. Give him nothing. But does Peter know about Hugh Warshaw? No one's supposed to. Esther's always kept her personal life confidential.

Thankfully, Peter straightens up, giving her just a little breathing room. "If I didn't know how bad you want to win," he says, "I'd think you weren't happy with the outcome. But we got everything we wanted, didn't we?" He touches her hair again, studying her face.

This is what he loves: to have her wriggling on his hook until he decides to let her go. And she's not the only one, to hear Avery tell it. But then, Esther knew that. She's his divorce attorney. She has to know all his secrets. More or less. She shudders to think what he's held back, what's remained in his vault.

"I'm very happy with the outcome," she says. "My work here is done."

"Is it, though?" That expression of his—half-smile, half-leer—has become painfully familiar.

She can't take another second of this. She's suffocating.

"Please move." Her tone is strong but she feels pitiful anyway. Just the way he likes.

"We've still got so much to talk about."

"Peter!" The voice rings out, upbeat and confident, as if the possessor couldn't be happier to see their host.

The voice is Avery's. Whose confederate is she really, Esther's or Peter's? Esther's gut says it's hers, but she can't be sure. In fact, what she wants most is to be away from these people and never have to wonder about any of them again. To leave them to their games.

Peter looks back and forth between Esther and Avery. Maybe he's not sure which one he wants to torture more, or whether he might be able to have a *ménage à trois*.

"Peter!" Avery says again. "Come here and talk to me! We've barely had a minute together all night."

Apparently, no one can say no to Avery because Peter turns on his heel and heads for her like a dog that's been called back. But he can still bite, of course.

Esther knows she should be grateful to Avery, and she is, but also she's humiliated. At needing to be saved. At needing to flee.

But flee she does, yanking the gigantic door open and racing out into the night.

She's filled with a terrible knowledge, way down deep in her bones: Peter isn't done with her yet.

FOUR

Dot comes up the hill, huffing and puffing. She's forever complaining that she needs to lose thirty pounds but doesn't want to do anything that might bring that change about, like exercising or switching up her diet. But Esther long ago stopped pointing that out and, instead, just smiles because her baby sister—forty-four years old to Esther's fifty-one—is so unabashedly herself.

They don't look much like sisters, and not only because Esther is rail thin, as disinterested in food as she is in exercise (except for tennis, which is less about exercise and more about competition). Esther is always polished while Dot has two distinct modes: bothered, and can't be bothered. Can't be bothered is far more frequent, and then Dot wears yoga pants with holey t-shirts, her sandy hair caught up in a bun, no makeup on her still unlined face. Dot's always been the prettier sister, with features soft and sweet. Esther's attractive in a way that's sharp and exacting, precisely calibrated to be taken seriously. She's been dying her hair black since she was twenty-five, though she's not trying to look twenty-five or arouse the desire of twenty-five-year-olds. But it is a lot of work, staying appropriately visible as a middle-aged woman.

"Where's your bag?" Esther says, noticing that Dot is holding her cell in her hand. Esther tries not to speak sharply to her sister, but seriously? Dot knows better than that.

"I forgot it. Sorry." She does look sorry.

Esther reaches into her purse. "I have an extra."

"Of course you do." Dot smiles, her faced sheened with sweat. She hands over her phone and Esther places it in a Faraday bag alongside the bag that holds her own cell. She made sure to buy the military-grade versions—not the ones available on Amazon—so that all radio signals will be blocked, her data is protected, and she can't be tracked. "Do we really need to keep meeting this way?"

What Dot means is, now that the Tramboni divorce has been settled, does Esther need to keep messaging Dot on WhatsApp a half hour before they meet with a location because that way, even if Peter does manage to spy on what are supposed to be fully encrypted messages, he wouldn't have time to get a surveillance team out to the location on such short notice, at least not without Esther seeing them.

"Yes, we need to," Esther says shortly. All precautions will remain in place until she knows for sure that Peter's moved on to his next victim.

It's been three days since the party and there's been no communication from Peter. But Esther hasn't relaxed for a second. Avery's already texted twice: once with *Howdy* and then with a waving hand emoji the following day. Esther has held off on responding. She needs more clues as to what Avery's really after. It could be camaraderie with another of Peter's victims, like Avery said, but there's also an outside chance Peter has roped Avery into one of his twisted games. Or could this be a game that Peter and Avery are playing together?

It's hard to imagine that Esther could matter that much to

either Peter or Avery, but one thing Esther's figured out about billionaires is that they're easily bored. With everyone catering and toadying, living in a world that bends to their whims, they can be drawn to any sense of challenge or opposition.

Even before Peter, Esther took precautions. After all, she's pissed off a lot of men in her time, some of whom were wealthy and powerful, though of course Peter's a whole other level of magnitude. For years, she's employed a cybersecurity firm to safeguard all her devices at the office and at her home. She also has her office, home, and car routinely swept for bugs. After Peter engaged her services, she upped the sweeping schedule from once a month to weekly. She has advanced video surveillance as well. Fortunately, Esther is taciturn by nature and, until recently, she hasn't felt much need to vent. When she does, she turns to Dot, in an undisclosed location, with Faraday bags.

This is the first time she's ever completely abandoned attorney-client confidentiality, referencing Peter by circumstance and by name. Because how could she disguise the details and still convey what she's up against, convincing Dot that not only is her paranoia warranted, it's the only sane course?

"Well, you know best," Dot tells Esther, her tone entirely devoid of sarcasm. "Esther knows best" is one of Dot's personal mantras.

Dot takes a seat beside Esther on the picnic bench. The field beyond is largely untended and untrammeled, dandelions running amok. That's why Esther picked it.

"How are July and Tyson?" Esther asks. She takes a swig from her metal water bottle. She's in running clothes and a baseball cap, her hair tucked up neatly and completely underneath it. It's a disguise of sorts. Esther never runs.

Unless she's trying to get out of Peter's house, that is.

"I still can't seem to motivate Tyson to work on his college essays," Dot says. "It's like he doesn't even care where he gets in."

"He doesn't. He knows he'll be fine anywhere."

Tyson is the all-around kid: pretty good at school, pretty good at sports, easygoing and popular. But none of that will get him into Stanford or even UC Berkeley, much to his mother's consternation.

"I just want him to be better than me." Dot sighs. She went to one of California's lesser state schools and has worked her way up from an administrative assistant to an executive assistant. In the San Francisco Bay Area, she'd barely be above the poverty line if she and the kids hadn't been the beneficiaries of her ex-husband's life insurance policy.

"It's a fallacy," Esther says. "Two fallacies, really. That kids need to surpass their parents, and that attendance at an elite college is a guarantee of a good life. Too often, those schools can't produce well-adjusted or even decent humans. Peter Tramboni went to Stanford."

"July's decided she's not into Stanford anymore. Now she only wants to go to Yale, like her Aunt E."

"I went there for law school, not undergrad. But whatever July wants, I'm sure she'll get."

Dot smiles and pushes a stray hair back from her face. "Since when did you become such a beacon of optimism?"

"July gives me hope, you know that."

July is fifteen, off the charts intelligent, and obsessed with STEM.

"I told July you actually met Avery Brengle." Avery is July's idol because she's not only a mogul but a brilliant coder, too. "Be warned, she's going to pump you for every detail when you next see her."

"Consider me warned," Esther says. "I'll be ready to tell her all about my brush with fame and fortune." Not all, of course. No one gets that, not even Dot.

Though Esther's told Dot about Peter, it's been an abridged version. On one level, that's because Esther needs to let off steam, but she doesn't want to make Dot worry too much. Dot has always been the emotionally fragile one and, besides, she has so many responsibilities as a single mother. There's no sense in spiking her anxiety when there's nothing she can do for Esther. Nothing anyone can do.

Esther's always been the tough sister, the protector. Always ready to take the bullet for Dot, and their dad had fired many. Given what Esther witnessed growing up and what she's observed in her line of work, she's never seen the appeal of marriage.

She's built her life on the pillars of autonomy and self-sufficiency. She felt sorry for her mother and sometimes for Dot, too, but no one should ever have a reason to feel sorry for Esther. She's never considered marriage, and she's never wanted to have kids. Those are pillars, too. But she loves her sister, niece, and nephew beyond measure, and there's nothing she wouldn't do for them.

Sure, her childhood has left a few marks but she's used those scars to propel herself. They've toughened her skin and made her realize she can survive anything. As a woman, projecting complete self-assurance is particularly important. Image isn't everything but it is a very large something, which is why she emphasizes impression management to her female clients right from the beginning. She makes sure they know how they have to carry themselves and that they'll need to be above reproach at all times. When they think no one's looking, someone is: the nanny or babysitter, their kids' teachers, even their own supposed friends (you never know who your friends really are until you're in a custody battle). The ex can have spies everywhere. Eyes everywhere. Oh, and there's no time for crying, unless that's going to move the judge in your favor. Don't simper; win.

"What was it really like for you to be at that party?" Dot asks.

"A living nightmare," Esther says flatly.

"But the nightmare is over now. You have to remember that." Dot reaches out and touches Esther's hand lightly. "The bad man's gone."

"I don't think so. I think he's in here." Esther indicates her chest.

"What do you mean?"

"He got me to act against my own principles, and my conscience. I put self-preservation above everything." Esther ordinarily meets all her clients at her office or at the courthouse; she makes sure to never see the children except in pictures or videos, the ones that are being submitted as evidence. But Peter had insisted on having Esther come face to face with his little boy, and it had been utter agony, knowing what was in store for that child.

"You acted for the greater good. What if you'd told Peter no and he'd gotten you disbarred? Think of all the families that would suffer then if they didn't have you."

Esther appreciates the sentiment, but she's never believed in the notion of lesser evils. Evil is evil, and it should be vanquished.

Because of Esther's high reputation in the field, she's able to carefully vet and select her clients, turning down as many cases as she accepts. Before Peter Tramboni she had only represented women in hetero divorces, and only took on cases where her instinct told her strongly that they were divorcing bad men.

Sometimes women come in talking about mediation and Esther shuts that down quick. There's too much of a power imbalance. Men are, frankly, better negotiators because they've been raised to please themselves first before all others, and the men her clients are married to in particular are generally skilled manipulators. Besides, Esther loves to fight. She's a very lucky woman, having found the perfect job: She gets to channel her personal history and competitive nature into a noble pursuit.

She was lucky, that is, until Peter brought her low.

"I feel"—Esther struggles to find the word—"exposed."

"I don't understand."

"I've always seen myself one way, and I liked that way, and then Peter..." Esther can't continue. It hurts too much, and she knows Dot would only try to refute it anyway. Dot can be unbearably loyal.

Esther also doesn't want to admit out loud just how much Peter Tramboni has gotten in her head. No man has ever dominated her like Peter has, and it's hard to leave it behind even now that the case is over. He used her to gain control over an impressionable child, a most horrifying thought. Under normal circumstances, Peter is the type of man she makes sure will never see his kids again. He deserves to be expunged. More than that, he deserves to be annihilated.

It also bothers Esther that Peter made her breach her professional ethics by telling Dot about him. No, he didn't make her. She actively chose. But what a choice. She felt she had to break confidentiality and talk to Dot because she couldn't hold it in anymore. Only it means lying to Dot, something she (almost) never does.

"I've never worked for any man before," Esther says.

"What a man to cut your teeth on." Dot smiles sympathetically. "Don't be so hard on yourself, E. You did what anyone would have done in your position."

"It was a devil's bargain, though. Now he's never going to leave me alone. This is never going to end."

The first time Esther met Peter was during the Stanton divorce, when she was representing Madeline against Peter's architect, Greg. She'd initially been intrigued as to what the famous Peter Tramboni was really like, but when she reached out to him for a sworn statement, she fully expected him to turn her down. After all, his time must have been far too valuable to waste on the divorce of an underling like Greg.

But to her surprise, Peter immediately invited her to his office at Nimbus. He was charming and witty and personable, offering to give her a tour of the building and the campus beyond.

"Did Greg Stanton design all of this?" she asked, surveying it from his floor-to-ceiling glass windows, embarrassed at how awestruck she sounded.

"No," Peter said dismissively, "I wouldn't let Greg near this place."

It was the first time she witnessed the scathing side of him, but unfortunately, it wouldn't turn out to be the last.

"Are you going to take my proposition?" he asked.

"Your proposition?"

He laughed. "Get your mind out of the gutter, Esther. I said deposition."

Her return laugh was uneasy, because she knew what she'd heard. It was the first time she'd experienced his gaslighting but, again, it would be far from the last. She couldn't know that then, though.

"It's not a deposition. Just an affidavit." She explained that he'd give a statement to a third party who would then notarize it.

He seemed disappointed. "I can't give it to you?"

"That's not how it works." She was starting to feel uncomfortable. She reminded herself that he was married to Bianca Tramboni, who was much younger and more beautiful than Esther, and that he was used to dealing with people of much greater significance. But she's never been one to ignore a warning sign and so she excused herself. Maybe that's what did it, that she declined his offer of a tour, that she ended the meeting before he could. She'd rejected him, and his ego must not have been able to take it. Because at their next encounter, he had the upper hand, and he very much wanted her to know it.

"I should go," Esther tells Dot, her mouth dry. She just can't talk about Peter anymore, though she can think of little else.

"How do I help you?" Dot's tone is plaintive. She's not used to seeing Esther in torment.

"You can't." She stands up, pecks a kiss on her sister's forehead, and heads back across the field. She pulls her phone from the Faraday bag and checks it.

Speak of the devil.

We need to talk.

That's his name as it's been entered into Esther's phone: *Devil.* And she knows what Dot would say, that she doesn't need to respond because she doesn't work for him anymore. But Dot's a wonderfully simple person, and she can't begin to grasp the complexities of dealing with a man like Peter.

Esther texts back: *May I ask what it's regarding?*

His reply is instant.

Cut the shit. You know exactly what it's regarding. My house. Tomorrow night. 8 p.m.

Before she can answer, he adds, *Come alone. Tell no one.*

FIVE

One case wraps up, another always takes its place, smooth as a conveyor belt. To change now would be like letting a terrorist win.

That's how Esther finds herself sitting across from a new client while her mind is entirely elsewhere. She can't stop thinking about what that text could mean. *You know what it's regarding*. She really doesn't, unless Peter's going to tell her that he'll soon be detonating a bomb at the center of her life. She did his bidding and now he's going to destroy her anyway for shits and giggles.

She has the absurd thought of reaching out to Avery Brengle and asking if she's ever gotten a text like that. Maybe Avery knows (or could guess) what Peter has up his sleeve? Esther finds herself wanting to trust Avery. That must be the true definition of charisma. People want to believe you, even when it's likely to their detriment.

At 8 p.m., Esther will find out what's going on, whether she likes it or not. No one stands Peter up.

Come alone. Tell no one.

Does that mean he knows what she's been telling Dot?

Could Dot be next on his hit list? Esther's been careful but maybe you can't be careful enough. Peter will always be two steps ahead. His reach is infinite.

No, he's not God. He's only the devil.

"I'm really happy that you called," the new client says. Kristi? Kristen? Normally, Esther's great with names, and great with first client meetings. Today is a notable exception.

Esther casts a quick glance toward her computer screen and sees that it's Kiersten. Then she looks back at Kiersten across her empty, spotless glass desk. The whole office is pristine, not a speck of dust anywhere, not a personal memento in sight. On the wall, it's only her framed diplomas: Harvard for undergraduate, JD from Yale Law. Why? Because Yale Law was harder to get into than Harvard Law. Esther likes to be chosen by the elite, unless that elite happens to be Peter Tramboni.

"I'd decided to wait just a little longer to see if you had an opening come up," Kiersten says. "You were definitely my favorite of all the lawyers I consulted with. You seem to have that killer instinct, you know?"

"I had a feeling about you, too." What Esther means is, she had a strong feeling about Kiersten's husband, Miles, who's a VP at Google. He's only thirty-one, a real golden boy, so on the rare occasions he hits Kiersten, he's careful to never leave a mark where others can see. That kind of premeditation makes him particularly detestable, from Esther's vantage point. He's also incredibly self-absorbed, controlling, and manipulative.

Kiersten kneads a tissue between her fingers as she speaks. She hasn't cried yet, but she will. She'd be pretty if she were less visibly distraught and had another ten pounds on her. Her energy is high-strung, like a wire stretched far too taut. But Esther doesn't hold that against her. She holds it against Miles.

Esther has a waiting list and could have called any number of potential clients but she called Kiersten because she wants to have a go at Miles. Esther needs a true irredeemable to fight right now, to wash the taste of Peter Tramboni out of her mouth.

"You have three children?" Esther asks.

Kiersten nods. "My oldest is five, and the twins are two and a half."

"Why now?"

"What do you mean?"

"Why divorce him now? You must have known for a long time what kind of a person Miles is. What he's capable of." Esther keeps her voice neutral, but Kiersten flushes anyway. "I'm just thinking of how to present this in court. We need a credible narrative."

"You don't think I'm telling the truth?"

"I know you're telling the truth. But this will go a lot faster if you don't answer my questions with questions. Please trust that I have a good reason for whatever I ask. I'm going to get you full custody."

Kiersten's shoulders relax slightly. "The other attorneys said they couldn't make promises."

"What I should say is, if you do everything I tell you to do, you'll get full custody because Miles is a monster."

"What?" Kiersten's frozen in disbelief.

"You might not see it now, but as this case unfolds, you will. He's not used to you standing up to him, and once you do—once we do—he's going to reveal an ugliness that you only suspected was there."

Kiersten pales. "I was hoping we could keep this civil."

"We will. We're entering a civil war."

"I just don't... what if..." Now Kiersten is using that tissue, dabbing at her eyes. "I have three kids."

"I know. You need to stay strong for them. I'm going to be right there to help you do that. I'm your partner."

Kiersten seems ever-so-slightly mollified, but also terrified.

"I can only imagine how hard this is." It's true, Esther has never been in Kiersten's position, and never will. "You keep thinking that if you play nice, he will, too. But I'm not going to let him take advantage of your kindness anymore." *Or of your fear.*

"Do you really think that's what's been happening in our marriage?"

"From everything you told me during our consultation, I'm sure of it." Esther leans in and holds Kiersten's gaze. "You're used to a partner who lies and manipulates you. That's not me. I'm going to tell you straight. I think you wanted me over the other attorneys because deep down you knew that Miles would never go quietly. I mean, look at what he did, forcing you to vacate the home and move into a rental even though you're the children's primary caregiver. That was a power move. He was showing you who's boss."

"I guess that's true," Kiersten says slowly.

If she'd been working with Kiersten at the time of the separation, Esther would never have allowed that. But now Esther can use it to her advantage, establishing a pattern of controlling and selfish behavior, with Miles putting his needs ahead of the children's.

Some of the more touchy-feely attorneys talk about how maturity is what separates the people in custody battles from those who figure out how to settle their disputes more amicably. Maturity is supposedly what allows a person to successfully collaborate with someone they once loved and now hate, that they can put away even the most virulent feelings for the sake of their children.

Bullshit. These women don't need to make any more compromises. They need freedom, and so do their children. That's what Esther gets for the Kierstens of the world. And don't get her started on all those people who hold the erroneous belief that a child needs both parents. Esther's parents stayed together and she would have been much better off if her father had left and never come back.

"Why now?" Esther asks again.

Kiersten closes her eyes and takes a long pause. "My five-year-old called me stupid the other day. Miles calls me stupid a lot, but never in front of other people, including our kids. But our daughter must have overheard, and if she overheard that, what else is she picking up?"

"You don't want her to learn that it's okay for a man to treat a woman like that. If she sees it enough, she'll think it's normal."

Kiersten nods, her head slumping in exhaustion.

"So, then you asked for the separation?" Esther asks.

Another nod.

"Were you surprised that he agreed so easily?"

"Not really. He's been sleeping with someone else for months. He doesn't even bother to hide it."

"California's a no-fault state. That means infidelity isn't grounds for divorce. But it does go toward a pattern. Lack of empathy, cruelty, emotional abuse, physical abuse. The children need to be protected from him. So do you."

People sometimes ask how Esther handles such a stressful job, what it's like to listen to horror stories all day, and she says that she doesn't let herself get swept up in the emotion. "Stay in your lane," is her advice to young divorce attorneys, "you're nobody's therapist." She can't control every element; she doesn't determine every outcome; she might not win every battle. But she wins the vast majority of the wars. The more extreme the case, the more important it is to present in the most moderate and reasonable manner, and to teach your clients to do the same.

"Start thinking about potential character witnesses now," Esther advises Kiersten. "Who'd line up to attest to your maternal bona fides? What relationships need damage control? Other parents, daycare providers, the staff at Mommy & Me classes, whoever you've got. Make your list now. Cases are won on thoroughness and consistency. You establish your credibility; you diminish his. It's not about one dramatic TV moment. It's a hundred little ones. And they all need to be documented in just the ways I'm about to describe."

This is where clients often get squirrely, where they protest that it sounds like an awful lot of work, and isn't it just a little bit paranoid, taking notes on every single interaction? But Kiersten is following along like a trooper.

"The best interest of the child is the standard when it comes to custody," Esther says. "That's based on the emotional bonds between the parent and child, on which parent can better provide reliability and stability, the parent's skills and judgment, and safety concerns, like domestic violence."

Kiersten is rapt, taking notes on her phone.

"It's not about what's true; it's about what we can prove. We have to be more prepared than the other side. I'm a big believer in targeted aggression, in delivering a knockout blow. That way, he'll know better than to come after you again, and he won't be dragging you back into court repeatedly between now and when your kids turn eighteen."

Kiersten nods intently.

"Get me what I need, and I'll get you the best result." Esther doesn't say what that is. It'll take a while for Kiersten to resign herself to the fact that Miles should be out of her kids' lives as well as hers, that eventually they'll have to go beyond full custody to eliminating all visitation.

So many divorce attorneys can't be bothered to prep their clients right from the start. They don't want to say outright just how much is going to be asked of them, as if that'll scare them off.

Esther loves those attorneys. They make her job a whole lot easier.

"Document everything, starting now," Esther says. "I

promise you, an ounce of prevention is worth a pound of cure. This is the best thing for you and your kids." Esther is really warming to this conversation. Somehow, as many times as she's said these words, it never gets old.

The war has begun.

Only when Kiersten leaves does Esther sink back into ruminations about Peter. Normally, she fights for justice but it's not personal. She doesn't get emotional. With Peter, though, it's different. She truly, viscerally hates him. She hates that she won the case for him. She even hates herself a little for not having the courage to tank the case. She should have made some costly mistake or left stones unturned. Not used all the dirt that Peter's PI team had dug up on Bianca.

Only Peter would never have let her get away with that. And Esther's never intentionally lost a fight in her life. But then, normally the monster is on the other side of the courtroom.

She stays late at the office, skipping dinner since she has no appetite. (She might look like Kiersten soon if this continues.) Finally, she can't avoid it any longer. She goes down to the parking lot beneath her building and gets into her Audi, taking a deep breath and steeling herself for the drive ahead.

After she's spent twenty minutes in gridlocked traffic, he texts: *Never mind, don't come.*

She texts back to ask: *What's it all about, can you tell me now?*

When she gets no reply—of course there's no reply; he wants her twisting in the wind—she opens her mouth and lets out a primal scream.

HOW MUCH LONGER? HOW MUCH FUCKING LONGER CAN THIS GO ON? HOW MUCH MORE CAN ONE WOMAN TAKE? HOW MUCH MORE CAN ESTHER TAKE BEFORE...?

WHY IS HE BLOODY DOING THIS TO HER? WHY HER?

IT HAS TO STOP!

HE'S A PSYCHOPATH, HE'LL NEVER STOP!

He has to be stopped.

SIX

"Fifteen–forty!" Hugh calls out from his side of the court.

"Match point!" Esther calls out from hers.

"Don't remind me," Hugh mutters. Then he raises his racquet and delivers a cracking serve... that lands so far beyond the lines that she doesn't even bother to call it out. It's endearingly Hugh: going for the ace with everything he has and, as usual, missing without a lick of shame or regret. She can't convince him to change his strategy and how hard should she try? This way, she beats him 90 percent of the time.

Yet those rare hits are what it's all about for him, the joy that comes from a bolt of lightning. Esther always says he was meant to be a TV lawyer since he lives for the *gotcha!* moment. Hugh always says she's the kind of grind that he avoided in law school. But somehow, here they are. A couple, sort of. An odd couple, definitely.

Their conflicting tennis styles reflect their personalities. She pairs patience with well-timed aggression, chasing down every ball, keeping her errors as low as possible so she gives nothing away, waiting for the right moment to pull the trigger and unleash a high-probability winner. Hugh's a kamikaze, thriving on the element of surprise with his unusual shot selections, going for as many winners as possible, even when he's out of position and it's a low-probability shot. He doesn't mind that she beats him most of the time. When he gets lucky and wins, he credits his superior skill, laughing when she rolls her eyes. He loves when she laughs, though. Loves that she's a tough audience.

If anyone actually knew they were together, it would likely inspire astonishment. Hugh with his electrified hair, ruddy skin, and slovenly clothing; Hugh, who had represented Greg Stanton while Esther had represented Madeline. They hadn't liked each other but they enjoyed sparring and now here Esther is, starring in her own romcom, except for the fact that their relationship exists in secrecy. No, confidentiality. It's not that Esther is embarrassed by her choice of partner; it's that she's a woman who's crossed the mid-century mark and her relationships are no one else's business. And wait, did she just call him "partner"?

Only in tennis.

Hugh tries for the ace again and Esther yells, "Out!" He's double-faulted the match away, and it's hardly the first time.

They slap hands at the net—they never embrace where prying eyes can see—and then sit on the courtside bench. She eats a banana while he gulps water.

"I'll get you next time," he says.

"Not unless you change your strategy."

"Never. I have to go down swinging."

He bumps her arm, accidentally on purpose, and she exaggeratedly pretends to wipe off the sweat, but really, she likes his nearness.

When Esther and Hugh got together, she hadn't been looking for him, or for anyone else. But she went to play at the tennis courts right up the street from her house, the ones at the Berkeley Rose Garden, and there he was. Somehow she wound up playing doubles with him as her partner and she found that he was quite talented at the net and a gentleman to boot. She wouldn't have guessed at either of those things. She'd always assumed he was out of shape but it turned out he was just always wearing shapeless suits. He's iconoclastic, defying categorization, and she's drawn to that. She appreciates their contrasts, and how she usually can't anticipate what his take on something might be.

Not that she'd ever ask him for legal advice. Or any advice at all, really.

She once charitably referred to Hugh as "morally ambiguous," and he countered, "I prefer the term 'morally agnostic.'" Whatever you call him, he's not prone to passing judgment on others. Still, there's no way she'd trust him with a secret that she'd sworn she'd take to the grave, especially when he sees her as being entirely above board. Or rather, as above board as anyone can be in the world of family law. She's not about to disabuse his favorable notions of her.

What they do agree upon, absolutely, is keeping their relationship discreet. No public affection, no meeting each other's families. No one needs to know what they've found in each other.

"You got another banana?" Hugh asks.

"You're a grown man. You should be responsible for your own bananas."

He waggles his eyebrows suggestively. She rolls her eyes, which makes his smile. Derision is his love language. Then she hands him the extra banana from her tennis bag.

"Much obliged." He peels it and takes a large bite. Then he asks a question she can't make out.

"Excuse me?"

He swallows. "Sorry. I was just asking about Peter Tramboni."

"What about him?"

"Well, how does it feel to have that case behind you?" Hugh pulls a bandana from his duffel and wipes at his face and neck.

She tenses up involuntarily. Her phone is in a Faraday bag but his must be in his duffel, naked. "I was happy to get the win," she lies, sounding about as authentic as a beauty pageant contestant. "But it's really just another case."

"You're telling me Peter Tramboni is just another client?" He lifts an eyebrow.

On the off-chance Peter is listening in, Esther says, "Who knows? It might open doors. It's great to be picked by someone of his stature." Hugh's eyebrow goes even higher. "All I'm saying is, it never hurts to raise your profile."

"Depends how you're doing the hoisting."

"So now you're a paragon of virtue? Please." She rustles around in her bag to avoid his eyes.

"Well, all *I'm* saying is, working with Peter Tramboni doesn't necessarily raise you. It might lower you."

Why does he sound so knowing? Now she's the one shooting him an inquiring glance.

"What?" he asks.

"You said that like you and Peter have some prior association."

He shakes his head. "Peter Tramboni and I don't exactly run in the same circles. The only thing we have in common is you."

"Are you saying that I was having sex with Peter Tramboni?" She's surprised by how angry she sounds. How angry she feels. So angry, in fact, that for a second, she'd forgotten about Hugh's nearby phone and the possibility of surveillance.

"I just meant that we both know you." Hugh looks surprised,

too. Esther isn't known for sudden bursts of emotion. Actually, she's known for its opposite, for preternatural calm and equanimity, in the courtroom and out. "What's going on, Esther?"

"It wasn't always easy, working for someone so demanding and exacting." Peter would like those descriptors; they're the ones Esther would actually apply to herself.

"And megalomaniacal." Peter would not like that one.

Again, she has the sense that Hugh is more acquainted with Peter than he cares to let on but many articles about Peter have stressed his perfectionism; some call it by its right name of egotism. Then there's the Silicon Valley rumor mill. Hugh's probably heard some stories in his day. But their relationship wouldn't survive if he took it upon himself to question her choice of clients. She expects him to respect her judgment and not to pry. So far, he's lived up to that.

"With a big case," she says, "you coast on the adrenaline. You don't really rest until it's over. That's when the crash comes."

"I just thought you'd seem happier that it's over. I know I am. Once you're not doing all those house calls, we'll have a lot more time to spend together."

"I am happy." She has to lie since Peter could be listening, and she doesn't mind lying because Hugh has just broken their implicit bargain, the reason they fit together and never fight. Esther doesn't talk about feelings and Hugh doesn't push. Who's he to tell her how she ought to seem? Does he also tell random women on the street that they should smile more?

"I'm here for you, no matter what. You get that, right?"

He tries to look deeply into her eyes, which would be uncomfortable under the best of circumstances. She's never done that kind of intimacy, and she's not about to start now.

"Yes, yes, I get it," she says, hoping he'll drop his gaze. But then hers grows ferocious. The last thing she's going to allow is another man to run a power play on her.

Hugh seems to sense the sea change and though he probably doesn't understand it, he backs down. He gets to his feet, hiking his duffel onto his shoulder. "My place or yours?" he asks.

"You change your sheets recently?"

He laughs. "Only for you, Esther. No one but you."

SEVEN

Stylist is doing her business; Esther has not been able to do hers.

Every time she tries to focus on the document open on her laptop, her brain goes walkabout. She's doing what she never does: ruminating on a past case. Because the past remains so horribly present.

She closes her eyes, trying to listen only to the soothing, meditative whir of the dryer. Then, instead of thoughts, she has a vision. It's of Peter Tramboni showing up unannounced, not at her office but at her home, her sanctuary by the Berkeley Rose Garden. He hadn't been waiting outside, she's sure of that, yet he knocked on the door less than five minutes after she arrived home. It was eerie, like he was the Invisible Man.

It had been over a year since the Stanton divorce and Peter's offer to give her a tour of his headquarters. During that time, she hadn't really thought of him unless he was in the news cycle, which wasn't infrequent. When she did hear his name or see his face, she felt an internal shudder, a hint of fear and relief. Now, with him smiling on her doorstep, she was feeling only the former.

"I love your house," Peter said. "What kind of architecture is it? Like Hansel and Gretel?"

"Storybook architecture." Esther didn't smile back, wanting to convey that she doesn't like surprise visits and that he's no Prince Charming.

"I wouldn't have pictured you in a place like this. No offense, but you don't seem to have a lot of whimsy in you." He couldn't have been the first to think it—she seems as if she'd like clean modern lines rather than asymmetry, a deeply pitched roof, gables, and two turrets, with climbing ivy and a deliberately overgrown back garden—but he was the first to say it. "I've always been fascinated by the distinction between how we present and what we're attracted to. Have you noticed how often you meet someone's spouse and think, *Really?*"

"Not really."

He laughed. "It's also true of their pets. And, obviously, their houses. People are tremendously inconsistent, Esther, don't you find?"

"Not really."

"What a consistent response. Very clever. Are you ready to invite me in?" Then before she could answer, he said, "I know. Not really. But you're going to want to hear what I have to say, and you certainly won't want your neighbors listening in."

Reluctantly, she moved aside. At least she was in her work clothes, with her bra on, and her house was always clean and fit for company, despite how rarely she entertained.

He looked around her living room with a delighted expression on his face. Like many of the rooms, it was irregularly shaped, mostly rounded, with an arched doorway. The walls were highly textured and hand-plastered, the windows mismatched and some leaded.

"See?" Peter said. "People are never what you think."

Unless they're worse. She couldn't believe that when she first met Peter at his headquarters, she'd been taken in, even for a moment. How had that happened, despite her exquisitely sensitive villainy meter?

"You want me to get to the point," he said.

"It'd be much appreciated."

"I'm getting divorced and you're going to handle it."

Her heart began to pound. She hadn't offered him a seat, and he seemed perfectly comfortable standing, issuing directives.

"My office is in Oakland," she said. "There are excellent family law firms much closer to you. I'm happy to make a referral."

"I know where your office is located. You'll be coming to me."

It was unsettling, the way he spoke as if it was a done deal, as if his wish was her command. "Unfortunately, my caseload is full."

"You'll make room for me." He smiled, much more coldly than earlier when he was complimenting her house. "Given what I know."

Her heart was in her ears now. It sounded like rushing rapids.

"You don't have a Nimbus account," he said. "Do you realize you're practically the only person on the planet without one?"

So much for the firewall that supposedly existed to block Peter Tramboni from his users' data, the one he always referenced during congressional hearings.

"No, I hadn't realized," she finally responded.

"I have quite a reach. There's not much that exceeds my grasp." He paused, his eyes roaming her face with a look that could best be described as rapacious.

She was disquieted in a way that she hadn't been since childhood.

"I'm not the right attorney for you," she said.

"I have an army of private investigators. Different firms that work independently on defined areas of inquiry. Once I have all the pieces, I fit them together."

In other words, he wanted to make sure that he was the puzzle master. He's that much of a control freak.

"I know what you did, Esther, and right now, I expect I'm the only one. But if you decline my case, that'll change."

She stared at him, eyes widening. Any number of incredible attorneys would jump at the chance to work for him, but he'd known that she wouldn't be among them. He came here intending to blackmail her.

"Do we understand each other?" he said.

"I don't know what you think you have on me but—"

So he proceeded to tell her. And he was right, which meant that he had all the power to use as he saw fit. She was now in his employ, and under his thumb.

The memory ends, but the residue remains. She opens her eyes and...

Speak of the devil. His face is on the salon's TV, which is tuned to CNN. For a second, Esther thinks she's hallucinating but no, he's always been all too real.

She reads the ticker tape along the bottom of the screen. Breaking news.

Stylist is looking at the screen too. This is no hallucination.

Peter Tramboni has been found dead, and it's being investigated as a homicide. He was done in by a single bullet to the back of the head. He died instantly.

If only he could have suffered longer.

EIGHT

Esther looks around to see who's seated on the cheap folding chairs. It's pretty much everyone from the divorce party, including Avery Brengle, plus all four ex-wives, half with new husbands, and three of Peter's children, ranging in age from eight to twenty-one. His littlest son, Stride, isn't there, though his mother, Bianca, is, front row center. She's been dabbing at her eyes nearly constantly though Esther imagines they're dry as dust. Or perhaps those are tears of joy. With Peter gone, Bianca now has full custody.

Hugh had argued for attending the funeral, saying that Esther really needed to put in an appearance. She'd found it strange—since when does Hugh care about appearances?—but then she was a bit touched because he knows that, traditionally, Esther does care.

Today isn't about impression management, though; it's about reconnaissance. She needs to figure out if her secret died with Peter.

"You really think this is what Peter would have wanted?" Hugh whispers to Esther.

Who gives a shit what Peter wanted? is what Esther wants to whisper back, but instead she shrugs.

"He probably didn't leave any instructions because he thought death could never come for him." Hugh looks around. "Because if he had left instructions, it wouldn't look like this. It would have been some processional fit for royalty, you can bet your ass on that."

Esther doesn't know how Hugh can speak so authoritatively but then, he does have a habit of playing fast and loose with facts. During the Stanton divorce, Esther had been amazed at how many unsupported assertions he could produce in a single legal brief.

But he's right, Peter would have hated this funeral. His mother had put it together, and who would have guessed that she'd be a total Woodstock hippie? She has straggly gray hair nearly to her waist and she's swathed in black tie-dye. The funeral is shockingly low-tech and low-rent, with red and white carnations displayed in front of a makeshift podium and photocopies laid out on every chair to explain that while Peter's body can't yet be cremated due to the ongoing investigation, he will eventually be laid to rest in his backyard. His ashes will be mixed with soil, and in that soil, a sapling will be planted. "My beautiful PETER will merge with the roots of the mighty REDWOOD," his mother had written.

As always, Esther is relieved she's not a mother herself. She could never wear the requisite blinders.

It's a gorgeous day, the sun glinting off Peter's man-made lake. Esther wonders who'll get this compound, what with all the ex-wives and kids. Or did he leave it to dear old Mom? She imagines that Peter's legacy will live on as they all thrash it out, fighting for dominance. The litigation would be a fitting tribute.

There's no minister or officiant, just a series of over-the-top eulogies. One by one, Peter's "friends," frenemies, competitors, and co-conspirators step forward to declare his greatness. They must have used a thesaurus to come up with myriad adjectives and similes describing his brilliance and determination. Some seem genuinely admiring of his ruthlessness. No one's said anything about kindness or humanity, though there've been a few well-placed references to his philanthropy. Everyone can agree that he's had a lasting impact on the world.

Peter's mother is sobbing too hard to speak. The ex-wives have remained silent. When it seems that everyone's capacity for grief and veneration has been exhausted, Avery walks to the front. Everyone sits a little straighter in collective anticipation.

Avery's in flowing white. Her auburn hair is down and flowing, too. She cuts a truly angelic figure as she surveys the crowd and says, "Peter Tramboni can lick my ass."

The air is instantly charged.

"You all know what he did to me, how he came after me. With Peter Tramboni alive, I could never get complacent. I could not rest on my laurels. I had to stay wily and cunning and one step ahead. No, two steps. Not just of him but of everyone, because he knew everyone. He had spies everywhere."

Her gaze has turned ferocious. She lifts her chin and looks at various audience members in turn. When she gets to Esther, does she linger just a few extra beats? Esther hopes so. And she hopes not.

"I can only be grateful for having known Peter. He sharpened me like a whetstone. He made me want to soar, so high that he could never reach me. But I'm angry, too, as so many of you must be. How dare he leave the world so early? How dare he leave us all behind?"

Avery's eyes seem to flicker with fury. It's like she's a revival preacher and expects a congregant to shout out the answer. Then suddenly, the spirit seems to exit her body. She sags a bit, as if she's the widow and it's all too much, and without another word, she finds her way back to her seat.

No one comforts her, if that, indeed, is what's called for. Avery is there alone.

Peter's mother stands up, turning around to face the crowd. "Thank you all for coming," she says, her raspy voice cracking, her face tear-streaked. "There will be a drum circle by the water later but first, we'll be celebrating Peter's life with refreshments in the ballroom."

That's how Esther winds up in Peter's ballroom for the second time in just over a week. Today, the walls are beige and unchanging. If the color morph function has been deactivated, does that mean the listening devices have been turned off as well? Or if someone's still listening, who is it? What do they know?

Esther won't be taking any chances. "It was a beautiful ceremony," she tells Hugh.

He raises his eyebrows incredulously but says nothing.

"And a lovely spread," she adds, indicating the tables that have been laid out with deli platters and cans of La Croix.

That's a bridge too far for Hugh. He says, almost roughly, "What the fuck, Esther?"

"Lower your voice," she hisses. "Show some respect. We're at a *funeral*."

"I know where we are." His voice has only lowered a scintilla. "I was the one who wanted us to come."

"I wanted to come," she says.

He moves closer and speaks so only she can hear. "You've been acting strange ever since you started working for Peter."

"That's not true. It was just very demanding—"

"So you said. Numerous times. That's practically all you've ever said." When he looks at her, his eyes are bright with tenderness. "I've never been able to figure you out. Maybe that's why I..." He trails off.

"Why you what?"

He shakes his head. "It doesn't matter. Are you actually in mourning? I thought you hated the guy."

"I never said that." Which is true. She tried to say as little about Peter Tramboni as possible.

"Everyone hated him. Couldn't you read between the lines of all those speeches? He turned some of the biggest names in Silicon Valley into lackeys and lapdogs. You think they took kindly to that? I bet the murderer was sitting in one of those rows."

"Shh," she says, though most likely, she's the only one who can make out his words. She's surely the only one paying him any attention, given the kind of wattage in this room. Avery Brengle is holding court not even ten feet away.

"You were spending a lot of time with Peter for a while there. Did you have feelings for him?"

Esther can't help it; she barks out a laugh. Then she instantly regrets it, in case the walls still have ears.

Hugh looks relieved. "Then what's going on with you? Why do you seem so messed up these days?"

"Let's not do this here." Or anywhere, really. She's not about to come clean to Hugh. "I don't want you worrying about me."

"Too bad, because I do."

"Excuse me," she says. "I'm going to find the restroom." She knows exactly where it is—where one of the many are—and heads in that direction. She surveys the party, which is not that dissimilar in tone to the one prior. People hadn't been entirely celebrating Peter's win then and they're not entirely celebrating his death now; both gatherings are about seeing, being seen, and FOMO. But today, there's good reason to fear. Peter was one of the chief power brokers in the Valley, and his death leaves a void that will have to be filled by someone (or multiple some-ones). Right in this very room, the jockeying for position has already begun, only it's operating on a frequency too low for someone like Esther to hear.

She sees Bianca Tramboni talking animatedly to Wife #2 and Esther spins on her heel. The last thing she wants is to come face to face with Bianca. Esther's still ashamed of the role she played in Bianca's recent custody debacle, though at least now justice has been served. Bianca's been reunited with her son.

"Esther!" a voice calls warmly. Definitely not Bianca.

But maybe it's worse.

NINE

Avery has broken free of the admiring throng around her to pursue Esther, who's just about the least powerful person here. It's utterly nonsensical, which means it's also peculiarly threatening.

Avery takes Esther by the arm as if they're old friends, or a geriatric person and her aide. "Come outside with me. I could use a smoke."

Esther wouldn't have guessed that Avery smokes, it doesn't seem in keeping with the Valley's communal obsession with immortality, but she's not about to comment. She allows herself to be carried along, ferried back outside and around to the side of the property where they have a view of the lake (and the future site of Peter's Mighty Redwood).

"It's all natural," Avery says, referencing the vape pen that she's just removed from her pocket, "in case you're wondering. And you're not going to get any secondhand smoke."

"It's okay. I'm not a health nut."

"I am. It's my nut of choice." Avery holds the pen up speculatively. "This also emits sound-blocking waves. You can never be too careful where Peter's concerned." First the lipstick, now the vape—what other gadgets has she got?

But what strikes Esther is that even with Peter dead, Avery is still taking precautions. So Esther hasn't been paranoid at all; she's been prudent.

"Now you can tell me what you really think of Peter," Avery says. "There's no attorney-client privilege anymore, right?"

Esther shakes her head. "That's not quite how it works."

"Tell me how it works, Esther." Avery grins. "You're one of those people I could listen to all day."

"I can't imagine why," Esther says truthfully.

Avery throws her head back and laughs.

In Esther's interactions with Avery, she's been deliberately and unremittingly dull. But maybe for Avery, that's the most fascinating of all, an encounter with someone who isn't trying to attract her attention. She's pegged Esther as an enigma and, unfortunately, Avery seems to love an enigma. There probably aren't many people playing hard to get with Avery Brengle.

"Just tell me," Avery nearly begs, "what did you think of Peter?" Her eyes lift at the corners, her merriment apparent. Is she amused by the death, the funeral, Esther's refusal to roll over, or all of the above?

Avery's demeanor suggests she just wants to be girlfriends but perhaps that's what she wants Esther to think.

Only Esther doesn't need to think at all. With Peter dead, she and Avery no longer have a common enemy. She can exit this conversation without looking back.

Much as Esther hates Peter, it's discomforting to see Avery's simple enjoyment at his demise. What Esther feels today is far more complicated.

"What I know is that Peter's dead," Esther says, "and I wasn't raised to speak ill of the dead. I should really get back inside now."

"To your boyfriend?" Avery looks eager for gossip.

"I'm fifty-one years old. I don't have boyfriends."

Avery chortles. "You are a riot, Esther. I'm going to call you soon, okay? We have so much to talk about."

No, they really don't. But there doesn't seem to be any point in protesting. Avery would just find Esther delightful again, which is a surprisingly irritating reaction. Esther is an effective person but she's never been a charming one, nor does she wish to be. Charm is fleeting and facile. Charm is for people like Avery Brengle and Peter Tramboni.

"Goodbye," Esther says, firmly.

"Goodbye!" Avery sings out in reply.

Esther heads for the house, shaking her head. It's well past time to go home. But inside the ballroom, Hugh seems to have vanished. Could he have left without her? No, he wouldn't do that.

Esther does another revolution of the ballroom, and then begins working on the bathroom circuit. Too late, she sees Bianca in a hallway off the kitchen. Bianca is instantly incandescent with rage.

"*You*," she seethes, coming close and backing Esther up against the wall.

Normally in a confrontation, Esther would stand her ground. Normally, she'd have words to defend herself. But she knows she deserves whatever it is that Bianca is about to say. The least she can do is listen as penance. Even then, it won't be nearly enough.

Esther is well aware of all the things Bianca could say. Esther had technically played by the rules but she hadn't been entirely above board; she'd reached into the grab bag of tricks that's typically reserved for bad guys. Only Bianca isn't bad. She's just young, callow, and self-centered. But Esther had painted her as neglectful, narcissistic, and emotionally abusive, a danger to her young son. Esther had done it at lightning speed, too, because she'd wanted to extricate herself from Peter ASAP.

Her conscience had bothered her throughout, and it got even worse after winning. But is there any point in saying that? Who would it be for, herself or for Bianca?

"I'm sorry," Esther says.

Bianca couldn't know it's the first time in Esther's career that she's apologized. In the legal profession, you never admit guilt.

Bianca's face is seared with disgust. She moves in even closer, her breath hot and fetid with deli meat. But that's not why Esther feels sick.

"You deserve to rot in hell, right beside Peter."

Esther doesn't entirely disagree, and perhaps Bianca can tell and that's why she takes pity and steps back. Or Bianca can't bear to be in Esther's immediate vicinity for a second longer.

"I'm sorry," Esther says again.

But Bianca has turned away as if Esther is beneath contempt.

Esther enters the bathroom Bianca recently vacated, locking the door behind her. She tries not to look at herself in the mirror as she takes deep breaths. In and out. In and out. Think of nothing. But instead, she's thinking of who might be watching on the surveillance cams, now that Peter's dead. Who's taking his place?

When she finally leaves the bathroom, she's still shaken. But she forces herself back into the ballroom, where she sees Hugh right away.

"I've been looking for you," he says. "Are you...?" He doesn't finish the sentence. Obviously she's not okay at all. In a demonstration of kindness and perhaps an acquiescence to Esther's preferred boundaries, he doesn't press.

"Let's get out of here," she tells him. She wonders where he was earlier when she was the one looking for him but she's suddenly as weary (and wary) of asking questions as she is of answering them.

She reflects on what Hugh said earlier, about how the killer is in their midst, and she knows he's right.

TEN

"Checkmate," Esther says, though she takes no pleasure in it. Frankly, she's not taking pleasure in anything these days.

"You got me again, Aunt E!" Tyson grins.

"Because you were barely trying!" July says, more uncomprehending than exasperated.

Tyson shrugs. He's sunny and handsome, with dark-blonde hair and blue eyes. "Winning means more to you two."

It's true, July cares a lot about winning, just like her aunt. Tyson takes after his mom, Dot: non-competitive and generous, happy when the victory goes to someone they love. Tyson dials up his performance when he's playing soccer and baseball, but that's in large part because he's doing it for the team.

"My turn," July says.

Tyson relinquishes his seat amiably. "Have fun. I've got a college app to finish." He starts to leave the kitchen and then turns back. "Love you, Aunt E."

"Love you, too," she responds. "Work on your middlegame." But she knows he won't. Working hard isn't in his wheelhouse, and it'll probably never hurt him either. That's not just because he's a male; it's because of the kind of male he is. He moves through the world with ease, whereas July is a scrapper.

The kitchen recently got a facelift, with new flooring, cabinets, and backsplash. Dot and her ex-husband bought the house in a gentrifying neighborhood in Oakland just before July was born and now it's worth quadruple what they paid. But the age-old question in the Bay Area real estate market is always, where would you go if you sold? You'd have to pay the insane prices somewhere else. So, after her ex-husband's death and with the money from his life insurance policy, Dot decided to stay put, renovate, and save up for the future, given that she's got two kids on the cusp of college.

When Esther looks around this house, it reminds her how much Dot's life has improved. That means everything Esther's done has been worth it, even if the secret did put her at Peter Tramboni's mercy.

July takes the seat across from Esther and starts placing her pawns.

"I'm sorry to do this, but I'm really tired," Esther says. "I don't think I have another game in me. At least, not the kind we play." Esther can sleepwalk through her matches with Tyson; not so with July.

July is disappointed, and she either doesn't or can't hide it. "Are you sure? I just finished that Jeremy Silman chess book and I want to measure my improvement."

"I'm sure."

"All right." July slumps slightly and then brightens. "Tell me about the funeral!" The only funeral July's ever attended was her father's.

"There isn't really much to tell. It was a pretty low-key affair." This, at least, is true, with the deli trays and canned water and no booze, and Esther tries to hew to the truth as much as she can with the people she loves.

July leans in, her eyes intense. It's a little unnerving, dealing with someone as sharp as her niece, even if she is only fifteen. She's got so much fire, energy, curiosity, and ambition. Her listening skills and her memory are second to none. If anyone is going to detect an inconsistency in Esther's stories, it would be July. "I just can't believe you're this close to an actual murder," she says.

"Not so close. I was just his lawyer."

"Tell me everything," July says. "Don't leave anything out. What was the security like? Where did you park? What kind of cars were people driving? Who were the people and what were they wearing? How—"

"Enough." Esther doesn't bang her arm on the table or anything, but July startles anyway. "A man's dead."

"Sorry." July doesn't sound sorry. She's breathing heavily, as if she's the one who's been wronged. "But he was a misogynistic piece of shit."

Now Esther is feeling startled. Has Dot said anything to July about what happened between Peter and Esther? That was supposed to be in confidence. "How would you know that?"

"I know what he's done to Avery Brengle. He kept dragging her back into court, and he says awful things about her publicly. That's why she had to countersue for defamation."

Esther relaxes slightly. So, July isn't offended on behalf of her Aunt Esther; she's offended on behalf of her hero.

"Can you at least tell me if you saw Avery at the funeral?" July asks.

"Yes, Avery was there. She was wearing all white. Her hair was down, and she basically looked like an angel."

"I bet she was there to dance on his grave." July looks tickled; Esther feels slightly nauseated, even though July is just being a hyperbolic teenager with a crush. "Did she have, like, any pimples at all?"

"I don't know. I didn't get close to her," Esther lies.

"Oh. But you talked at the divorce party, right? Did she

have any pimples then? I forgot to ask." July struggles with her skin, the most common site of eruptions being her forehead and her chin. "She's talked about how she sometimes breaks out when she's under stress."

"No. Her skin was perfect."

July sighs, lovelorn. Then her dreamy eyes sharpen. "Tell me again about your conversation last time. I need every detail."

"I'm tired, July. And I already told you. No one at that party or at the funeral was interested in me. I'm small potatoes."

"Do you really think Avery's a snob?" July seems to be holding her breath.

Esther reassures her again—just like she did a week ago—that no, Avery is lovely, bright, and charismatic. She just happened to know everyone at the party and they all wanted their time with her. She couldn't spare much for Esther.

"Did she say hi to you at the funeral?" July asks.

"She waved from across the room."

"That is so cool!"

Esther smiles in spite of herself. To be young and capable of swooning—even at fifteen, Esther wasn't like that. She needs to protect all the facets of July, make sure her niece gets to have everything and be everything.

In the self-absorbed way of teenagers, July has unceremoniously moved on. She wants to describe her latest creations with the 3D printer she got recently; she's obsessed with it. And Esther reminds herself that Dot wouldn't be able to afford things like 3D printers for her kids if Esther hadn't made certain choices. If she hadn't amassed certain secrets.

It's all been worth it.

Every.

Single.

Thing.

ELEVEN

At 8:37 a.m. on Sunday, Esther's doorbell rings. She checks the security app on her phone and when she sees the video of the man on her porch, she reminds herself to stay calm and breathe. She has nothing to hide. Or at least, that's the image she needs to project. There's no reason to panic. She's been expecting him. It makes perfect sense that the investigating officer would want to interview the dead man's most recent divorce attorney.

Only she didn't expect him at 8:37 a.m. on a Sunday, and that's why she has to hurriedly yank a robe on over her pajamas and pull a brush through her hair before racing downstairs. The doorbell trills again. At least Hugh isn't here. She doesn't want the police to know any more of her private affairs than they absolutely have to, and she certainly doesn't want Hugh overhearing the interrogation.

"Interrogation" is probably too strong a word. She'll just answer some routine questions (or not answer them, that's the beauty of attorney-client privilege) and politely send the officer on his way.

She opens the door and blinks out into the sunshine, blandly innocent.

"Good morning," he says. "Are you Esther Kahn?"

"I am. And you are?"

"Detective Zelnik from the Santa Clara police department. Could I come in and talk to you a minute?" He looks to be about forty. He's tall, dark, and neither handsome nor unhandsome; it's an eye of the beholder thing.

She opens the door wide and then shows him to the living room. She can see that he's taking in the fairy-tale asymmetry, same as Peter once did.

"Could I get you a coffee?" she asks. "I could really use one myself."

"No, I'm good, thank you."

She sits down on a settee that's covered in brown velvet, and he takes a seat on the red fabric couch opposite her. She waits for him to begin, her expression pleasantly neutral. The last thing she's going to do is voluntarily reveal herself, unprompted. Anything he wants to know, he'll need to ask.

"I'm here about Peter Tramboni," he says. "Given the manner in which he died, it's being investigated as a homicide." She watches Detective Zelnik; he watches her back. A question is clearly in order. "You represented Mr. Tramboni in his recent divorce case?"

Finally! "Yes, I did." She's not giving anything away there. It's a matter of public record.

"Did you have a personal relationship with Mr. Tramboni prior to working together?"

"I did not."

"You'd never met him socially?"

"No. Before he retained my services, I had met him one time before. That was in connection with another divorce case I was working on." Esther keeps her gaze level and open.

Detective Zelnik nods slowly, like she's said something very interesting. "What divorce case was that?"

"I can't say because it would violate confidentiality on that other case. I can say that I met with Mr. Tramboni once at his office to discuss him filing an affidavit that could potentially be beneficial to my client."

"Did he file the affidavit?" She nods. "Sounds like you were quite persuasive. Was it beneficial?"

"Hard to say."

"Did you win that case?" Detective Zelnik looks truly curious.

"I did."

Another slow nod. "Mr. Tramboni must have been very impressed by what you showed him during that one meeting at his office since he chose you over all the other firms in the Bay Area."

Esther tips her head slightly, neither confirming nor denying. She's going to need to teach this detective how to phrase things in the form of a question.

"If you could be forthcoming, it would make my job a hell of a lot easier."

"I've answered everything you've asked, insofar as I'm legally permitted."

His expression sours the tiniest bit. She can imagine what he's thinking: *This is why I hate lawyers. Arrogant bitch.*

"I'm required to be circumspect. As you know, attorney-client privilege continues after death."

"His death or yours?" She stiffens, and he must see that because he adds, "I meant that as a joke. It's just, you know, gallows humor."

"Do you have reason to believe I might be in danger?"

"No, not at all. Like I said, it was a bad joke. Sorry about that." Now he seems chastened. Good, she likes them off-kilter.

"I'm sorry I can't be as forthcoming as you'd hoped. I'm a person who does things by the book, Detective, and with a high-profile case like Peter Tramboni's, I'm going to be extra careful. I'm sure you understand." Even now, Esther can't escape the sense that Peter could be listening in. If anyone's listening in his stead, she's prepared to show that she'll carry Peter Tramboni's secrets to her grave.

"What can you tell me?" the detective asks.

"Very little, I'm afraid."

"Well, let's start there. In the time that you worked with him, shortly before his death, did Mr. Tramboni ever seem afraid?"

She shakes her head. "Not once. He was used to putting the fear of God into people, not experiencing it himself."

Detective Zelnik's expression turns avid. Wait, did she say too much? No, Peter's fearlessness—and ferocity—was also a matter of public record. Detective Zelnik must have already read up on Peter and interviewed plenty of people—including the most logical suspect, Bianca Tramboni.

Esther finds herself wanting to keep talking, to clarify or amend, but she knows that's how people get themselves into trouble. The detective's job is to gather data and draw conclusions; her job is to give him as little as she can for free. It's an adversarial relationship, and she can't forget that for a second.

"The Tramboni custody battle got pretty intense, is that right?" Detective Zelnik says.

"I can't comment on that."

"You can't tell me what Mr. Tramboni revealed to you. But you can reveal your impressions of him, and of the case, right? That's not information he controls."

He controlled everything.

"It's a fine line, and as I mentioned, I'm being careful not to cross any lines. You must already know that Mr. Tramboni was the plaintiff in multiple lawsuits, some of them lasting for years and costing millions of dollars in legal fees. If his heirs are anywhere near that litigious, then I'd prefer to keep my name out of their mouths."

"I can understand that." Detective Zelnik smiles ruefully. "But it means you're not much good to me."

"Unfortunately not."

"Well, since I'm here, might as well learn more about you." He proceeds to inquire about everything from how she got into divorce law—"family law," she corrects—to when she bought her house to whether she has personal debt to her political affiliation.

It feels peculiar and invasive. She can't tell if he's behaving strangely or she's just being paranoid. Or is he behaving strangely because he can tell she's paranoid?

Then he asks where she was the night of Peter's murder, and if she owns a gun.

"I was home, and of course I don't own a gun," she says, trying to keep her heart rate steady even though she's starting to feel like a real suspect.

"Why of course not? I'd think a woman in your line of work would want to take precautions. Do you?"

"Do I what?"

"Take precautions."

Is he... flirting?

"I carry mace and an alarm that I can sound. I'm always very aware of my surroundings." *And of who I can and can't trust. You, Detective Zelnik, are on the No-Fly list.*

"But what if someone breaks into your home while you're sleeping?"

"I have a very extensive—and expensive—alarm system."

"You have an answer for everything, don't you?" He's not smiling. "Unless the question has to do with Peter Tramboni."

"I've tried to be as accommodating as I can while still protecting myself."

"Why do you need so much protection?"

"I believe you're the one who said I need to take precautions.

Aren't those the same thing?" Sometimes she enjoys verbal jousting, but this is not one of those times. She wants him to get the fuck out of her house. She's been cooperative—well, given the appearance of cooperation. But maybe Detective Zelnik doesn't fall for appearances and he's intuited that she's hiding something.

A number of things, actually.

"Do you have any further questions for me?" she says. "I'm supposed to meet a friend at the tennis court soon."

"The one right up the street? At the Berkeley Rose Garden?"

"No, I'm meeting her in Oakland." She doesn't like how concerned he is about her whereabouts, past and future.

"Well, I'll let you get to it." He clambers to his feet with a smile. "Thanks for talking to me, Esther. Is it all right for me to call you Esther, or is it Ms. Kahn?"

"Esther's fine."

"Have a wonderful day. I'll see myself out."

Esther is left wondering if he'll be watching her, in which case he'll realize she was lying about meeting a friend. Once he discovers one lie, no matter how small, he'll go looking for others.

Just to be safe, she gets into a tennis outfit complete with visor and carries her racquet bag out to her car. She doesn't see Detective Zelnik on the street but that doesn't mean anything. She didn't always see Peter coming either.

The detective is reminding her uncomfortably of Peter and his power games. There was that one particularly flirty moment with Detective Zelnik where he seemed to be taking pleasure in his authority. Had he been intentionally abusing it, though, with all those personal questions?

Peter got off on slow smiles and innuendo. "I know you hate me," he once told her, "and I love that."

He also loved making her come to his office and to his home, summoning her at the last moment. He didn't care how many hours she spent in traffic even though she charged him for every single one. It bothered her that he didn't care about the money; it bothered her that she had no way to bother him. She couldn't punish him and, instead, he was using her to punish Bianca.

She still can't even imagine the extent of the games he played with Bianca and his other wives, but the detective's job is to find out. And he's right, Esther isn't going to make it easy on him.

Detective Zelnik had shown up unannounced the first time, just like Peter had. He'd made himself at home, just like Peter had. Had made it clear that he was the one in charge, just like Peter had.

All these men barging in, probing for her weaknesses. Wanting to bring her down.

In the end, Peter Tramboni failed, and this detective will, too.

TWELVE

"I don't know how you find these places so close to home," Dot says, gazing out at the field of wildflowers alongside a stream. "I mean, we're within spitting distance of a major city."

"Three major cities," Esther says. "Oakland, San Francisco, and should we count San Jose?"

"Spitting distance isn't what it used to be. With traffic these days, it's always at least an hour, maybe two, getting from Oakland to either of those."

Dot doesn't have to educate Esther on local traffic patterns, especially after the way Peter Tramboni yanked her all over the Bay Area like a puppet on his string. "Eat a muffin." Esther gestures toward the box of pastries on the blanket. She picked them up on the way to further the pretense that this is a picnic.

But neither she nor Dot is fooled—it doesn't help that their phones are securely in their Faraday bags—and it's not long before Dot is complaining gently. "I just wish we could act normal again, don't you?"

"Sure, I wish a lot of things, but I live in reality."

Dot doesn't respond, though that expression of hers...

"Go on. Out with it."

"I'm not sure you've fully taken in the new reality. Peter Tramboni is dead. He can't spy on you anymore unless it's from the sky. And we both know he's not in heaven."

Dot's always been way too optimistic, sure a storm has passed the second the thunder stops rumbling. And naïve, don't forget naïve. Esther has taken pains to keep Dot that way despite the enormous personal cost. But Dot never asked for that type of kid-glove treatment so Esther bears no resentments. She just can't take Dot's safety evaluations very seriously.

"I miss hanging out with you at your house or mine."

"I still spend time at your house." Esther tries not to sound defensive; she knows Dot would never attack her. "Just the other day, I was playing chess with Tyson and July."

"But you're tensed up the whole time. You barely say anything."

"If you want me relaxed, this is what it takes." Esther gestures toward the field. "I'm enjoying nature."

"Can we at least try being normal again?"

Absolutely not. Esther is not about to abandon her precautions, especially not with the detective sniffing around. In fact, he'd told her outright that she should stay vigilant, in her line of work. He claimed it was gallows humor but maybe he knows something, and she really is in danger.

"Don't be stubborn, okay?" Dot says. "Just because it's not your idea, that doesn't mean it's a bad idea."

"That's not what this is about."

"What's it about then?" Dot's gaze is full of concern. "Tell me, why are you still so tormented? You kept saying you wanted to be free, and with Peter gone, you are. You don't have to think about anything he put you through."

But Esther still needs to think about what she did. While she trusts her sister implicitly, there are things Dot can never know.

"I had a visit from a homicide detective," Esther says. "I'm fairly certain I'm a suspect."

"In Peter's murder?" Dot is aghast. "That's the craziest thing ever! You've never been violent in your life. Why would you kill Peter *after* you'd won the case for him, when the blackmail was over?"

Because Peter had made it clear that their association was far from over. Esther shifts uncomfortably. She doesn't like when Dot talks about the blackmail. It reminds her that she'd lied to her sister about what Peter had on her.

"Surely you're not the only person Peter ever blackmailed." Dot leans in conspiratorially. "Don't tell July I said this, but I think Avery's the killer. That speech you said she gave at the funeral—how weird was that? I don't think it even qualifies as a eulogy. I mean, what was she saying, that she wished Peter was still alive so that he could sue her for another decade? Of course she wanted him dead!"

"But if she'd killed him, why would she give a speech like that and call so much attention to herself?"

"Because she can't not call attention to herself. Everything she does, people are going to be watching, and following. Maybe that's how she likes it. She could be a narcissist, just like Peter was. You do realize women can be narcissists, too?"

Esther isn't used to being condescended to by Dot, and she doesn't like it a bit. "Leave the speculation to me, all right?"

Dot nods, instantly chastened. "You're right. This isn't my area of expertise."

No, her area is scheduling, coordinating, and organizing the professional life of a VP of operations, which sounds in practice like it's quite similar to what she does as the mother of two teenagers with myriad extracurriculars (multiple sports for Tyson, various STEM and social justice clubs for July). Dot's too nice and doesn't know how to say no to anyone about anything so her personal calendar is completely out of control.

"All I'm saying is, there must have been lots of people who wanted to kill a man like Peter Tramboni," Dot says. "I can't even imagine the size of the suspect list. Peter was as bad as Dad."

Esther looks at Dot, astounded. "You really think of Dad and Peter as equals?"

"Dad was an insurance agent. He could only be a tyrant to you, me, and Mom. Given the chance, he would have been just as bad as Peter." Rarely does Dot sound this authoritative about anything.

"I guess I've never looked at it that way."

"We're stuck seeing Dad every Christmas. You don't have to see Peter for another minute. You got lucky." Dot breaks into a crooked smile.

Could she be onto something? Has Esther been minimizing their father's crimes—meaning, the true bogeyman is still at large while Peter no longer constitutes any kind of threat?

No, Dad's just a feeble old man who's never dared to say so much as a harsh word to July or Tyson. He barely says a word anymore, period. The only power he has is that which his children accord to him, and Esther refuses to assault herself with memories. She hates the way everyone's always talking about trauma these days. She never uses that term in reference to her own upbringing, and even as a kid, she never felt like a victim. Despite everything, she managed to chart her own course.

But with Peter, it's a different story. She did feel like a victim. She still does.

Better to think about Dad. About what she's risen above, not where she remains mired. "Dad was a bully but he was never violent," she tells Dot.

"Sometimes words are worse. He wanted to have the final say about everything, to reign supreme. Don't you remember how unpredictable he could be, that he'd get activated by something and then he'd just barrage us, talking about how worthless we were for what felt like hours?"

"I tuned him out."

Dot hadn't been able to do that, which was why Esther often interceded. Their father would be yelling at Dot and Esther would do something undeniably stupid in the other room, like dropping and breaking one of his prized possessions, and then he'd turn his wrath on her like a fire hose. But he was really more pathetic than fearsome.

Esther always knew that the problem wasn't her inadequacies; it was Dad's sense of his own powerlessness in the world. That knowledge served as a sort of carapace or superhero cape, rendering her untouchable. But Dot had been much more fragile, treating the cruel things he said as truthful proclamations or predictions.

Their mother stood by, utterly helpless and useless. She didn't work outside the home and was entirely dependent on Dad for money and approval. So Esther needed to be the one to step up and she vowed that she would never find herself in the same position as her mother.

"Dad just had a bad temper," she says. "I'm not excusing his behavior, but he never had it in him to methodically terrorize anyone. Look at him now. He's so frail and weak."

"Which is how I like him."

Esther hasn't admitted it out loud but part of why she dislikes the holidays is because she doesn't want to see their dad as this lifeless husk. It makes no sense, really. She's a devotee of righteous indignation and karmic justice, if you can't get it any other way. She should view her father's current condition as fair punishment. Instead, she winds up feeling sorry for him.

"Being depressed and demented isn't the same as making amends." Dot pushes back her hair. "But anyway, enough about him. Your nightmare's over, E. You were afraid that Peter would just keep coming back for more, and now he can't. The cage door is open and all you need to do is walk through it. You're free."

Esther forces a smile. "I have to go," she says. Hugh is going to pick her up soon. He said he wanted to whisk her away for a surprise overnight. It's sweet but doesn't he know by now that Esther hates surprises?

"Off to see your mystery man." Dot's tone is light.

"He's not a mystery. He's just not important enough to talk about in detail." Esther calls him Small—as in the opposite of Big, from *Sex and the City*. When she and Hugh first got together, she had no idea it would last so long. She didn't anticipate actually liking him. And if she'd provided Hugh's full name and Dot had started Googling... well, Hugh's online footprint is not exactly inspirational. As the older sister, Esther is supposed to set an example. Dot hasn't dated anyone since her divorce over six years ago.

"You and Small have been seeing each other for months. Isn't it time he met the family? Or at least got a name?"

"It's still casual. Don't confuse longevity for intimacy." Esther stands up and gives Dot a hug. "Take the pastries with you. And love up Tyson and July for me, will you?"

"Absolutely."

Esther gathers up her blanket and heads for the car. Once inside, she opens up the Faraday bag to retrieve her phone. She finds yet another message from Avery, on top of the two unreturned texts from yesterday.

Let me buy you lunch

There's never a period or a question mark; even a semicolon would be welcome as an inflectional cue.

If Avery were a man, it would be harassment, wouldn't it? Well, Esther believes in equal rights, which means this is harassment. But as with a powerful man, calling Avery out is unlikely to yield a positive result.

Esther could ignore this text, too, but that hasn't been a winning strategy thus far. Avery seems tantalized rather than deterred. So instead, Esther texts back about how busy things are and that she'll be in touch soon. She hopes Avery will take the hint, that bluntness won't be required.

The last thing Esther needs is to make another billionaire enemy.

THIRTEEN

"Incredible, right?" Hugh says. Even though his voice is slightly distorted by the noise-cancelling headsets they're wearing, his excitement comes through loud and clear.

It almost breaks Esther's heart. She can tell he's never been on a helicopter before but, unfortunately, she has. The thrum and vibration of it is indescribable and all too memorable. She's viscerally recalling her last experience of being 500 feet above the ocean. At least the company is better this time.

"Incredible," she affirms, with a big smile. A fake smile, but in his exhilaration, Hugh doesn't seem to notice.

He turns his head back toward the window. His hair is too wild, wiry, and leonine to be contained by the band of his headset. He and Esther are both wearing mandatory life jackets and he thoughtfully brought an extra pair of sunglasses for her. It's a beautiful day, as still and cloudless as the day of Peter's funeral.

The pilot comes onto the headset to check if they're okay and to point out a few landmarks, like Angel Island. From this vantage point, the island looks like a sprawled-out tortoise, its shell of varying gradations of green, with light-brown arteries that must be hiking paths. The water surrounding it on all sides is prismatic shades of blue, from cornflower to teal. It's spellbinding, and yet what she wants most is to touch down.

"Are you okay?" Hugh asks. "You look a little ill."

"Motion sickness," she says, which is a lie. She has an iron stomach and the flight has been smooth. Much smoother than the one she took with Peter.

But then, she suspects Peter had been showing off/torturing her, having his personal pilot do sudden maneuvers. It was a much windier day and Peter claimed that was the reason for the sharp turns, dips, and altitude changes. She hadn't wanted to go up for her first helicopter ride with him, hadn't wanted his imprimatur on what could otherwise be an awesome (and awe-inspiring) experience. But he said that as his attorney, she needed to see his many real estate holdings from the air.

Nonsense. To adequately represent him, she didn't need an aerial tour of the Tramboni Center or the Tramboni Clinic for Pediatric Cancers, or, further afield, his houses in Los Angeles and San Diego. They were still early in their working relationship and Peter must have been hoping that she would be starstruck enough to overlook the blackmail or perhaps even start to think he'd done her a favor by allowing her in his orbit. He insisted on calling their association "a mutually beneficial opportunity." While she didn't contradict him—on anything—she wasn't going to verbalize enthusiasm either. She remained stoic throughout, which clearly bothered him. He must have wanted her oohing and ahhing. But she had a strong suspicion that had she faked her enthusiasm, he would have known and that would have drawn ire, too. Peter liked trapping people in no-win situations. She'd been a hostage, no matter how gilded (and aerodynamic) the cage.

She thinks of what Dot said about how the door is finally open so all she needs to do is walk out. What if Peter's greatest trick was getting people to buy into his pretense of omnipotence so completely that even after his death, they'd continue to torment themselves eternally? If that's the case, then he's at their mercy, his existence predicated on the infinite loop inside their heads. What a weak and vulnerable form of immortality. Pathetic, really.

If Esther's fear truly is the only thing penning her in, then she has the power to vanquish him once and for all. She's in control.

If only she could believe that.

Then as now, the flight had been objectively spectacular. Since helicopters fly so much lower than airplanes, Esther's able to see the land masses below so distinctly, both coast and city, like everything's outlined in kohl. There was an intimacy to the landscape, and it made her painfully conscious of the radiant heat of Peter's body beside her.

Looking back, she realizes that his fatal flaw was on full display, the one that led directly to his downfall: Peter loved flying close to the sun, keeping people close who hated him but were afraid to betray him. It must have felt like the ultimate power, and the ultimate thrill. But in the end, he'd miscalculated. Everyone has their breaking point.

"Are we turning back soon?" Esther asks Hugh.

He shakes his head. When he shifts toward her, his smile is so massive that he looks slightly deranged. "We're going to Gaia."

"Where?"

"Gaia Island. There's a boutique hotel with only five rooms and its own helipad. Lifestyles of the rich and famous, huh?"

"Oh, wow," she says. At least she'd never been there with Peter.

"We're going to stay overnight and then take a helicopter back in the morning." He observes her, his eyebrows furrowing. "You don't seem happy. Is it because of the motion sickness?"

"It must be." Because this is a wonderful thing that Hugh has arranged for her. The fact that they'll be on an island with no escape—well, she won't need to escape. She squeezes Hugh's hand. "Thank you."

"You're very welcome." He beams. "This hotel is going to be a world apart. It's a place where you can really detox."

"A detox sounds perfect." Perfectly improbable. But she appreciates his kind intent, even if the thought of gratitude is, in itself, exhausting.

"That's Gaia," the pilot announces. "Prepare yourselves for the landing." Esther knows from her one previous experience that it'll all happen quickly, unlike on an airplane where descent can take twenty minutes. The helicopter is constantly slowing as it angles toward the helipad and within a minute or two, the propeller has stilled.

Hugh is giving her another boyish smile, seeming almost dazed. She's never seen this side of him before.

During their descent, she could see that the hotel is comprised of five circular bungalows, each with their own patio and unobstructed ocean views, each topped by a living roof of grass and multicolored flowers. She can feel that Hugh wants her to be impressed and she tells herself that's a normal desire, that it doesn't make him Peter-like at all. Still, it's disconcerting that her second helicopter ride also features a man wanting to be validated by her enthusiasm.

A very different man. One she cares about, who quite evidently cares for her.

"I can't wait to see what this place is like," she tells him.

"It's going to be majestic."

"Glad you're keeping the bar low," she jokes. When he doesn't smile, she feels a surge of nerves. She can't even imagine how much he spent for this one night and what he's hoping it's bought him.

No, that's not how Hugh is. That's how Peter was.

Esther's been steeped in Peter for months, so maybe it's

only natural that it'll take some time to purge him. Yet since his death, she only feels more saturated. Corrupted.

The pilot has come around to their door and opened it. Hugh is thanking him profusely and she joins in.

"Phenomenal!" Hugh declares. "Just phenomenal."

"It really was." She smiles weakly.

As their overnight bags are set beside them, two uniformed staff members appear, a man and a woman. The man immediately seizes their bags and the woman proffers drinks on a platinum tray. She seems to have significantly more teeth than one would expect and she's determined to show every one of them in a concerted act of hospitality.

"Welcome, Mr. Warshaw and Ms. Kahn!" she says. "We're thrilled to have you!"

"We're more thrilled to be here," Hugh says. Esther's not sure if she can get used to this new, more effusive Hugh. "Virgin?" Fortunately, he's referencing the cocktail, not the woman.

"Yes. Mr. Warshaw, yours is passionfruit and non-alcoholic champagne. Ms. Kahn, you have passionfruit and Prosecco."

Hugh takes a sip from his flute. "Mmm!"

The woman's smile manages to broaden further, which Esther would have thought was impossible. Esther sips her drink. It's way too sweet but she adds her own murmur of approval. There's an air of unreality to this entire exchange. She's not sure what she expected when Hugh talked about whisking her away but it wasn't this.

"Hector can get you settled in the Robin House. You have a private outdoor deck with oversized soaking tub, and Mr. Warshaw has arranged for an in-room couples' massage. Dinner will be at six p.m. on either the deck or the dining room table, if you'd prefer."

"So, everything will be happening at the Robin House?" Esther asks. "There's no restaurant or bar on the island?"

"There's no on-site restaurant, though our chef has worked at Michelin-starred restaurants all over the world. Our wine cellar is second to none. Your room has a telephone with international calling but just as a reminder, there's no Wi-Fi or cell service and the rooms have no televisions. There's nothing to distract you from one another and from the abundance of nature."

No distractions. Jesus, what was Hugh thinking?

"Our guests tend to be high-profile and they prefer seclusion."

"Seclusion," Esther repeats. She looks at Hugh. "More like sequester!" She assumes he'll laugh but again, she's shot down. She'd rather have a Radisson and regular Hugh instead of this humorless doppelganger. She gets the feeling he's disappointed in her, and also maybe a little embarrassed, as if she's been rude to their toothsome cruise director. But Esther isn't the problem; this whole situation is weird, and why hasn't Hector spoken yet?

Hugh drains his glass and replaces it on the tray. "Could you deliver a bottle of Prosecco to the room, please?"

"Absolutely." The woman looks between Hugh and Esther. "I just want to assure you that you'll have full privacy and discretion during your stay. You won't be seeing any other guests, and the staff will be as unobtrusive as possible. If you'd like to hike, please use the map provided so that you stick to your assigned path."

"We can't go bushwhacking?" Esther says.

"No, I'm afraid not. For the safety and comfort of our guests, we'll need to ask you to restrict yourself to just your path. But I can assure you, they're all equally beautiful."

That's a lot of assurance in only a few minutes. Esther casts a glance at Hugh to see if he finds all this peculiar but he seems transfixed by Toothy. Maybe he already knew all this and it reflects his taste. Or maybe he thought it would reflect Esther's. She has been pretty secretive lately.

Esther feels chastened. Hugh's trying so hard and she's

barely tried at all. For too long, her energies have been elsewhere.

"Hector will show you to the Robin House," Toothy says. "He can answer any additional questions you have."

So, Hector can speak!

"Thank you so much," Hugh says. "Could I get your name, please?"

"Ayanna."

"It's wonderful to meet you, Ayanna." Hugh turns toward Hector. "And wonderful to meet you, Hector."

"Yes, thank you," Esther says, and then she and Hugh are following Hector along a path—their path?—to Robin House. She's thinking how context is everything, that the same descriptions can connote romance or fear.

Privacy.

Seclusion.

No distractions.

No escape.

FOURTEEN

As Hector opens the door to Robin House, even Esther can't help a sharp intake of breath. The outer wall is glass so that the ocean beyond and below is showcased in every room. The entire structure is curvaceous and cylindrical, sumptuous and sexy. There are marble floors and high ceilings made of warm yellow-brown logs, with a double-sided fireplace for the living room and the bedroom. Outside is a teak deck large enough for a dining room table that seats four, two massage tables, and lounge chairs.

"What kind of sunsets do you get here, Hector?" Hugh asks.

"They're otherworldly, Mr. Warshaw," Hector answers.

Hugh nods authoritatively. "Then we'll have dinner outside. Could you please arrange for that, Hector?"

Esther wishes he'd stop using Hector's name. It seems to underscore the master-servant vibe of this whole interaction. Why not just call Hector "Jeeves"? Also, shouldn't Hugh be asking her where she prefers to eat? She would have said yes to outside but has never liked when anyone speaks for her, and he should know that by now.

While this whole experience has ostensibly been designed

for her pleasure, it feels like it has almost nothing to do with her, like Hugh barely knows her. But then, she doesn't make that easy for anyone.

As Hector withdraws, Ayanna appears with the bottle of Prosecco in an ice bucket and two fresh champagne flutes. Hugh says, "We'll only need one of those glasses," and Ayanna apologizes. Hugh waves a hand, graciously willing to absolve her. She asks if she should open it now, and Hugh says yes. Ayanna executes with the most subtly refined pop and pours it into the glass, which Hugh takes from her and hands to Esther.

Esther doesn't want to refuse because it would be like chastising Ayanna but she also doesn't want to encourage the sort of patronizing behavior that's passed off as chivalry. So she says, "Thank you," before setting the flute down on the nearest surface.

Hugh looks slightly hurt at the micro-rejection. She doesn't usually think of him as sensitive—quite the opposite, in fact. She also doesn't usually think of him as being eager to please. If the two go hand in hand, then she'd rather he didn't try to please her at all. Their relationship has always been about two adults responsible for seeking their own satisfaction. But she's not going to remind him of that now, when he's in such a seemingly fragile state.

Why is he in this state? What's changed?

Ayanna leaves them alone and Esther crosses the room to stand beside him so they can admire the view together. He immediately holds out his hand so she'll accompany him onto the deck. It doesn't take much convincing, though he doesn't normally escort her as if she's Lady Di. That's the thing: They're just not themselves here. Is that what Hugh wants, for them to become some other couple? For a night, or longer?

Until recently, Esther never wanted to be anyone but herself.

Once outside, she inhales the briny air and looks around.

The expanse of ocean is before her and while she knows that the other cabins (or bungalows or cottages) are beside her, the arrangement is ingenious. Through terracing, all guests have unrestricted views of the water stretching out to the horizon and entirely restricted views of one another. No one's in Esther's line of sight and she imagines she's not in any of theirs. She's aware of the palliative effect that should have on her nervous system, that relaxation should be imminent. After all, there are no visible threats.

But for months now, Esther's life has been ruled by invisible ones. And the overall oddity that is Gaia Island—an island she's never even heard of—is setting her on edge (both literally and figuratively).

When she looks at Hugh, he's smiling with his eyes closed, his face upturned toward the sun. The lack of concordance between the two of them feels somehow telling, though she tries to ignore it. Instead, she listens to Hugh's generic exclamations and trite observations; she mimics his contented sighs. In other words, she's play acting, which is one of the main reasons she's avoided committed relationships for so many years. She doesn't want to owe anyone inauthenticity, or have them in her debt either. The performance of gratitude is exhausting, and she's already depleted enough these days. What she really wants, more than anything? Autonomy and freedom. But that's not really on offer.

To truncate the moment, she asks if he wants to take a walk. "Maybe from another vantage point, we could see clear to Sausalito? Or even to San Francisco? I can't tell where we are exactly; I'm all turned around."

"I can grab the map," he says.

"No, let's just go."

He doesn't move. "That's against the rules."

"Since when do you play by the rules?" She means it to be teasing, but his jaw tenses. "You must have spent a fortune on this place. I don't want to be told which paths I can and can't follow."

"I signed a pledge."

"*What?*"

"Not a pledge, exactly." He sounds slightly defensive, and he's still looking at the vista, not her. "It was more like a code of conduct that all the guests agree to adhere to."

"Or what? They'll sue you?" She can't believe what she's hearing. This is just too bizarre.

"It's an honor system. It's for our protection, and for the other guests'. We all came here to be alone and if we go traipsing—"

"Since when do you use words like traipsing?" Who is this man? This whole experience, this place, it seems engineered for rich control freaks like Peter Tramboni. If she had to guess, she'd say his personal helicopter has landed on that helipad before. She can practically smell his noxious cologne now.

"This is for you," Hugh says, a touch plaintively. "So you can feel safe again."

"I've never said that I don't feel safe."

"Sometimes you look like you're about to jump out of your skin."

As if to prove his point, there's a knock on their door, and she does, indeed, jump. He doesn't say "See?" but he might as well have.

She knew this was a bad idea. Dot knows never to surprise Esther on Christmas or her birthday; instead, Esther gives a list of things she wants and Dot and the kids buy presents from it, like a wedding registry.

So maybe Esther is, in her way, as much of a control freak as Peter was.

"I'll get the door," Hugh says. "It must be the massage therapists. I guess we don't have time for a hike anyway."

Esther wishes he'd asked her ahead of time about all of this.

What people tend to forget about surprises is that they require intimate knowledge of another's preferences and proclivities. And their dislikes, of course; those are just as important. Often the workaround is to incorporate the elements of generic romance, as if everyone enjoys an expensive hotel and seclusion and massages and roses (not that she's seen roses yet but she fears a bouquet will be arriving soon).

It's not Hugh's fault. How could he know that while she loves a blowout, she hates a massage? They seem to be in the same category of pampering, and the specific topic of massage has never come up. People's choice of creature comforts are as individual as their taste in bad reality television. She'd never expect anyone to know that she hasn't missed an episode of *Real Housewives of Orange County* but can't stand *Real Housewives of Beverly Hills*.

But, by now, hasn't Hugh figured out that Esther's very particular about who touches her and how, and under what circumstances? Doesn't he know that an inviolable principle for her is that people should give consent about what happens to their body and never feel coerced, not even by someone else's eagerness to please or by a setting as opulent as this one?

Because she can't very well say no, can she? Not when he's gone to all this trouble and expense, not when he's trying so hard.

Everything about this getaway feels forced, effortful, and exposing: of him, of her, of their differences, of all that they don't know about one another, of all that Esther doesn't want known about her. It also feels imposing, as if Hugh is trying to make his desires hers.

And now he's coming onto the deck with two women in tow, thrusting the champagne flute at her once again. The massage therapists are both slight with disproportionately large hands, smiling like it's their job. If only their job ended there, but instead, Esther has to disrobe, climb onto the massage table with a white sheet laid over her, and submit.

Esther's therapist says she's "fluent" in many styles, including Swedish, deep tissue, shiatsu, Thai, and reflexology.

"Dealer's choice," Esther says. "Whatever you think."

"How much pressure can you tolerate?"

"A lot." Esther downs the Prosecco and when she glances over at Hugh, she sees that he's giving her an approving look. Why is "romance" so full of paternalistic bullshit?

She winds up face planted as her massage therapist shifts the sheet and does some exploratory probing of her back. "You have some pronounced knots," the therapist says. Her tone is neutral. Professional. Yet Esther feels judged anyway. She wants to shush the woman. That's private information, quasi-medical and none of Hugh's business.

For the next hour, she's subjected to a systematic pummeling set to a soundtrack of Hugh's appreciative noises and sighs as if he's riding on a cloud.

Esther has always found couples' massages to be oxymoronic. These are essentially separate and presumably gratifying experiences that are being had feet away from one another, face down, with other partners. That's not soothing; it's awkward.

For Esther, massages are a source of socially approved torture. She's confined to a table while her thoughts run amok, with no unifying theme or principle. She can't think about work. She can't very well devise strategy or compose legal briefs in her head when anyone else would be doing what Hugh's doing. Massages force her to acknowledge her own deviance through a simple truth.

ESTHER KAHN DOES NOT KNOW HOW TO RELAX.

There, she said it. And in the regular course of events, her propensity to go, go, go is rewarded. It's called ambition. It's called drive. It's even called noble when it's about the protection of vulnerable women and children. But the fact is, Esther is incapable of tranquility. Even tennis—her most relaxing of pursuits—is about challenging herself. It's about winning.

How much longer is this woman going to pound and knead Esther like dough?

Finally, mercifully, it's over. Esther goes to get her purse, the sheet wrapped tight around her. She tries to give an additional tip but it's waved away. "I'm just glad you enjoyed it," the therapist says, beaming with pride, and Esther wonders what it's like to be so dense or easily fooled. It could be a blessing, moving through the world with ignorance and trust, taking interactions at face value. Who knows? Esther's never tried it.

Hugh is dousing his massage therapist in superlatives and seeing both women off in just his boxer shorts without a hint of embarrassment. Once the door is closed behind them, he turns to Esther with a broad smile. "Maybe a soak in the outdoor tub before dinner?"

"Okay," she agrees, because what else is there to do, marooned here without cell service, Wi-Fi, or a TV?

He disappears inside and then returns with two plush white robes and the Prosecco. He picks up her glass, refills it, and hands it to her. Again, without asking. She accepts, without thanking him.

"We could soak until dinner," he says, "and then put the robes on while we eat." He gestures toward the panorama.

"Or we could just get dressed."

"Where's the fun in that? We eat in our clothes all the time. Have you felt these?" He holds a robe out to her and she fingers it obligingly. "How soft is that?"

"Pretty soft," she says. "Like a chinchilla gave her life."

"Humor me."

There's no point in squabbling. He seems to have abandoned all modesty since arriving, parading around in his underwear in front of nubile twenty-something massage therapists. Does he think flashing the help is the height of luxury?

She sets the champagne flute down along the rim of the soaking tub, drops her sheet, and lowers herself into the water. It's not as warm and enveloping as she'd expected; she'd guess the temperature is eighty degrees. Hugh follows her in, and she braces herself for another round of his adulatory exhalations.

"I love that it's not actually a hot tub," he says.

"It's nice."

He casts her a sideways glance. "You're more lukewarm than this tub. Is there something wrong with this place?" What she hears, between the lines: *Is there something wrong with you?*

"No, it's beautiful. I'm just adapting."

"What do you mean?"

"You were mentally prepared for all this... splendor." With how sensitive he's suddenly become, she has to choose her words carefully. "I'm just catching up, that's all. Maybe I was imagining something else."

"What were you imagining?" He leans toward her like they're about to have a heart to heart.

"I don't know." She hadn't even paused to imagine what their overnight would be like; she's just been in survival mode. Perhaps he's seen that, even though she hasn't told him, and this is his attempt to support her. He's a good man, and she's no good at this. "I'm sorry."

"For what?"

First Bianca Tramboni, now Hugh. This is as close as Esther has ever gotten to an apology tour. "For not being more fun to be around. For not being more excited." She gestures toward the view. "Any woman would be lucky to be here. Any human."

"But you don't feel lucky." She can see that he's hurt.

"That's not it."

"What is it then?"

She stares fixedly at the ocean, until he finally does the

same. But there are no more pleasurable noises coming from his quadrant of the tub.

Another knock on the door. "That must be dinner," Hugh says, climbing out of the tub and shrugging into his robe. She grabs a towel and hurries inside. While she hears Hugh interacting with Hector, she debates what to wear. Getting fully dressed feels like a hostile act so she decides on silk pajamas, with a bra on. But when she returns to the deck, she sees that Hugh is unhappy with the compromise. If he'd always been like this, personalizing her every choice, they wouldn't have lasted a month.

A cart has been rolled out to the deck, and Hector has set the table in record time. It feels more geriatric than luxurious to Esther, like she and Hugh have reached the point of needing in-home care rather than being able to go out to a restaurant. But Hugh obviously feels differently, and she's determined to turn this night around.

Hector removes the silver domes and launches into a spiel about the farm-to-table menu that incorporates seasonal vegetables grown on the island. Esther has never cared much about food so she keeps tuning in and out (*sunchoke... ponzu... kohlrabi... fonduta... galette...*). Hugh looks rapt; he even has questions about sourcing.

Now Hector is addressing only Esther, explaining the wine pairings for each course. They include grenache, tempranillo, viognier, and a tawny port for dessert. He has much to say about the particular grapes, regions, and vineyards of origin.

"Will there be a quiz on this later?" she asks playfully.

Hector looks abashed rather than amused. "Since I won't be here for all the courses, I just wanted to make sure that you—"

"I was kidding. You're doing a wonderful job," she says. She picks up slight disapproval from Hugh, as if she's the one who's gauche when he's the one who's naked under his robe. She just doesn't get any of this. He must know by now that Esther cares little about food and she certainly doesn't need four bottles of expensive wine all to herself.

Hector retreats, and Esther and Hugh are left to their own devices. Or without their own devices, is more like it. It's still early, only six, so the sun hasn't set yet, which means the view hasn't changed since they've arrived, and it's not that Esther is bored with it, per se, but what more can they say about it?

Esther digs into her food, which is predictably delicious, and Hugh launches into a series of equally predictable comments about the view and then the food. Does he feel inadequately appreciated for having planned and executed this? Is he fishing for compliments? Or is it that they have nothing else to say to one another?

He wasted this on the wrong woman, is the sad truth of it.

"Thank you for going to so much trouble," she says.

"You're worth it." He sounds downcast. Disappointed. The beauty of their relationship to date has been that they're undisappointable. That's the meaning of casual, isn't it?

He keeps pouring her new glasses of wine from new bottles to match the courses, asking what she thinks of the pairing. "I need to live vicariously through you," he says.

"You really don't want to do that." She takes a sip. "It tastes like berries and spice, maybe?"

"You said that about the last one."

"My palate's shit. But the wine's good." She tries to make conversation: art, politics, and eventually the weather. He tries to respond. By contrast, she can see how effortless it's always been before when the expectations and the stakes felt low.

Neither of them brings up Peter.

So much is going unsaid, and she has the sense that it's not only on her side. More than once, she suspects there's something he wants to tell her, that it could be why he was pushing first Prosecco and now wine, but he always diverts at the last second. Can he tell she'd rather not know? If he has secrets, he can keep them to himself. She's got enough of her own.

If she and Hugh are incapable of keeping it light anymore, then it's possible this relationship has run its course, like all of hers eventually do.

But normally, she doesn't care.

The sunset hasn't yet arrived when Hugh suggests they go inside. He leads her to the bedroom; she's unsteady on her feet. She regards the massive bed.

"This isn't a California king," she says. "It's bigger."

"It must be a Texas king."

"Is that a real thing?"

"It is. Check this out." He pulls her down beside him. "Do you feel that?"

"Umm, yes?" It feels different than the mattress she's used to but not in a way that she could describe or quantify. Or maybe the slight sloshing is internal, from all she's had to drink.

"It's a waterbed."

"Like 1975?"

He tells her he read all about it on the website. "The contemporary waterbed is better at temperature control and contouring. The sense of floating will relax your muscles quickly and completely. You're going to forget everything once you sleep on this thing. And do some other things." He waggles his eyebrows.

She wishes he wasn't self-parodying, that there wasn't a note of Pepé Le Pew coming at her. She lies flat on the bed, anticipating the tell-tale seventies shipwreck sensation but instead, she's greeted by the most placid undulation. She smiles. "It's kind of amazing."

"It kind of is." He lies down next to her, taking her hand. "Do you want to...?" She nods determinedly.

When Hugh moves in to kiss her, though, all she can think about is how off it has felt between them since they arrived here, or maybe before. The thrill is gone and in its place is a note of resignation. Also, she's feeling a little seasick.

Still, she lubes herself through sheer force of will and a series of reliable fantasies that pre-date men, that go back to when she was a little girl exploring her body, not even knowing what sex was. She's going to get through this encounter; she has to.

Is it to protect Hugh's ego? Is it to prove a point to herself, or to Peter? Sometimes she has the strangest feeling he's still somehow watching her from beyond the grave. He wouldn't get into heaven but hell may very well have a viewing box. Or he could have paid for proprietary rights to a technological advance, a simulation of life after death, his brain hooked up to a virtual reality machine. She wouldn't put anything past him.

Hugh finishes and she rolls away. That's what she has to remind herself: Everything ends.

Night is beginning to fall, the sky turning into a riot of color before their eyes. Hugh is on his side, facing her. "Do you know what I feel for you, Esther?" His voice is soft yet urgent. "How much I admire you?"

"I don't want admiration." It comes out sour.

His expression turns pained, and that's when it clicks. She understands why he planned this whole excursion. She's denied being personally involved with Peter but Hugh hasn't believed her.

He thinks he's in competition with her dead billionaire lover.

He must have sensed that she's pulling away. And she senses that he's not going to let her go as easily as the others have.

FIFTEEN

Hugh is snoring louder than Esther's ever heard him. You'd think he was the one who'd had all those glasses of wine instead of her. How many glasses had he poured? Esther never buys the good stuff. She doesn't like to spend money when her appreciation will be disproportionate to the price difference.

Someone once said that the way you can tell the quality of vodka is by the hangover the next day. The better it is, the less you should suffer. Esther hopes that's true with wine, too.

Except that she's already suffering. It's pitch-dark outside, and she can't see the ocean anymore. Instead, superimposed over the glass is a reflection of Hugh, supine, and Esther, upright. She hadn't thought to bring a physical book on her romantic overnight, and since her devices are useless, she's left with only her thoughts.

And a headache that's quickly gaining strength. She didn't think to bring aspirin either.

But maybe Hugh did?

Esther goes into the bathroom, looking for what Hugh calls his "dopp kit," a holdover from his stint in the military many years ago when, really, it's just a toiletry bag. But it's not by the sink, or in the recessed medicine cabinet, or on top of the toilet. Esther doesn't see it anywhere that she'd expect, though his toothbrush and toothpaste have pride of place on the counter.

She tiptoes back into the bedroom area, grabs her phone for light (which is all it's good for at this resort), and then oh so quietly opens his suitcase. Why he has an entire suitcase rather than an overnight bag, she has no idea. Perhaps it's another military holdover. Always be rucking. Not that it matters. What matters is that her head is truly starting to pound.

It occurs to her that she could call the front desk and ask that they bring her an aspirin. Sure, it's the middle of the night, but they're in the middle of the ocean dealing with a clientele high maintenance enough to require their own dedicated hiking trails.

Esther's just about to close the suitcase when her eye catches on something silver and glinting. What the...?

She moves closer for inspection, then recoils. Hugh brought a gun.

To their romantic getaway.

On a secluded island.

Esther is shocked, though she tells herself she shouldn't be. She knew that Hugh owned a gun, and she's never before asked details, like, "Do you bring it on romantic getaways?" But she knew he had it, and he knew she disapproved of him having it in a sort of kneejerk liberal way, and it never seemed to merit further discussion.

If he was going to bring it on vacation, should he have told her about it? What's the etiquette?

That's probably not the right question to ask. She's definitely had too much to drink, and this is not her preferred state for dealing with a situation this fraught. This potentially lethal.

She's thinking crazy. No one's going to get shot.

But why is the gun here, then? This is America. Guns get fired all the time. People die all the time.

She sinks to her haunches and glances back at Hugh, still sleeping soundly. She needs to decide what she's going to do, whether to wake him up and...

No, she's not going to do that. Not because he needs his beauty rest or because he was generous enough to take her on this trip but because there's no point. She's a lawyer, by trade and constitution. She doesn't ask questions unless she already knows the answer. After all, he could easily lie and say he brought the gun for Esther's protection, given that Peter Tramboni has already been killed and that lately she's been so jumpy. Is that what he called her earlier? He said she sometimes looked like she was about to jump out of her skin, that's what it was.

It might not even be a lie if he said that. It's entirely possible that he did, in fact, bring the gun for Esther's sense of safety and peace of mind. But if that's the case, why didn't he tell her about it?

Maybe he thinks that he and Esther are in danger; he could be feeling paranoid himself. That's what an association with Peter will do to a person. But then, Hugh didn't have an association with Peter. It's by proxy, through Esther. Perhaps Esther's paranoia is contagious, and Hugh's caught it.

She double-checks. Yes, the gun is still there. She wasn't imagining it.

She has to think rationally about Hugh's motives. He must have brought the gun to protect himself and/or Esther, or to protect himself from Esther.

Is it possible she's been acting so strangely that Hugh thinks she's a danger to him? No, if that were the case, he would never have planned to go to a secluded resort with her. He wanted to be alone with her.

Very alone.

While it seems almost unfathomable that Hugh would want to hurt Esther, she can't entirely rule it out. This does seem like the kind of island and the kind of set-up where rich people would go to hide their crimes, and the bodies.

She has really lost her marbles. How many glasses of wine did she have, really? And what was in that wine? Could Hugh have...?

No, he could not have. Hugh did not slip something in her drink. He has his flaws, of course, and he has seemed hypersensitive during this trip, but he's not a psychopath. He's not Peter Tramboni.

She should just wake him up and ask him. There's probably a very simple explanation.

That she won't believe anyway.

The problem is, Esther is a fundamentally untrusting person. Whatever Hugh says, she won't be able to take him at his word. She needs proof.

And she needs to make sure he can't get his hands on that gun.

Just for safekeeping, that's what she tells herself. She reaches into the suitcase, heart pounding, and lifts the gun up by two fingers. She doesn't even know what it looks like for the safety to be on, or how she'd check for that. If only she had access to the internet, she could find out in no time at all. But she's trapped here with only a landline. Even if she called the police, by the time they arrived by helicopter, it would be too late.

Too late for what? She's acting like a lunatic. Hugh would never hurt her.

Besides, she's not defenseless. She's the one with the gun.

He lets out an especially loud snore, and she does another jump, her terror mounting. What if she had dropped the gun and it discharged, or if she accidentally pulled the trigger?

She turns it over, gently, in her hands. Then she watches Hugh sleep.

SIXTEEN

Esther looks down at her phone where the alert has just come in from her assistant: *Detective Zelnik is here to see you. Should I ask what it's regarding?*

Esther messages back: *No. Five minutes, then send him in.*

She stands up from her desk, shakes out her arms, and rolls her head around. She does a little shadow boxing. It's her routine before going to court, her most common battlefield. A mentor suggested it many years ago and said that while it may initially feel ridiculous, it's quite effective. You want to engage your whole body, not just your brain, before going to war.

She doesn't entirely mind the interruption, with its accompanying jolt of adrenaline. She should have been drafting a brief for Kiersten's case that would begin the process of exposing Miles for the degenerate that Esther knows he is. But her brain seems to be on strike. It's determined to return to two nights prior, to the island. To the gun.

She's still in shock about it all. Not just the discovery of the gun, but her reaction. After she'd looked back and forth between Hugh and the gun, Hugh and the gun, Hugh and the... she'd finally carried it with her and gotten back into bed.

The only illumination was from her phone, which she was using as a night light because she was afraid to turn on the bedside lamp. If she'd woken him up, she'd have to let it all play out. She didn't want to know what he'd say, or what she would. She hadn't been ready to find out.

So, there she sat against the headboard, feeling the weight of a rather handsome silver revolver, acutely aware of its violent potential. She was scared of that, yes, but also the teensiest bit excited by it, too. It was a different form of empowerment than she typically sought.

She wondered if that was why Hugh had brought it. Did he want to feel powerful, too? Was it akin to Viagra? It's not like she's never been called emasculating before, or a worse derivative.

He might have been bringing it everywhere with him since Peter's death because of Esther's behavior; maybe he's taking his cue from her. Or he'd *always* brought it everywhere with him, for as long as Esther's known him, and nothing's changed at all.

If only she was the type of woman who could simply ask. The type who could simply believe the answer.

She absolutely didn't want Hugh to wake up and find her there, his gun in her hand, since she hates those sorts of dramatic scenes. Those aren't the kind of fights that she spoils for. Yet, she also half-hoped he would wake up so that she could cease to be alone with her speculation, so that he could tell her something so undeniably credible and sensible that she would be able to put the whole thing—and herself—to bed.

Minutes passed, the snoring was unceasing, and, both relieved and disappointed, she placed the gun in the nightstand on her side of the bed.

She found herself reviewing everything she knew about Hugh, from when she'd first heard about his reputation to when they'd been opposing counsel for the Stanton divorce to when they ran into each other at the tennis courts. All the time they'd spent together, all the conversations and the sex they'd had, and really, not once had she found him suspicious. He'd always struck her as a man who plainly enjoyed her company. But all along, could there have been more to it? Has he been biding his time and there's some larger, diabolical plan? Could that plan have even involved Peter Tramboni?

It sounded certifiable. But that didn't make it impossible.

After a sleepless night, she snuck the gun back into his suitcase, right where she'd found it. Hugh woke up in fine spirits, looking like a man who'd gotten a massage and gotten laid and afterward slept in a Texas king waterbed on a semi-private island. They ate breakfast on the deck and she listened to his stream of banalities with only the occasional interjection, studying him all the while.

When he'd finished eating, he tried to entice her back to bed. She couldn't believe it. Was she really that good of an actress or that good of a lay or was he that bad at reading the room or that indifferent to it?

She declined, of course, saying that as beautiful as the island is and sweet as it was of him to arrange all this, she should get back ASAP. She didn't say why; he didn't ask. But within minutes, he was attempting to entice her onto their private trail. All she could think was that if she went on that trail, she and Hugh would be completely alone, hundreds of yards above a teeming ocean where no one would happen upon them and very likely no one could hear a scream.

Farfetched as she believed (and continues to believe) it is that Hugh would want to hurt her, she still couldn't (and hasn't) ruled it out entirely. So she said no to hiking and they took a largely silent helicopter ride from parts unknown back to the road well-traveled.

There's a knock at the door. Esther opens it and sees Detective Zelnik standing beside her assistant. "Come in," Esther says, with a formal smile. She reseats herself, gesturing to the chair opposite her desk, ready to gather more information than she'll give.

He takes a long minute to walk around the office, head bobbing slightly as if he's taking mental notes. "It's very Zen in here," he comments.

There aren't exactly tiny Buddhas dotting the surfaces. In fact, nothing dots the surfaces. He's mistaking clean for Zen. What an idiot.

He finally sits across from her. She imagines his self-guided tour was as much to intimidate as to pick up clues. By her design, all he'll have learned is that Esther's the consummate blank slate. But then, he must have known that from their first meeting.

She stares at him, eyes wide, expression open, politely curious, one professional interfacing with another. In other words, she's portraying a woman with nothing to hide. She has to remember that he can't see what she doesn't show. He can't know that internally, she's still disoriented by the Hugh situation, or that an hour ago, she received another text from Avery. Esther can no longer say that Avery can't take a hint; clearly Avery can't take an overt direction. Esther's basically said "don't call me, I'll call you" but Avery just keeps coming. Is it paranoia if everyone's after you?

"What can I do for you, Detective?" Esther asks pleasantly.

"Don't worry, I'm not here to talk about Mr. Tramboni's motivations. Let's focus on yours."

Esther's cooperative expression doesn't change, but he's going to need to ask a question. She will not crack; she will not spill.

"Why did you take Mr. Tramboni's case?"

"I work in family law. He was getting a divorce."

Detective Zelnik tilts his head with a smile that says he's not buying it, but again, he's going to need to insert a question here. "He's not your usual client base, is he?"

"My client base is people getting a divorce so, yes, he was."

"But he's a man."

"Yes, he was." She will not flinch; she will not swerve.

"Let's be real. You don't normally have male clients. Why would you make an exception for Peter Tramboni?"

She allows a small smile that then gives way to a finely tuned sadness. "Because Peter Tramboni wasn't just any man. He was fascinating."

She'd planned this line and practiced its delivery. Hope for the best, prepare for the worst. She never wanted to see Detective Zelnik again but knew there was a decent possibility that she would. Her gut had told her she is a suspect, though it's doubtful she's his Number 1. At a minimum, Bianca and Avery must be higher on the shortlist.

"Come on, Esther." Now he's smiling at her, like she shouldn't kid a kidder.

"I'm not sure I understand, Detective. What are you saying?" If he thinks she's a liar, he'll need to come out and say it. She refuses to fill in other people's blanks.

"It's just surprising, that's all. That you'd break your streak for Mr. Tramboni."

"People are surprising." If he doesn't know that by now given his job, she surely can't help him.

"You're saying that you decided to work with Peter Tramboni because he 'fascinated' you?" The detective places a slightly incredulous emphasis on "fascinated."

"Mr. Tramboni fascinated the entire world. Why would I be any different?"

"Your reputation says that you're different."

"What's my reputation?" It's a bit concerning that he's been asking around, both in terms of what it means for her placement on the suspect list and what it means for her reputation itself. Did he speak to other attorneys about her? To judges? She's worked tirelessly to protect her standing in the legal community. How dare Detective Zelnik monkey with that, and so callously. He's been barely stifling a smirk this entire conversation.

But she has to keep her anger in check. Anger makes people say too much.

"You must know your reputation," he says.

"I know what I hope people think of me. I know what they should think of me. But that doesn't mean they do."

"They think you're incredibly ethical and dedicated and principled. And the principle that you're most dedicated to, as far as they know, is defending women and children from predatory men." He's watching her closely. "Are they wrong about you?"

Ah, finally. A question. "They're largely right. But I'm also human. When Mr. Tramboni came to me, it was an offer I couldn't refuse." She regrets that she just said that; it dances too close to the truth. Too close to the blackmail. But she can't backtrack; she needs to keep going. Backtracking and overexplaining makes detectives assume guilt, which is ridiculous since innocent people get nervous, too. Esther will provide context; she will not ramble. She'll give Detective Zelnik nothing that he doesn't earn. "Like the rest of the world, I'm fascinated by the uber-rich. I'd read profiles about Mr. Tramboni before—"

"You'd also met him before," Detective Zelnik cuts in. "Had you been intrigued by him then?"

"Yes." Esther tries not to let on her discomfiture that he just scored a point.

"So why didn't you take him up on it when he offered to show you around his headquarters? Why didn't you want to spend more time with him then?"

Shit. Esther hadn't revealed that detail to Detective Zelnik, so how did he know it? Had Peter revealed it to someone who then told the detective, or had Peter documented it in something the detective had gotten his hands on?

Peter documented every slight. Esther knows that better than anyone. It's part of what allowed him to prevail so swiftly against Bianca.

"It's a long drive back from Silicon Valley to my office," Esther says. "Otherwise, I would have loved to stay."

"Were you attracted to Mr. Tramboni?"

"Not attracted. Intrigued. And when he showed up to ask me to handle his divorce, I was flattered, as anyone would have been. He could have worked with any attorney and he chose me." Wait, is she overexplaining? She's a little bit off her game since the detective blindsided her with that detail. It suggests he knows more than he's shared, that he might be able to contradict any lie she tells.

"Did you have a sexual relationship with Mr. Tramboni?"

"Absolutely not. That would have been extremely unprofessional." And revolting.

"But you would have had a sexual relationship with Mr. Tramboni, if you weren't working for him?"

"No. Like I said, I wasn't attracted to him."

"The case ended a week before Mr. Tramboni's murder."

Is Detective Zelnik pitching a scenario, with a motive for Esther to kill Peter? The case ended, Esther would have been ostensibly free to be with Peter, she propositioned him, he turned her down, and in a rage she shot him in the back of the head at close range?

It's preposterous. The detective must be able to see that. Only he's watching her. Waiting her out.

"What's your question?" she says. Unfortunately, it comes out just the slightest bit testy.

He's gotten to her, and he knows it. He likes it. These fucking men. "You worked closely with Peter, didn't you?"

"I worked as closely with him as I do with all my clients."

"Do you make house calls to your other clients? I've been told that you were a frequent guest at his home."

"I was paid for my commute time and the time we spent working at his house. They were all billable hours."

"You didn't answer my question. Do you make house calls to your other clients?"

"No. But let's be real, Detective Zelnik." Hadn't that been his turn of phrase earlier? "Peter Tramboni's time was literally more valuable than anyone else's on the planet. In that way, he's not just another client. So I made things more convenient for him."

"Fair enough. Did Mr. Tramboni pay more than your other clients?"

"No. That would have been unethical. I have a set hourly rate."

"So he wasn't actually worth more to you, as a client, from a financial perspective. And working with him could have done harm to your reputation, couldn't it?"

"In what way?" She usually plays smart but sometimes dumb is the better tactic.

"People see you as a defender of the downtrodden. Mr. Tramboni is the opposite."

"The opposite of what?" She's going to make him say it: Peter Tramboni is the predator when Esther has built her reputation defending the prey.

"The opposite of your usual client."

Detective Zelnik seems hesitant to insult the victim. She wonders if that's always the case, if they try to portray the victim as an upstanding citizen, if they hesitate to speak ill of the dead, or could Detective Zelnik feel a little bit like Esther does? That even beyond the grave, Peter Tramboni still has eyes and ears everywhere. "I'm just trying to understand why someone like you would work with someone like Mr. Tramboni. Frankly, it doesn't add up."

So maybe he doesn't have evidence against Esther; he's going by his instincts. But if he also has loads of documentation by Peter still to sift through, she could be in real trouble. She needs to do something unorthodox. Something she hates. She's going to have to be vulnerable. While lying.

"I look back and it doesn't exactly make sense to me either, Detective. Normally, I would never work for someone like Peter Tramboni. Normally, I'd be on the other side of the case. But I guess we all have our weaknesses and our susceptibilities. I was flattered to be chosen, and I was curious to get a peek behind the curtain. Can you imagine seeing what goes on behind the scenes for one of the world's most powerful men? It felt irresistible."

Detective Zelnik nods slowly. She thinks her gambit worked but she's not quite sure. "It could have opened a lot of doors for you, too. That's what happened for Greg Stanton. One minute he's a nothing architect, the next he's a... what do you call it? A starchitect."

Is this a non-sequitur, or a trick to get Esther talking about the Stanton case? Or is Greg Stanton one of the suspects?

"I can understand wanting to tap into that Silicon Valley referral network. You start working with the billionaire set, you can definitely raise your rates sky high. Was that part of the appeal?"

"It crossed my mind."

"I wish you could tell me what it was really like behind that curtain. I bet you saw some wild stuff." He grins like they've become friends.

"I just can't say." She tries to sound regretful.

"I get it. You do have an impeccable reputation, Esther. You know what I heard the most? That you're tough. No one can ruffle you or rile you." He fixes her with a stare. "You're a real straight shooter. When you shoot, you don't miss."

"Everyone misses sometimes." Her heart speeds up a little.

"Whoever shot Peter gave herself the best chance of success. He never saw her coming."

Could Esther, in fact, be the Number 1 suspect? Or is this just how he talks to everyone, including Bianca and Avery? There have to be some men in the mix, too.

He's just trying to make her nervous. Nervous enough to say something stupid. Which will never happen.

Unless it already has. Once he leaves, Esther will play back the recording she's made of this conversation, along with the recording she made of his last visit. She'll check for any inconsistencies in her story, see if she needs to do damage control.

The problem is, she doesn't know who else he's talking to, or what kind of documentation he's gotten his hands on. It's hard to prepare when she doesn't know exactly what she's up against. This isn't like litigation where there's a discovery process, a whole phase where each side is legally required to show their cards. This is more like poker, a game of incomplete information, and Detective Zelnik seems pretty good at bluffing.

And if he keeps digging, will he find out the whole truth? In investigating Peter's murder, will her other crimes come to light?

SEVENTEEN

You think no one knows who you really are?

As soon as Esther reads it, the text disappears.

It's a Sleight, which means that the sender can choose to reveal their identity or not. In this case, the sender remains anonymous.

You think no one knows what you've done?

Until now, Esther hasn't really thought much about Sleight. Sure, harassment has increased ten-fold since Avery Brengle's app came along but Esther's threat rate has remained the same. That's because domestic violence is generally just that: domestic. Even the most violent exes tend to keep it in-house.

These messages are in-house, all right. Esther only got home a few minutes ago, which reminds her of Peter's first impressively timed appearance on her doorstep. Is someone staking out this place? Is Esther being watched?

She races to the windows, makes sure all the blinds are shut, double-checks that her security system's activated and has been all day, reviews the footage from the perimeter of her house. Nothing's amiss, but her heart is beating wildly.

Given Detective Zelnik's most recent visit, paired with the trip to Gaia Island, and the extremity of Esther's secrets, she's feeling pretty raw. This is not the moment she wants to manifest an actual stalker.

She hates even thinking this, but could the Sleight messages be from Hugh? He arranged that whole weekend getaway, spent a ton of money, and he must have been able to tell she wasn't into it at all. Maybe he's afraid she's not into him. He could be sending her the messages to turn her into a damsel in distress, to get her running back to him for protection. Or he's trying to punish her for hurting him.

Most trolls are harmless. Hers might have a gun.

No way. Hugh isn't some misogynistic control freak. Is he?

She can read people. Can't she?

Esther stares at her phone, from which both messages have disappeared without a trace. She goes pale. Because it's never before occurred to her that Sleight is essentially writing in high-tech invisible ink.

Invisible ink, just like she told him once upon a time, when she was in the position to issue threats of her own.

EIGHTEEN

"This was not unexpected," Esther tells Kiersten over the phone. In fact, it's exactly as Esther predicted: Since Kiersten's husband, Miles, is an abusive narcissist, it was only a matter of time before he upped the ante.

"I can't believe he badmouthed me to the kids," Kiersten moans. "We said we were going to keep it respectful."

"What he says and what he does often fail to match up. You know that. You've been dealing with his inconsistency and gaslighting for years." Esther drums her fingers on her empty desk. She doesn't have patience for the denial today.

These women need to stop fooling themselves about the men they've married. Hell, they have to stop fooling themselves about the men they're dating so they can avoid marrying these turds. Not that Esther is blaming the victim. She's made it her mission to help the victim. But sometimes it can get frustrating, telling these women over and over what they already know, deep down. What they've always known.

Esther flashes uncomfortably on Hugh when, normally, he never intrudes on her thoughts during working hours. She remembers that during the Stanton class, she hadn't liked him at all. No, it was more than that. She'd found him untrustworthy. Unsavory, even. Yet once they became personally reacquainted, her Spidey sense had never tingled. Maybe that means he really is a good person. A good person who makes a bad first impression. A good person who just happens to feel safer when he's carrying a gun.

Or Esther is as prone to denial as all the women she's been trying to save.

"... Miles was an hour late bringing the kids home, and he didn't answer my texts," Kiersten says. "I was so worried."

"Just as he wanted you to be." Esther tries to focus only on Kiersten and Miles, pushing Hugh out of her mind. "All your frantic texts showed him that his ploy was working. He was getting under your skin."

"He didn't even fight me on the idea of the separation. I don't get what's changed."

"At first, he was probably thinking about all the freedom. You'd have the kids, he could have all his nights to be with other women without having to make the slightest attempt to cover his tracks. But then it dawned on him: You're all right without him. Now he's furious. A narcissist wants to be indispensable."

"What does it really mean, to be a narcissist?"

Has Kiersten never heard of Google? Does she really expect Esther to hold her hand every step of the way?

"It means he doesn't give a crap about you or your kids, not really. You're just extensions of him. Pawns to be manipulated. Toys he can play with. He wants you all under his thumb and whenever he senses that you're not, he's going to do whatever it takes to regain the upper hand."

That's not Hugh. Esther's practically sure of it.

There's a shocked silence on the line.

"Sorry to be so blunt but you're paying me in fifteen-minute increments. If I were you, I'd Google personality disorders.

Start reading the checklists. It'll all click into place. But in the meantime, have you been documenting like I told you?"

"Yes." Kiersten sounds terse.

Is she actually offended on behalf of her ex? Usually, Esther handles these situations with more delicacy but Kiersten has caught her on the wrong day.

"I'm going to take care of you and your kids. I can promise you, I have your best interests at heart."

"I know that," Kiersten says quietly. Then she sighs. "I thought it would be hard but I didn't think it would be brutal. That I'd have to be brutal."

Good girl. Now she sees.

"He got away with a lot in your marriage. He's not going to get away with it in the divorce."

"Thanks, Esther." Kiersten sounds a little relieved. "I knew you were the one. So, what do we do now?"

"I'm going to have a conversation with Miles's attorney about the conduct we're seeing. I'll make it clear that if this becomes a pattern, I'll compose a motion that'll light his hair on fire." Esther has the reputation to make good on her threat; it's now been independently confirmed by Detective Zelnik. "Most divorce cases are decided by who's prevailing on the motions."

"How do motions work, exactly?"

"Let's say I file a motion. It will be followed by a hearing where I'll present written evidence like affidavits, and Miles's attorney will present his written evidence to try to counter it. Unless there's a trial, there's no oral testimony from witnesses. So you don't need to worry about your kids or anyone else getting hauled into court. You won't have to say a thing unless the judge asks you a direct question, which is quite rare. It's all me."

"And then?"

"Then the judge makes his ruling on the motion. It becomes a court order, and those types of orders will determine the custodial and financial arrangements. It's supposed to be temporary until the final verdict but usually they last a long time since litigation moves so slowly. And just so you know, I'm very good at winning my motions."

"I want him to see the kids. I mean, they love him."

Well, sure, they love him *now*. They don't know any better. Not yet anyway.

"Let's see what happens, how Miles behaves over time," Esther says. The thing for you to know is that whatever parenting plan is ordered by the court, even if it's supposed to be temporary, it's quite hard to disrupt. Judges value stability. So let's say the trial is a year away. Then that means the temporary order is in effect for an entire year and if it's going well, most judges won't want to mess with a good thing. So every time we win a battle, we're even more likely to win a war."

"Do we have to go to war?"

"I'm not afraid of it and you don't have to be either. That's part of how he kept you under his control for so long, isn't it?"

Fear of change is the most powerful fear there is, for most people. Esther, though, isn't most people.

"Probably," Kiersten says, heavy with sadness.

"But here's something else to consider. Most divorce cases don't reach the trial. That's the rarest resolution, actually. Sometimes the two parties negotiate a settlement agreement before that, which honestly is not that likely with someone like Miles. The most likely outcome in your situation is that someone gives up the fight. They're financially and emotionally drained and they just don't have it in them to continue." Esther does a meaningful pause. "You're not going to be that person, Kiersten. He is."

"I don't know, Esther. He sounds ready to go to war. He even said"—she lowers her voice—"that you must be a fucking bitch."

Esther laughs. "Is that all he's got?" She's surprised he's

going there quite this early but what it tells her is that this is going to be fun. She could really use some fun these days. "He keeps that up and he'll be paying your court costs in no time."

The loser often pays the winner's attorney fees and court costs. Esther loves handing men their asses while they have to write her checks, often in installments for years.

Could one of those men be sending her the Sleight messages? Or could it be Miles, firing off warning shots?

If it's not Hugh (and Esther hopes to hell it isn't), then her gut says that it's more likely someone connected to Peter's murder. Maybe it could even be Detective Zelnik, looking for a way to crack her wide open. Law enforcement supposedly hates Sleight but it can be a tool for them, too. Or maybe it's Bianca Tramboni, still stewing over what Esther did to her in the custody battle. Now that Peter's gone, she needs a new target for her vestigial fury.

Esther forces herself back to the present, back to Kiersten. But after she's wrapped up their phone call, she can't help circling back to the suspects, trying to ascertain how much danger those Sleight texts really pose.

She's interrupted by a knock on her door. Her assistant knows better than this, that Esther prefers to be texted.

So, who's there?

NINETEEN

Esther doesn't say, "Come in." She doesn't say anything at all. Instead, she watches the door slowly open.

Her assistant enters, whispering excitedly, "Sorry to bother you, and normally I would have texted but... *Avery Brengle is here!* Do you actually know her?"

"We've met once or twice," Esther says, irritated by the fangirling and by Avery's hubris. "Did she say what she wants?"

An ecstatic head shake, followed by a smoothing of the hair. "I just can't believe she's here!"

"I can't either." Esther's going to need to deal with this, once and for all. Stalked by a billionaire—who would have thought? Get rid of one and another rises to take his place.

But not *stalked* stalked, right? Avery couldn't be behind those Sleight messages, could she? One clue is that the messages use punctuation marks, which she never does in her texts (just like Tyson, July, and the rest of the younger generations). She's probably smart enough to impersonate an elder, though.

"Send her in." Esther quickly smooths her own hair. Not because she cares about what Avery thinks of her appearance but because it's always been a comforting gesture. Her hair never frizzes or frazzles. There's order amid chaos.

Esther's assistant exits the office, leaving the door wide open in her wake, her body language that of a twelve-year-old girl having a Taylor Swift sighting, which makes Esther think of July. If July knew Aunt Esther was being pursued by Avery...

She'll never know. Because it stops today. It stops here.

Avery glides in, shutting the door behind her. She's wearing a variety of mismatched knits that totally obscure her shape, and a loosely woven beret. In Esther's day, fashion existed to show off a trim physique. Esther just doesn't understand Avery, on any level. Nor does she need to. What's aggravating is that Avery seems so determined to understand Esther. Is it possible that a billionaire CEO needs to get a hobby?

Esther remains seated, her expression stern, like Avery is a misbehaving adolescent.

Avery barely gives the office a glance—in stark contrast to Detective Zelnik's lengthy appraisal—as she takes the chair opposite Esther. She smiles brilliantly. "Well, hello, Esther Kahn!"

It's as if she has no idea how egregious it is for her to show up like this after Esther's made her disinterest plain. Esther spells out in her written contract with clients that if they ever stop by without an appointment and it's anything less than a life-or-death emergency, they'll be charged triple her rate. That's how much she hates an uninvited guest.

"Hello, Avery," Esther says coolly. "As I've mentioned repeatedly in my texts, I'm quite busy. What can I do for you?"

Avery bursts out into delighted laughter. "You are such a character, Esther!" As if Esther exists for Avery's amusement, as if she's here putting on a show.

Esther is momentarily stumped. What do you even say to someone who seems incapable of recognizing—or caring, or believing—that they aren't wanted? Avery has an ego to rival Peter Tramboni's. No, actually, Avery's is much stronger. Peter felt rejection acutely and retaliated whereas Avery seems somehow inoculated against it.

Now Avery takes a moment to survey the surroundings. "You really are a closed vault, aren't you?" She sounds admiring.

"What can I do for you?" Esther repeats, edgier this time.

"Always so proper! I love that about you." Avery leans forward. "How about a little game of I'll show you mine? I can tell you're a woman who can keep a secret."

Esther feels her hackles going up.

"I'll start."

"Don't," Esther says. "I have work to do. I'm expected in court this afternoon."

"What time do you have to be there? I'll get you out on time. I'm sure you're already overprepared." Avery consults an extremely ugly and oversized orange watch. "You want me to set an alarm? I can make it sound like anything. Literally, name a sound, and it can come out of this baby, hyper realistic."

"I don't understand what you want from me." It's the most revealing thing Esther has said, and Avery smiles as if they've grown instantly closer. "You're giving me too much credit. I'm a middle-aged lawyer. No more, no less."

"We have a connection, Esther. You must feel it."

Esther shakes her head. What she feels is invaded.

"I want to tell you my Peter story and hear yours. As women, we need to look out for each other. I can tell you believe that, too, from your divorce practice."

"Family law," Esther corrects. "And we don't need to look out for each other now that Peter's gone."

"Gone but not forgotten. I still have the scars. Don't you?"

How ironic, that Avery claims she wants to support women

when her behavior replicates the same sense of violation that Esther experienced with Peter.

But Esther isn't about to say that. It would be playing Avery's game. Esther isn't going to show hers.

"I'm not interested in comparing scars," she says. "I don't see the value."

"Because women your age were told that you had to be all stiff upper lip just to get ahead, right? You have to act like a man to compete in a man's world?"

It's so patronizing that Esther refuses to answer. She can't believe she's being reduced to an agist trope by someone who wants her friendship. But is that really what Avery wants? Or does Avery want a trauma compatriot? Whatever it is, she'd best look elsewhere.

"Sorry to offend you," Avery says, so suddenly chastened that Esther nearly gets whiplash. "But I want you to know what Peter put me through."

Avery starts talking about how she first met Peter. She was a junior engineer working for Nimbus and she couldn't believe he took an interest in her. At first, it seemed entirely professional, like he was just amazed by how her brain worked, and—honestly?—she'd heard that for years, being a STEM prodigy since early childhood. Then she was a gawky, acne-beset teen, and then a young woman with outsized ambition, which meant her romantic and sexual experiences had been limited. So it took her longer than it should have to recognize what was really going on with Peter. She was naïve, she'll admit that, thinking that since he was married (he'd been on his third wife then), she was safe. She was just his protégé and her meteoric rise had nothing to do with sex and everything to do with the fact that she'd always been destined for success.

But then Peter and the third wife split up and while he said Avery didn't have anything to do with that, not directly, he had developed feelings for her. She felt the same, didn't she?

No, she didn't, and, stupidly, she told him so outright. She said that she was so grateful for his mentorship and support but that was it. He looked stunned and hurt. He said, "Well, thank you for the candor," and then he beat a hasty retreat. It had been awkward but surely not shattering. Not friendship ending, or career ending, right? Not for a star as bright as Avery.

Peter turned exceedingly cold. He made it clear that he could end her any time he wanted. He had been documenting all her frailties and failings this whole time—he actually showed her some of what he'd written—and it was actionable. He could fire her right then, if he so chose, and make her unwelcome at any other company. "I could end you," he repeated, "but I won't. You're too good, Avery. Too precious." He ran his hand along her cheekbone, and she was paralyzed with fright.

From that point, Avery was dancing on a knife's edge, doing her best to avoid having sex with him and avoid pissing him off. He had her reporting to him directly; she was his immediate subordinate, and there was no oversight. Everyone knew HR was a joke. In a lot of ways, #MeToo itself had turned out to be a joke, creating the illusion of accountability with very few true changes. After all, Silicon Valley is rife with sexual harassment and abuse by CEOs but there's been no reckoning, has there?

"No, there has not," Esther confirms softly.

"Peter and I had sex a few times. I channeled a coma patient. He was angry, demanding to know why I wasn't attracted to him. I said of course I was attracted to him, I'm just not a sexual person. It's all my fault." Avery is reciting it almost as if it happened to someone else. "I never forgot what he said. That he could end me. Sometimes I can still hear him."

Esther relates.

"Worst of all was what he did next." Avery closes her eyes. "He took it upon himself to be my sexual tutor. He told me he'd go down on me for 'as long as it took' so I started faking orgasms in record time. But he didn't believe them, so he'd keep going."

"That's horrifying." Esther doesn't want to imagine. Thankfully she and Peter never had sex. His terrorism remained psychological throughout.

"I should thank Bianca. If Peter hadn't met her, I don't know how much longer it would have gone on. But according to Peter, Bianca was everything I wasn't. He liked to go on and on about how in touch with her body she was and how good she was in bed. He wanted to humiliate me, but that wasn't what I felt at all. I'd never been so relieved in my entire life."

"Because he'd moved on to his next victim." It takes Esther a second to realize she'd said it out loud, and that she shouldn't have.

Avery's eyes light up. "Exactly. Which is a disgusting thought to have, but Peter forced women to have all kinds of disgusting thoughts. To do all kinds of disgusting things, and wish disgusting things on other women just so it'd stop for them."

Despite herself, Esther feels a bit of solace. She's being understood and validated by the youngest self-made female billionaire in the world. But then she thinks about how Avery got there, by creating an app that abets stalking. That's not just wishing disgusting things on other women; it's wish fulfillment.

Avery's now sharing the next chapter of her story, the part where she ascends. While still working for Peter, she'd secretly designed the app that would become Sleight. She knew she couldn't tell a soul. The employment contract she'd been required to sign was incredibly rigid where intellectual property was concerned. It made it sound like any idea she'd ever had would belong to Nimbus.

"It ought to be illegal, a contract like that," Avery says.

Esther agrees but only makes a non-committal noise.

"I worked at Nimbus twelve hours a day and worked on Sleight every other waking hour to build my prototype. I never breathed a word of it to Peter or anyone else there. When I turned in my notice, I said it was for burnout, that I needed to take care of my mental health."

"I can imagine how well that went over."

"Uh-huh. He was furious. He barred the exit and kept screaming about what an ingrate I was and how my life would be ruined. It was the only time I really thought he might hit me. I had to beg for my release. I cried like a baby. He finally let me out but he said that I'd live to regret it, that no one blindsides Peter Tramboni."

"Did he really use his full name?" Esther wants to roll her eyes but then she remembers that she and Avery are not bonding.

"He really did." Avery does roll her eyes. "I tried to laugh about it later but, at the time, it was terrifying. I mean, I was terrified for a long time, especially when I went to a female venture capital firm for funding instead of to him."

"I remember when that was announced. You were the talk of the Valley."

"In all the profiles, I praised Peter to the sky but he was still humiliated. Everyone could read between the lines. Why hadn't my mentor been my investor?" Avery pauses to do some breathing. "Sorry, I still get worked up."

"No apology needed."

"It was a really hard time. I mean, I was so excited about what I was about to achieve but Peter would not go quietly. First he tried to sweet talk his way in, and then bully his way in, and then he started making threats about what he could release to the press, the public, my investors. Not to mention that he could bury me in litigation."

"When all else fails, blackmail."

"Exactly. I stood firm and so did my investors. They said they knew all about his tricks and they believed in me. Some of them thought I should come forward, try to have a #MeToo moment, but I didn't want any part of that. I'm not an activist. I don't want my legacy intertwined with Peter's; I don't want to be known as the woman who brought him down. Since I was five years old, I've wanted to build shit. I've wanted to run shit."

"And now you do." But at what cost?

"So he sued me. His lawyers argued that he owned everything because I'd come up with it at Nimbus. But they kept trying to settle, which showed weakness. He was willing to take a mere fifty percent stake in the company that I'd built."

"Generous of him," Esther murmurs.

"Only by then, I could afford great lawyers, too. I intended to take the fight all the way. I countersued for defamation. It was on."

Peter would have taken it all the way, too. It was like a twisted marriage: Avery and Peter litigating for as long as they both shall live.

"It sounds like a cliché, but Sleight really is my baby. I gave birth to it, I nurtured it. Peter was all smoke and mirrors. He wasn't even a good coder. He was just a thief, and he wasn't going to get his hands on my jewels." Avery smiles suddenly. "But he wanted to. He kept coming to see me against the advice of counsel, trying to make side deals, propositioning me for sex. He said our friendship meant more to him than anything. Sometimes that man was completely divorced from reality."

"Because he thought he could make his own."

"See, Esther, you get it."

Esther says nothing, not wanting to encourage Avery further. This will be the last time they talk.

"My lawyers told me to get a restraining order. They wanted to bring up Peter's conduct in court, the history of harassment, but then I'd have to talk about it publicly. I know I have nothing to be ashamed of, but still. At best, I would have been painted as a victim and at worst, a gold-digger, someone who manipulated and profited from Peter's obsession. That was the gossip at Nimbus while I was there. In the Valley, they love minimizing your talent, making you out to be a bitch or a cautionary tale. I don't want to be reduced. Not in any way."

"I can understand that," Esther says.

"Besides, I wanted Peter to keep coming to see me. I was the one manipulating him, trying to get insider information." Avery leans in to share a secret. "Peter wasn't as smart as he thought he was. He loved the cat and mouse too much; that was his Achilles' heel."

Esther had seen his love of it but she hadn't known how to weaponize it against him. She probably wasn't as smart as Peter or Avery.

"Is that how he was with Bianca?" Avery asks. "And with you?"

Esther says nothing. But really, Peter wasn't the same with Bianca. He didn't seem to hold her in as high esteem as he did Avery and Esther. He hadn't been trying to hang onto Bianca; he'd wanted to erase her completely from his life and his son's life, which was Esther's specialty though it had always been applied in reverse. She eradicated men like Peter; she didn't take orders from them.

Esther already knew the Avery story. Peter's sequence of events matched, only his version was tinged with umbrage. He claimed that Avery had wanted to have sex with him, only it was to further her career. He thought he was the one who'd been used.

Peter had enjoyed talking about Avery with Esther, lingering on all the details, including how he'd tutored Avery in the sexual arts. He said it was because Esther needed to know, since she had asked who could hurt him in the custody case, who could depict him in an unflattering light. It was a standard question she asked all her clients, and with Peter, the list had been long.

Peter liked spending time with Esther, telling her his power-mad anecdotes, gauging her reaction. He described his power games with other women while playing one with Esther. That meant he got off twice. Esther kept her disgust to herself because she could see that he enjoyed that, too.

"Tell me how he was with you," Avery says.

"This isn't appropriate. I was his attorney."

"It's just us. You can trust me."

"I really can't. Attorney-client privilege survives death." But even if Esther could, she wouldn't want to. Avery didn't want to be a victim, and neither does Esther.

"You can trust me, Esther. We'll form our own support group: WAPT. Women Against Peter Tramboni."

Is Avery serious? It's hard to tell, but she's not smiling.

"I'm sorry, I don't need support," Esther says.

"There's nothing wrong with admitting you've been hurt and that you could use help. That takes strength."

Enough is enough. No more millennial wisdom.

"I didn't ask you to come here, and I don't need any help." Esther stands up. "I'll thank you to leave now."

Avery stands up with another of the delighted laughs that Esther has come to despise. "I can definitely see why Peter was drawn to you."

"I wasn't having sex with Peter." Esther is shocked by her admission. While it's true, she can't believe that Avery goaded her into revealing anything.

"Good to know," Avery says, on her way out the door. "Enjoy your day in court!"

Esther wonders again if Avery could have sent those Sleight messages, though it doesn't really seem like her style. Not because of the punctuation but because Avery seems to relish being in your face—well, Esther's anyway.

Still, Avery has to have some kind of hidden agenda; everyone does.

It suddenly occurs to Esther that since Peter got off on talking to her about Avery, the reverse could be true. What had Peter told Avery about Esther before his death? Could Avery know the whole truth?

TWENTY

"Checkmate!" July chortles. She's a shamelessly bad winner, but Esther likes that her niece is so uninhibited, that she doesn't feel the need to cloak her desires or feign humility.

Esther fully expected to lose tonight. For one thing, July's been studying up, determined to finally best her aunt, and for another, Esther's still preoccupied with Avery's visit. She feels a little bit guilty, concealing it from July. But if Esther opens the door, July will walk right through it, and all sorts of unpalatable questions will follow. July will understandably want to know why Esther holds allure for a person like Avery, which would then lead into their shared history of harassment. Esther isn't ready to warn July about the existence of men as evil as Peter Tramboni.

Esther pushes back from Dot's kitchen table. She goes to the alcohol cabinet and takes out a bottle of whiskey and a tumbler. Without a word, she pours herself three fingers' worth.

"That kind of day?" July asks. Esther neither confirms nor denies. "You can talk to me, Aunt E. I'm not some kid. I just beat you at chess."

The fact that July thinks beating Esther at chess is an indication that she's ready to play confidante is proof that July's critical thinking has a ways to go.

"You've been acting strange lately."

Like Esther needs one more person to tell her that. She's been avoiding Hugh since they got back from their trip. If he thought she was jumpy before... "I'm fine."

"Is it about Peter Tramboni?" July tries again.

"I'm tired, that's all. I know you can stay up all night without any wear and tear, but my energy is finite."

"Alcohol's actually a depressant. It can disrupt your sleep."

"Good to know." She has the defiant impulse to pour herself another drink, but she has to drive soon. Besides, July is just a kid, even if she'd like to convince the world otherwise.

She still needs protection, and so does Tyson, and so does Dot. One of Esther's biggest fears is that whoever's coming after her will realize that the ultimate revenge would be hurting her family. She doesn't know how she'd survive the guilt if she put them in the line of fire.

All this started because she wanted to make sure Dot and the kids were taken care of. Esther's actions were for their benefit, even though they were never supposed to know what she did. All her wrongs were for the right reasons, only they allowed Peter to sink his hooks into her, and now maybe someone else is going to pick up where he left off. That's what the Sleight messages suggest.

"I've been thinking about my dad," July says, and Esther almost chokes on her drink. "He's the only person close to me who ever died."

Esther stares at July, not liking where this is going. The dead need to stay in their graves. "You've been thinking about him why?"

"Because of Peter dying."

"Peter means nothing to you. You didn't even know him."

"You were close to him, though, weren't you? I mean, you worked closely with him. You were always driving out to see him."

"He was a client," Esther says sharply. "Nothing more."

"I didn't say he was more." July looks slightly petulant, as if she's been falsely accused. "I wasn't even trying to talk about Peter. I was trying to talk about my dad. God!" She stands up and storms out of the room.

Saved by a bout of teenage hormonal sensitivity. Esther sags against the counter, relieved the conversation's over.

Dot walks in, saying, "What was that all about? Do you want some tea?"

The whiskey bottle is still out and uncapped, though Esther's glass is now empty. Dot makes no comment.

"I should be heading home soon." Esther hasn't said anything about Avery's visit or about the Sleight messages. She doesn't want Dot to worry, or to have to listen to Dot's fevered speculation. Dot loved Nancy Drew books when they were kids. "Did you know July's been thinking about her dad?"

Dot leans against the opposite counter. "Must be something in the air. I've been thinking about Dale, too."

For fuck's sake. "Do you think the kids miss him?"

"Tyson doesn't say much either way. You know how he is. Nothing fazes him. But July—I think she's conflicted. On the one hand, she's so dismissive, saying things like, 'Dad brought nothing to the table.' On the other, she seems to feel his absence far more acutely than Tyson does, like on holidays or when she gets an award."

Esther happens to agree that Dale brought nothing to the table. "I never knew July felt that way."

"Regardless, July and Tyson have it a whole lot better than you and I did. Not to toot my own horn but at least they have one solid parent. You and me... well."

Esther knows just what Dot means. Their dad had been a weak person, so weak that he had to bully his family, and so had Mom, who'd been submissive to him. Dot deserved a role model with strength, and that's what Esther has spent her whole life trying to be. But then Dot turned around and married Dale, a man who was more sponge than human.

Esther shouldn't throw stones, though, considering what's coming to light about her choice in men. Hugh's sending another inane text right now: *Just wanted to see how your night's going.*

What had the island done to him? He and Esther used to have a tacit agreement to only text when they actually had something of note to say, or to make a plan—i.e. when they had a reason to take up one another's valuable time. But over the past few days, he's been "checking in." He even used that phrase once, which irritated Esther to no end. She can't tell if he's feeling insecure and seeking reassurance or doing damage control. If he sent those Sleight texts, then all bets are off.

"What's with the face?" Dot asks.

"I don't have a face."

Dot laughs. "Hate to break it to you but we all do. We're expressing all the time."

"Gross."

Dot laughs again.

"Small's just asking how my night's going. He should know better than to bother me with questions like that."

"I think it's sweet. Maybe he wants to take your relationship to the next level."

That's one interesting explanation for the gun. "I'm not looking to go steady."

"What are you looking for?"

First Avery, then July, and now Dot? Hell no. "It's getting late, and I've got an early meeting."

"It feels like you're holding something back," Dot says,

capping the bottle and putting it away. "What happened on your overnight date?"

"What is this, *The Bachelor*?"

"No, really, what happened? Every time I've asked, you've deflected. Did you and Small have a fight?" Esther shakes her head. "I looked up that hotel. Do you know how much it costs a night?"

Esther doesn't, but she can guess. "That was the problem. Being in a place like that sets the bar impossibly high." She takes her purse from the back of the chair. "But it's fine. Small and I are fine."

"See, you're deflecting again. And running away."

"I'm not. There's nothing to tell. My life is really incredibly boring." Now if only Esther could convince Avery Brengle of that.

Dot looks none too happy about Esther's exit but she doesn't protest. After all, the idea that Esther knows best is the cornerstone of their relationship.

Esther reminds Dot to set the state-of-the-art home security system that Esther pays for, and Dot says yes, of course. Esther knows when she's being humored, though. Dot thinks the threat is gone. Dead and buried. Well, Esther will let her sister sleep soundly for as long as possible. She'll only tell Dot about the Sleight messages if she absolutely has to.

As Esther walks down Dot's front steps, she has the distinct sense that she's being watched. She holds her mace and alarm tightly, scanning the street. There's no movement but that doesn't mean anything. If it's a professional, then they're paid to avoid detection.

When she pulls out into the street, she's sure no one's tailing her. But once on the highway, she notices a car that keeps changing lanes every time she does. She gets off at the exit for her house and the car continues driving but that doesn't mean anything either. They've confirmed she's going home, and another pro could very well be waiting for her there.

She takes a deep breath, assimilating this new information. It's not just messages anymore. Which means she doesn't have a troll; she officially has a stalker.

They don't know who they're messing with.

Unless they do.

TWENTY-ONE

Esther barely slept all night, finally dozing off close to daybreak, and now she's late. She didn't even have time to stop at her office, instead going straight to the courthouse. She's running behind, running on empty, running up the stone steps, and that's when she spies a most unwelcome sight. It's Bianca Tramboni, huddled under the eaves.

She's wearing a skintight lime-green pantsuit and python stilettos, looking just as unhappy to see Esther as Esther is to see her. But that's probably an act. After all, what are the odds they'd bump into each other? It seems far more likely that this meeting has been staged.

Bianca fared poorly in the divorce but she's still a wealthy woman. She could certainly afford to hire a private security firm to intimidate her enemies, stealing a page from her late husband's book. Given the suspicious timing of this encounter, Bianca must be behind last night's surveillance as well as the Sleight messages. Esther has her stalker.

"What are you doing here?" Bianca asks irately.

"I work here," Esther responds, with a degree of calm that she knows people find enraging. "And you?"

"There's some custody paperwork that needs handling, seeing as circumstances have recently changed. Don't you dare try to stop me from raising my own son, Esther."

"I don't have any mandate or intention to stop you. As far as I'm concerned, your case is over. It was never anything personal."

Bianca snorts. "So that's just how you do business, huh?"

She might really be there to sign paperwork but it's apparent that she's still holding a grudge.

"You've got your son now," Esther says. "If I were you, I wouldn't court trouble." She tries to move past Bianca and head inside. Bianca blocks the path, tiny but formidable.

"You took all the details and stories from my life completely out of context," she says. "You either helped Peter or looked the other way while he muzzled all the witnesses who would have been on my side. You managed to convince the judge that I was the danger to my son when Peter was the ultimate danger." Bianca's eyes flash with anger. "No, actually, you're the ultimate danger. Because you're still going."

"Tread lightly. You have your son to think about." Esther means this as a kind warning. She doesn't want to do Bianca any more harm but she will, if pushed.

"And who do you have to think about?"

Is that some kind of a threat against Dot, July, and Tyson? "Tread lightly," Esther repeats. Then she suddenly sidesteps Bianca, dropping her shoulder and angling her body so that they narrowly avoid a collision.

"Detective Zelnik is looking into you!" Bianca shouts after her. "He knows you're guilty as sin!"

Does Bianca actually know anything, or is she just talking out of her ass as she did so often during the custody case? Part of why her attorney pushed for a settlement was because he didn't want to put her on the stand. She was a wild card, unable to contain herself.

But she's not stupid. If she's got private security firms looking into Esther—the same ones Peter used—and is feeding information to Detective Zelnik, then Esther could be in real trouble.

A few minutes later, the next Sleight message appears, and disappears:

I SEE YOU ESTHER you've done bad bad things

TWENTY-TWO

There's no doubt in Esther's mind that her stalker is Bianca "Rot in Hell" Tramboni. During the custody case, it was proven that Bianca is vengeful and lacks impulse control. And with the timing of that latest Sleight message—*I SEE YOU*—it's like Bianca is daring Esther to try to take her down.

Well, Esther's never backed away from a challenge, unless you count Peter's. Someone needs to tell Bianca that she's not the opponent her late husband was.

While Bianca hates Esther, the feeling is not mutual. Esther did, in fact, do very bad things to Bianca while under Peter's thumb. But Esther can't allow this kind of behavior to continue unchecked. If Bianca thinks she can get away with this now, what'll she do next?

Esther shoves down her thoughts of Bianca, enters the courtroom, and mounts a persuasive argument on behalf of her client. After the judge has ruled in her favor, Esther hightails it out of there and straight to the police station.

"I'm here to report a crime," Esther tells the man behind the desk. "I'll need to speak to an officer right away."

"What's the crime?" he asks, with only the barest trace of curiosity.

"Stalking."

He nods, unimpressed. "Over there." He gestures toward the waiting area where ten chairs are arranged in a horseshoe. Nine of them are occupied, some by people with questionable hygiene. One older man with only half his teeth offers a welcoming leer.

"I'm going to give you my cell number and you can call me when it's my turn. I'll be in my car." She turns over her business card and scribbles on it.

The man lifts it up. "Esther Kahn," he reads aloud. "You're a lawyer?" He seems slightly more interested now.

"I am." She taps on the desk. "Call me. Soon." Then she marches out the front door.

She's not sure if being an attorney will speed up this process or slow it down but it's not like she can conceal that particular detail for long.

She settles into her car, puts in her ear buds, and starts listening to a tennis podcast. She should hit balls by herself tonight against the backboard. Get in a rhythm, enter a Zen state, release all this tension she's carrying. There's no need to stress herself out, now that she's identified the perpetrator. She knows practically everything about Bianca Tramboni, via Peter. The past is the best predictor of the future, and despite how Esther presented Bianca's history in legal briefs and in court, Bianca isn't actually dangerous. She has no history of violence, and she cares deeply about her little boy.

So why is Esther here? Why not just let Bianca flame herself out?

Because Esther believes in justice. People should get what they deserve, not what they can get away with.

Esther's halfway through her second tennis podcast when she receives the call. Walking back inside, she sees seven of the same people in the waiting area. So being an attorney does have its privileges.

Privacy is actually not among them, though, as she discovers when she's taken to an officer's desk nestled among others. There aren't even dividers or screens. She can hear everyone on their phone calls or chatting about lunch plans; a woman is being condescended to while seeking a restraining order against her ex-boyfriend.

"Could we speak somewhere without so many ears?" Esther asks. "The perpetrator in my case is quite high profile."

The officer shakes his head. He's burly and looks like he'd lose any foot race. He's made for deskwork. "Sorry. But I'll talk low, if you want."

"Yes, I'd appreciate the discretion." She scoots her chair closer. "Could I have your name, please?"

"Officer Connors."

"It's good to meet you, Officer. I'm Esther Kahn, and I've been practicing family law for twenty-five years. I've seen a lot but I've never been in a situation quite like this. I'd really appreciate your help."

"I'll do my best, ma'am." Officer Connors's face remains impassive, but not especially cold. He could be workable. She hears the hint of a repressed Southern accent.

"I was"—Esther lowers her voice further—"Peter Tramboni's attorney in his recent divorce." The officer's eyes widen in recognition. "For brevity's sake, let's say that Mr. Tramboni was the decisive winner. While his ex-wife contested the prenuptial agreement, citing coercion and manipulation, the agreement was upheld. Not only that, Mr. Tramboni was granted full legal and physical custody of his four-year-old son. Bianca Tramboni was humiliated and enraged."

"Are those legal terms?"

"Ask anyone who knows her, or knew about the case. At

Mr. Tramboni's funeral, she accosted me. Her direct quote was, 'Rot in hell.' Then the stalking began."

Stalking is a crime that's about a pattern of malicious and willful behavior, not simply a one-time event, so Esther makes sure to highlight Bianca's repeated verbal attacks, the multiple Sleight messages, and the surveillance.

"I know the law, Office Connors," Esther concludes. "Stalking involves credible threats with the intent to place someone in reasonable fear for her safety. Bianca Tramboni's actions meet that standard."

"Do you have any evidence that the Sleight messages came from Mrs. Tramboni?"

"Of course not. That's why she used Sleight."

"Ma'am, were there any witnesses to the confrontations that you said occurred at the funeral and on the courthouse steps?" His expression is carefully neutral.

"I'm a person of integrity, with an impeccable reputation. If I say it happened, it happened." She tries to keep the affront out of her voice. "Aren't there cameras around the perimeter of the courthouse? You should be able to verify that today's confrontation occurred. You'll see how aggressive her body language was."

He nods mildly, not committing to doing any such thing. Not committing to doing anything, actually.

"Once I file this report, will you be following up on it?"

"Ma'am, I can assure you, I always do my job. I've got a pretty good reputation myself." This is the first "ma'am" that smacked of mockery. This conversation is going south, fast.

That's the problem with the justice system. People don't want to do their jobs and then when you call them out, they're even less likely to want to do their jobs. What's an ordinary person to do?

Esther's not used to being an ordinary person. She's used to working the levers, expertly. She doesn't want to need anything from the lout in front of her, but unfortunately, that's the position she's found herself in.

"Bianca Tramboni should know that she can't just get away with this," Esther says.

"Mrs. Tramboni recently lost her husband, correct?"

"Incorrect. It's her ex-husband who died, and she despised him. He'd taken everything away from her, including their son."

"And you helped him to do that, correct?"

Esther knows the police have an unfortunate tendency to blame the victim; she's just never approached them as the victim before. "I did my job. It wasn't personal."

"I'd imagine it was personal to Mrs. Tramboni, ma'am."

"Are you saying that she should get to stalk me with impunity? Are you refusing to investigate on some sort of moral grounds?"

"No, ma'am. What I'm saying is that Mrs. Tramboni's obviously been under a lot of strain recently and it's possible that spilled over when she found herself face to face with you on numerous occasions—"

"On the first occasion, she told me to rot in hell!" It comes out too loud, and Esther glances around, seeing that the two neighboring officers are listening in.

"From what you've told me, I can't prove any direct or credible threat. We don't know for sure that there's been surveillance of your person or your property, let alone that it was ordered by her, and there's nothing tying her to the Sleight messages. Two heated conversations isn't exactly a pattern."

"Two is a pattern! The first time, one could argue she ran into me accidentally. The second time, it had to be intentional. How did she know I would be at the courthouse, if she wasn't having me followed?"

"She had her own business at the courthouse, correct?"

"That's what she said. Don't you think you should investigate whether it's true?"

He adopts a look of infinite patience. "I will be filing this report, as you've requested, and I'll determine what the relevant next steps are."

She stands up. "So I'm on my own, *correct*?"

"I'm a professional. I take my job as seriously as you take yours." With indignation, his Southern accent has become more pronounced. "And in your line of work, a whole lot of people could have sent those messages, couldn't they? Nobody's got clean hands in a custody battle, least of all the lawyers."

"That's an incredibly judgmental and inappropriate thing to say."

"My apologies. But there's an expression where I come from. It's one you might have heard before, about how chickens come home to roost."

So there it is. She never stood a chance. He's bigoted against her profession and thinks that whether the stalker is Bianca or someone else, Esther is getting what's coming to her.

"Will you be questioning Mrs. Tramboni?"

"I can assure you, I'll be looking into this matter, ma'am. But I'll need actual evidence before harassing a widow."

"She's not a widow!" Esther fumes. "The Trambonis were divorced when he was murdered! Don't you get it? She was a big loser. He's dead and she still wants someone to pay. That's why she's stalking me."

"As I said, I'll need actual evidence, not just your feelings or theories."

Has Esther crossed over into some other dimension? She's the queen of documentation! She barely ever expresses a feeling, not even to those closest to her!

It's infuriating, being treated this way. She could try to go over his head and file a complaint but then she'd just confirm the stereotype he has about lawyers. She'd prove herself to be combative and litigious, if she hasn't already in this interaction.

She's seen this happen all the time. She provokes it all the time. Get someone's goat and they'll become so frustrated that they act out the other person's low impression of them. In this case, Esther is coming off belligerent and irrational. She can't believe it. This troglodyte is beating her.

"I'm a highly rational person," she says. "I deal in facts."

"I'm sure you do. You also deal in spin, do you not?"

"I don't cry wolf. I've received threats before but this is the first time I've ever shown up at the precinct. I deserve to be taken seriously."

"I've said numerous times that I'm taking this seriously. I'm not sure what else I can do." He looks up at her, full of innocence.

To her mortification, tears prick her eyes. "I want this on record. I want my visit here documented."

"It certainly will be, ma'am."

She walks off, first ignoring the stares and then the laughter between Connors and his pals, but they follow her all the way.

TWENTY-THREE

The police are worse than useless; they're actively siding with Bianca. Esther shouldn't be surprised, she's certainly heard more than her share of stories from her clients who've experienced domestic violence, but somehow, she *is* surprised. She assumed she'd waltz in there with her expensive suit and credentials and that would be enough to garner respect. Instead, Officer Connors had behaved as if she were beneath contempt.

She stares at the dashboard of her car, debating what destination to program into her GPS. From the divorce file, she knows where Bianca Tramboni lives.

Esther's not just any stalking victim. She's Esther Kahn! She eats assholes for breakfast! Wait, that sounds disgusting. But the point is, she can absolutely handle Bianca.

The question is, how? She'd issued a veiled threat on the courthouse steps only to have Bianca up the ante. Maybe she needs to pay a visit to Bianca and be more explicit. After all, Bianca gained custody by default, because her ex is dead, not because she earned it. If she's behaving in a manner that's unstable—lurking, stalking, engaging in verbal attacks—then that could very well represent a danger to her son. It would also be consistent with the findings in her custody battle. A call to Child Protective Services just might be in order.

Yet Esther finds herself hesitating. Could she really go there, after what she's already put Bianca through? Part of her understands Bianca's self-righteous fury and the desire to have a target for it. Bianca really thinks Esther's evil, and can Esther fully blame her for that?

Still, she can't just let a stalker off the hook. Even if Bianca's been bluffing and doesn't really know what Esther's done, some professional had been waiting outside Dot's house last night. That is, undeniably, a threat. Esther doesn't want people knowing where Dot and her family live.

So it's decided. Esther just needs to make a house call. Give Bianca a taste of her own medicine.

As Esther's driving back to her office to obtain the address from the Tramboni file, a flurry of Sleight messages come in. When she's stopped at a red light, she reviews them with rising concern.

They have a different flavor than the previous messages. They feel more specific. They're parodying what one client once called "Esther words"—meaning, they're the words she advises her clients to use with their exes to sound rational and collaborative while forcefully setting boundaries ("comfort," "security," "accountability," "transparency"). It's hard to refute terms like that, and if the ex tries, then they'll be the one to look shitty to the court.

But Peter hadn't listened to Esther's advice. He said, "I'll communicate with Bianca any damn way I please. I'll do it my way, and I'll prevail."

That means Bianca's never been exposed to Esther words.

This type of sarcasm also doesn't feel like Bianca. She's been purely vicious both times Esther's run into her since Peter's death.

Despite Esther's certainty at the police station, it's suddenly looking a lot less likely that Bianca's the Sleight stalker. Which makes it a lot more frightening. Esther's going to need backup suspects, and she's going to have to do her own investigating. Officer Connors could not have made it any clearer that he could not care less.

Could it be a disgruntled client of Esther's? No, her clients are generally walking away satisfied. But it could be the angry ex of one of her clients. Why now, though?

The timing makes it seem like it's connected to Peter's murder but that could be a coincidence. Unless it's Avery...?

Avery has seemed awfully knowledgeable about Esther, and the most recent Sleight messages suggest someone who's quite familiar with Esther's work. Avery admitted at their first meeting at the divorce party that she'd been looking into Esther, so at a minimum she probably commissioned a background check. At a maximum—well, Esther doesn't want to even think about that.

But why would Avery want to torment Esther? That seems about as likely as Avery wanting to befriend her. Frankly, they're both absurd prospects.

What if the murder's a red herring, and Esther's stalker is a lot closer to home?

Hugh knows Esther's language. While they're not in the habit of discussing trade secrets, he was on the opposite side of the Stanton divorce, and Madeline used that exact verbiage with Greg. Perhaps he's the most obvious suspect.

Or is he the least likely, since he's always been firmly on her side? For all Esther knows, that gun on the island was for her protection.

The husband of a former client has a lot more motive than Hugh does, that's for sure.

While she hasn't yet been able to rule Hugh out, she has no reason to rule him in, either. The lack of evidence to convict or exonerate is maddening. Esther hates living in the gray.

Her plan just changed. She's still driving back to her office but instead of looking up Bianca's address, she'll be reading through her current case files. That's where she'll find men who fit the stalker profile (which Hugh does not) and who have recent beef with her (which Hugh does not). The suspects will be those who have a pattern of angry, abusive, punitive behavior that's being redirected toward Esther.

Now she won't have to keep it professional; she's about to make it very personal.

TWENTY-FOUR

Esther's never kept in touch with former clients. They're not friends, after all; she doesn't want to be on anyone's Christmas card list. The way most divorce attorneys know what happens with their clients is that they keep getting called back over the years every time there's some new conflagration. Esther's method is to settle matters such that no one wants to tangle with her clients (or her) again.

She pulls up in front of the slightly rundown Victorian duplex in San Leandro where Kay Emerson now lives with her teenage daughter, Naomi. The divorce had cost Kay and her then-husband Rex a lot in both money and spirit, and they'd had to sell their beautiful Oakland home, split the proceeds, and decamp for cheaper environs.

Esther sighs. She's not looking forward to the family law edition of *Where Are They Now?*

She looks down at her phone, at Hugh's unanswered text. It came in more than an hour ago: *You're avoiding me.*

She's been parsing his texts ever since they got back from Gaia, hoping he'd reveal himself as friend or foe. If he'd slipped up in some way—for example, mentioning the stalker to her though she hadn't told him anything—then she'd have some clarity. But there's been nothing like that. He seems like a man who cares about her and is feeling increasingly rejected and dejected. Still, appearances can be deceiving.

She needs to quit procrastinating and see him in person. Hopefully, he'll be able to convince her, once and for all, that he's innocent.

She tells herself that she's been lying to him for months about Peter, anyway; how is this any different, really? But she knows that it is. He'll be happy to see her, seeking reassurance, and she'll be conducting a secret investigation.

Another sigh, and then she forces herself to respond: *Come over tonight for dinner.*

He immediately sends back fireworks emojis. She feels even worse. Now she's forcing herself out of the car and walking toward front steps that are visibly bowed. Up close, the duplex is in significant disrepair, with large ribbons of peeling paint and spiderweb cracks in the windowpanes. Esther hopes that Kay rents rather than owns.

Esther's starting here because the Emerson divorce had been one of the ugliest she's ever been affiliated with, which is really saying something. There'd been dueling calls to Child Protective Services, with each parent alleging neglect and abuse, lining up their opposing witnesses until the entire community felt pressured to take a side. Every aspect of their lives and their daughter's life were subject to intense scrutiny. The documentation... well, even Esther had to tell her client to give it a rest and take a vacation. But Kay Emerson had been obsessed, convinced her child's future hung in the balance.

Esther certainly understood Kay's compulsion. Rex Emerson had been egotistical, flamboyant, and hyperbolic. He took every problem his daughter had and tried to link it to actions and inaction by her mother. He turned every unfortunate situation to his advantage, seeming to passionately believe in all his embellishments and confabulations. In his mind, he was blameless, and faultless. He was a noble warrior.

The case went on for three years, far longer than Esther's usually did, and Kay eventually prevailed. Rex and Kay had both been fighting for sole custody, and for a while, it was 50/50, and then it eventually settled on 80/20, in Kay's favor. It had gone all the way to trial, which cases rarely do, and so Kay's victory was one that would last. Not even Rex was fool enough to restart the entire process. By that point, everyone had been litigated out, including Esther.

While Esther hasn't heard from Kay or Rex for the past two years, Rex still made her stalker list because of his personal qualities, particularly his flair for the dramatic and his capacity to justify aggression with a misplaced sense of righteousness. It's possible that he never recovered from the loss and has developed a taste for vengeance.

The case had been one of the most exhausting of Esther's career, and as she stands with her hand poised on the door knocker, all energy seems to vacate her body. Her feet feel leaden, like they're welded to the sagging floorboards. Does she really want to see these people ever again?

Of course not. But she can't live this way; she needs her answer. So she does a quick rap with the door knocker followed by a hurried greeting and then Kay ushers Esther inside. With no hug, to Esther's relief. The living room is narrow and sparsely furnished, light pouring in through large windows to illuminate the original mahogany accents as well as a plethora of swirling dust motes. There was grandeur once in this architecture but the property has been mistreated and disregarded. The wood is discolored, scratched, and scuffed. The chandelier is missing multiple crystals and half the bulbs are burnt out.

Kay fits the surroundings. At almost fifty, her skin is weathered and her light-brown hair is shot through with gray. She's wearing yoga pants and a black t-shirt with a distended neckline. She sits down in a papasan chair, tucking her socked feet under her, and gestures toward the threadbare brown corduroy sofa, where Esther sits.

Kay has retained the no-nonsense manner Esther always appreciated. There's no offer of food or drink. "How are you, Esther?" she asks.

"Just fine. How about you, Kay? How have the last two years been treating you?"

"Not great." Kay squints at Esther. "I was surprised to hear that you wanted to check in. When the trial ended, you seemed well and truly done with me."

"It wasn't an easy case. I really wanted the best for you and for Naomi."

Kay nods slowly. "Yeah, that didn't happen."

"What do you mean?"

"Naomi's a drug addict. She'll use just about anything, with just about anyone. I don't even want to think about what she's willing to do to get more."

Esther remembers pictures of chubby, sweet-faced Naomi, though none are displayed in the living room. "I'm so sorry."

"She's not living with me right now."

"She's with Rex, full-time? You should have called me if custody was in jeopardy. I would have—"

"No, she's in a locked facility in Utah. That's where we had to send her because she was running away from the local programs, going back out on the streets and prostituting herself."

Esther is shocked. Kay had struck Esther as an excellent mother, and Esther had assumed that would be enough to avoid worst-case scenarios like the one Kay is describing.

"It's not your fault," Esther says. "Considering who Rex is—"

"He's been great, actually."

"Seriously?" Esther is even more shocked.

"I wouldn't have predicted it either. But we were thrown together by Naomi's first drug program. We said we didn't want to meet together and they basically said, 'We don't care what you want; here's what you have to do. Otherwise, your daughter's going to die.'"

"That's... blunt."

"It was the wake-up call we needed. Rex and I hadn't sat in the same room for over a year and there we were, being told that despite having tried to sever all ties, we were in this together. The custody battle had caused more damage than either of us realized. Naomi started using drugs to numb out from the stress of shuttling between two hateful parents."

"I don't know about hateful—" Esther begins.

"I do. I know a lot about hateful. I look back and I think of how reckless I was. I refused to negotiate with him and instead was always game to go in front of the judge. But it was risky, wasn't it? I wouldn't even try joint decision-making with Rex; I was willing to just roll the dice and leave it to an outside authority who didn't really know us or Naomi. With all those CPS reports we filed, it's amazing either of us were awarded custody. I mean, the judge could have decided to put Naomi in foster care."

"I would never have let that happen."

Kay gives her a dubious look. "You're a hard worker, Esther, but you don't control everything. And at the end of the day, Naomi's my child, not yours. I should never have taken those kinds of chances with her life."

Esther is tempted to defend her work—she's no renegade!—but that's not why she's here. Better to just get through this as efficiently as possible. No relitigating anything, especially not her conduct.

"I followed all your instructions to the letter," Kay continues. "No badmouthing, and document everything. But Naomi's a smart girl. She saw that I was stressed and preoccupied. She could tell that Rex and I hated each other. Knowing that she had both of us inside her, she started to hate herself. She just wanted to escape. At least, that's what her drug counselors surmise. She doesn't really open up to them that much."

"It sounds like a pretty reductionist theory to me. Blaming the parents when Naomi needs to take personal responsibility. She's not a little girl anymore."

"But you believe in blaming the parents. Or at least, one parent." Kay looks at Esther with a face full of pain. "I hated him, just like you wanted me to."

Now wait a minute... "Your feelings were your own. They were based on his behavior."

"I don't have room for feelings toward Rex anymore." Kay looks down, picks at an already bloodied cuticle. "I have too many about Naomi, and about myself."

"Do you think Rex has room for feelings?" Like about a certain opposing attorney? "He was pretty angry with how the case turned out. He seemed to think he was the true victim."

"You might be surprised by how much he's changed."

"I'd love to see for myself," Esther says.

"Let me text and see if he's able to stop by. I bet he wouldn't mind showing you the kind of father he really is."

This is almost too easy. Esther feels a bit guilty for manipulating a mother who's so obviously tormented. But she can't do anything for Kay or Naomi now; she has to help herself. Besides, this visit could prove cathartic for Kay. Isn't it good for people to talk it all out? People who aren't Esther, that is.

Kay busies herself with her phone and then looks up. "He'll be here in about fifteen minutes."

Esther and Kay engage in small talk until his arrival. Rex looks the same, redheaded and freckled, in a loud print shirt and skinny jeans that belong on a Gen Zer. While Kay was letting him in, Esther took the papasan chair, leaving the couch for the formerly married couple.

"Well," Rex says, "this isn't awkward at all!" One side of his mouth lifts sardonically.

"Kay caught me up on what's been going on with Naomi," Esther says. "I'm really sorry." This is intended as a pleasantry, not an admission of guilt. Like Kay said, Esther can't control everything.

"There's no need for condolences. She's not dead." Rex isn't glaring at Esther, but his gaze isn't especially friendly either.

"She's only fourteen," Kay says. "There's plenty of time for her to turn things around." Esther has the impression Kay's been telling herself that often.

"Absolutely." Rex nods his head with great authority, which Kay seems to appreciate.

It's one of the things Esther remembers vividly, his penchant for definitive gestures to accompany his definitive statements. No matter what he said—how contrived or farfetched or just plain dishonest it was—he never lacked conviction.

"Are you two back together?" Esther asks.

They both burst out laughing. "God, no," Kay says, though Esther can feel there's a certain fondness between them, perhaps a sort of foxhole camaraderie.

"Well, it's great that you're co-parenting so well," Esther says.

"I just wish we'd done it years ago," Rex says. "I wish our attorneys had encouraged us in that direction. But I get that it's just the system. It's how you people do things."

The Rex that Esther knew was constantly launching into tirades and casting stones, seething and glaring, seemingly incapable of taking someone else's perspective or recognizing his own faults. Maybe he really has changed. But his transformation may have come too late. Who knows whether Naomi will ever recover?

Esther feels uneasy. She used to think of this case as an unqualified victory. Defeat one bad man, move on to the next.

She never promised happily ever after. She's not a miracle worker, just an attorney.

She wishes their family all the best, says she'll keep Naomi in her thoughts, and then hurries out of the duplex.

She does hope Naomi is getting the help she needs but Esther doesn't intend to think about the Emersons any more than she has to. And right now, she doesn't have to. She can rule out Rex.

The stalker search goes on. Unfortunately, the man coming over for dinner tonight might be her prime suspect.

TWENTY-FIVE

"Enchanted forest or haunted wood?" Hugh jokes. "You be the judge!" His nervousness is palpable.

But what does it mean? Esther has no idea what criteria or rubric to use in a situation like this. She doesn't know how he should be acting or how she should, which details are clues. He could be nervous because he can feel she's been pulling away and he doesn't want to lose her, or it could be because he's been leading some sort of double life. All she knows for sure is that she hates this.

She continues to doggedly spoon the takeout Chinese onto plates. She rarely lets anyone in her yard, it's her own special landscape, and while she realizes she's never told Hugh that, she's still slightly annoyed by his reaction. Maybe this was actually a test. She wanted to see if he could appreciate a place like this, where the beauty is gnarly and overgrown and even a bit forbidding.

He's clearly failed.

He must sense her displeasure because he adds hastily, "I love it, though!" She doesn't believe him. But does one white lie mean he's a stalker? Maybe, maybe not.

And then there's Avery, continuing to swim in the suspect pool. An hour ago, Esther received another infernal text: *Still here*

It seems less like a threat and more of a reassurance, as if Avery is saying she hasn't been scared off by Esther's hard exterior. But Esther isn't a nut to be cracked; all she wants is to be left alone. Could Avery possibly be missing that, or does she simply think she knows better, from one trauma survivor to another?

Then not even a minute later, a Sleight message had come in: FUCK YOU ESTHER

No period on the end.

And could that timing have been coincidental? Or could Avery be that much of a two-faced psychopath that with one side of her mouth she's sweet-talking and with the other she's attacking? That message was the most openly aggressive yet, or at least, it's a rhetorically different form of aggression. Highly direct, which seems to be Avery's style.

"You're so far away," Hugh says. He's sitting across from her at the picnic table and pats the bench beside him. "Could you come sit by me, please?"

"I'm left-handed. You're right-handed. We'd keep bumping arms."

His eyebrows furrow. "Something's changed. Is it because of the resort? I'm sorry I didn't gauge your taste correctly. Next time I'll know that you don't really like to get away from it all."

"It's not about the resort. That was very sweet of you. I've told you that how many times now? I've thanked you how many times now?" Her tone is verging on testy.

It's probably wrong tactically. She should be ingratiating herself so that he'll feel guilty and want to come clean. Or at least act normal, posing innocuous questions with potentially revealing answers. She may not know how to do a police interrogation but she certainly knows how to do a cross-examination.

She knows how to trip up a man. Yet sitting across from Hugh, she's drawing a blank. The fact is, she doesn't want to do this. She cares about him more than she ever meant to. Maybe that means it's gone on too long.

"Well, you're very welcome." Hugh's smile is tight as he reaches for his fork. "I just thought that since you like to keep secrets, I'd take you to a secret island."

She stares at him. What's he saying, exactly?

"It's been a while now, Esther. Why can't people just know about us? What do we have to hide?"

Oh, so he was referencing their relationship.

"I'm not suggesting a press release or that we go Instagram official or whatever the fuck. But lately it seems to me that it's more work to stay private than to be public. We don't have to eat in a rabbit warren when we could be in a restaurant."

"I love it back here." It's true, she does, though she realizes she could stand to install a few more outside lights. If someone did breach her perimeter, they'd have way too many spots to hide.

He smiles with what seems to be true affection, but how can she know for sure? "Come on, Esther, let's do this thing. Let's be like any other couple."

"I've never wanted to be like any other couple." Or any other individual, for that matter. She's comfortable in her skin, living according to her rules. Now Hugh wants to change them. Why? And why now? Those are the questions any police detective is supposed to ask when considering a motive.

"Why now?" she says, trying to sound casual.

"Why not now?" he counters. "I'm not trying to marry you. I'm not saying you should introduce me to Dot and the kids. We don't need to go out of our way to do anything. We just need to stop avoiding the light of day. I'm too damn old to be anyone's dirty secret."

"Who said anything about dirty?" She's trying to make a

joke but really, her head is spinning. She feels like he's just given her a big clue that she doesn't know how to interpret.

"Just think it over, okay? We don't need to decide anything tonight."

"Okay." She looks down at her plate in consternation. Her stomach's in knots.

He starts eating, then pauses as if he's just remembered something. "Funny coincidence. I got a custody evaluator assigned to one of my cases. Guess who it is?" He looks at her expectantly.

"No idea."

"Just guess."

"Raymond Yee." In no mood for games, she plucks a name out of the air.

"Raymond Yee? What the...? No, it's Wilfred von Holten. Mr. Sweater Vest himself. What, you don't remember the case that brought us together?" Hugh looks slightly hurt, and that kind of thin-skinned reaction takes her right back to the island. Back to the gun.

"I remember the Stanton divorce." It had also brought Esther and Peter Tramboni together.

She reaches for her highball glass. It's only got one finger of whiskey; it's here for an emergency as she's not normally much of a drinker, especially not in front of Hugh. He's been sober for years but she likes to show respect. She still doesn't understand why he seemed so determined to get her drunk on Gaia Island.

He's watching her closely. No, actually, he's watching the glass. Is he yearning for a drink because he's innocent, or because he's guilty?

She doesn't want to stress out Hugh to the point that it could have an impact on his sobriety. But she doesn't see how she can rule him out as a suspect without asking some direct questions. Maybe that's the best way, to just go right at him and observe his reaction. Or could she actually believe whatever it is he says?

It occurs to her that that is, in fact, how many people approach their relationships. When they have fears or doubts, they approach their partners with candor and trust. But Esther's never had a true partner, has she? She's never been that way with anyone in her life. Not even with Dot.

"Where were you today?" Hugh asks. "In the afternoon?"

Wait, is Hugh seriously questioning her whereabouts? "Excuse me?"

"I called and your assistant said you were out of the office."

"She's not supposed to be giving away that much information. She should have said I was unavailable and taken a message." Esther's assistant doesn't know anything about Hugh, thinks he's just another opposing counsel.

"It wasn't much information."

"Why were you calling my assistant instead of calling or texting me directly?" Esther finishes off the whiskey.

"Because all week you've been acting like I'm an interruption. Like I'm an annoyance. So I was trying to find a time that's convenient. I was trying to be nice, for Christ's sake." He stares at her, aggrieved. "What the hell do you think of me?"

"It was a crazy week. I just..." She can't believe that he's turned the tables, that now she's the one floundering. Either he's got a real knack for playing the good guy, or he actually is one. How on earth is she supposed to know the difference?

He hesitates. "There's something I need to tell you, and you're not going to like it. Should I just come out with it?" Esther forces a nod. "A detective paid me a visit. He's investigating the Tramboni murder. From what he said, I gathered he'd already questioned you."

"Yes, he already has." Twice.

"I'm loyal to you, Esther. One hundred percent. I gave him nothing."

Hugh has nothing to give. Esther's been circumspect throughout their entire relationship. It's her way of life. But his wording suggests that he'd held something back.

"What did the detective want to know?" she asks.

"He was looking for hearsay. What did I know about the Tramboni divorce case? What were your feelings about Peter Tramboni? Like I said, I gave him nothing."

"But he already knew about you and me?"

"I assumed you'd told him."

"No, he never asked about that." So someone else told him. But who could that source have been? She'd hoped that Detective Zelnik would have moved on to other suspects by now. Instead, he's digging deeper.

"Do you have an alibi for that night?" Hugh says.

"I was home alone."

"And you obviously don't have any reason to kill Peter." She has the sense that Hugh would like to be reassured about that.

"Of course I had no reason to kill Peter. He was loathsome, but anyone who worked closely with him would have that same impression. Did you tell the detective what I felt for Peter?"

"I don't know what you felt for Peter. I don't know what you feel for anyone, including me." Hugh runs his hand through his hair, making it stand on end.

Esther can tell that he wants to ask more. No, he wants her to volunteer more.

When it's apparent that's not going to happen, he says, "So where were you this afternoon?"

It's not the moment to say, "None of your business." She wants him in her corner since he's on Detective Zelnik's radar. Telling the truth could ensure his continued trust in her. "I was meeting with an old client."

"Why didn't you just have her come to the office?"

"It was a social call. I've been thinking that I'd like to follow up on some of my old cases. You know, see where they are in their lives now."

He looks at her with mock horror. "What are you, a masochist?"

"Do you keep in touch with your old clients?"

"For the high-conflict divorces? Sure. Because most of them are still current clients. They keep turning up like bad pennies. The kids are a little older so now they need to battle it out over karate lessons or sleepaway camp or some other pretext. Cha-ching!"

She feels a note of revulsion. This is why she thought he was a bottom feeder when she first went up against him.

Which is a definite clue.

"I get it," he says. "You're better than me."

"That's not what I said."

"You might get the quickest settlements in the West but that doesn't make you a saint." Does his sudden anger make him a sinner?

She can't do this anymore.

She stands up, holding her still-full plate. "It's good to see you, and I appreciate how you handled the situation with Detective Zelnik, but I should call it a night."

"You're not inviting me in?"

"I have an early day tomorrow."

"So do I. But I want to sleep next to you. Okay, Esther? We can go right to sleep." He's turned pleading, which would be unattractive under the best of circumstances.

"You can take the rest of the food home." She sets her plate down in order to pack up the containers and put them back into the paper bag from whence they came.

"If you're mad, you need to say it."

"I don't need to do anything. And I'll never have a man dictate to me. I really think you should go."

While it's not the smartest move, given that Hugh must still have Detective Zelnik's business card, Esther just can't be smart right now. She walks out of the garden and into the house. She'll clean up after he's gone.

She hides in the shadows near her kitchen window, peering out at him. He's still seated, hunched over. When he stands up, she half-expects him to follow her into the house. Not that she wants that, not at all, but then why is she a little bit disappointed when she sees him walk toward the front gate?

She's alone again. Which is what she wanted, right?

Regardless, it's what she needs.

But with her stalker on the loose, who knows what she's going to get.

TWENTY-SIX

Love to see you sweat, Esther

It's just after 5 a.m. when the latest Sleight message comes in with its distinctively ominous ping. Esther's lying in her darkened bedroom, but she's been awake much of the night, thinking back over her conversation with Hugh, dissecting every word, revisiting choice moments from their relationship, still no closer to a conclusion.

She sits bolt upright, slapping on the lamp. How does her stalker know she's awake? Could they have bugged her bedroom with a night vision camera?

No, there's no way. She had the place swept two days ago and, besides, she has security cameras. There haven't been any intruders.

Her stalker must have been making an educated guess. Anyone receiving anonymous threats would be feeling the heat. They'd start to panic; they'd make mistakes.

But Esther is not going to let her haters win. Detective Zelnik's mandate is to catch a murderer; hers is to catch a stalker. She isn't sure if the perpetrators are one and the same, though it would be great if they were. She's always valued efficiency.

Esther reminds herself that her stalker hasn't really demonstrated any specific knowledge of her crimes, that it's all been innuendo designed to make her mind run amok. She's supposed to fill in the blanks and torture herself. She refuses to play that game.

Peter's game?

No, Peter's dead. He can't play anymore. But someone might have adopted his rules.

Esther's gut says that Bianca doesn't fit the profile. So maybe it's Avery, or Hugh, or one of the ex-husbands that Esther still needs to investigate.

She can't allow herself to get sloppy, not when Detective Zelnik is nosing around. He clearly hasn't taken her off the suspect list (if anything, she seems to have risen higher, given the time and resources he's devoted). He must be reasonably good at his job since he was able to find out about Hugh. She didn't kill Peter Tramboni but there are other crimes.

She hauls herself out of bed and down the stairs. While she generally doesn't do much cooking, she can make a mean French toast, varying the spice blend every time. Perhaps some garam masala, anise, and cinnamon would help awaken her appetite.

She sets to work rather joylessly but at a certain point, the muscle memory, the scents, and the sound of the sizzling pan act on her. It's the first positive anticipation she's experienced in weeks.

She eats both pieces of French toast with gusto, and then makes another. She's enjoying her defiance—*see, Stalker? I'm not sweating, I'm savoring!*—and realizes she's lost track of time. She's even lost track of her phone. It must still be upstairs. But it's barely 6 a.m., and there's nowhere she needs to be right now.

Esther closes her eyes and breathes in deep, hoping she can

retain some small measure of peace through her next former client visit with the Tillmans.

Julianne Tillman always struck Esther as soft: in temperament, in voice, even in appearance (her hair, skin, and waistline). She seemed to take it for granted that there was more kindness than cruelty in the world, and justice would always prevail. That presumption had rankled Esther, as it could lead to complacency. (Julianne's documentation had often been subpar.) Esther's first order of business had been to get Julianne good and calloused.

As Esther washes up the breakfast dishes, she wonders how much will have changed. Kay and Rex Emerson had certainly offered up a few surprises.

An hour later, Esther pulls up in front of a well-tended Craftsman in a neighborhood adjacent to hers. Julianne loved that house. She'd desperately wanted to hang onto it in the divorce settlement; it had been her one non-negotiable, though Esther had pushed for others, particularly around custody. Julianne had been raised in a nearly identical house, with a warm and loving upbringing that had predisposed her to see the best in everyone. That included her ex-husband, Xander. One of Esther's biggest challenges had been smashing Julianne's rose-colored glasses so that she could finally see the truth.

Now, sitting in Julianne's cozy living room with a mantel full of pictures above the fireplace, Esther realizes that being too soft is no longer a problem. Julianne isn't merely calloused; she's callous.

Her son, Phil (named after Julianne's father), recently turned five, and he has a little play table set up just feet away from the plaid sectional where Esther and Julianne are seated. The Tillman custody battle wrapped up about a year and a half ago, with Julianne scoring a major victory. Yet you wouldn't know it from the level of vitriol and bitterness Julianne is spouting—loudly, and unprompted—about Xander.

"Are you sure we should be talking about this here?" Esther asks, gesturing discreetly toward Phil.

"He's totally absorbed in coloring. He'll barely hear us, and anyway, he doesn't care."

One of Esther's most important admonitions to her clients is to never badmouth the other parent in front of the children. But Julianne isn't her client anymore.

"Are you sure?" Esther repeats, lowering her voice in the hope that Julianne will do the same.

"It's fine." Julianne doesn't take the hint about volume control. "So what can I do for you, Esther? Do you need a recommendation? I'm happy to provide one. I sing your praises to anyone who'll listen."

Esther is a bit unnerved. She's not sure she wants credit for the scene before her, though Phil does seem taken with his coloring. He's carefully selecting each crayon and humming as he works.

"That's very kind of you," Esther says. "I'm just checking back in with my old clients. Seeing how the co-parenting is going."

"Co-parenting." Julianne snorts. "With a man like Xander, co-parenting is impossible. He's impossible."

"What do you mean?" Esther knows she should get Julianne talking about Xander; after all, that's really what she came here for. She's investigating a suspect. But Phil is only feet away.

"He's a narcissistic sociopath, just like you said."

"I'm not sure I said—" Esther glances over at Phil. Even though he obviously won't know what those words mean, can't children pick up tone? Julianne is beyond contemptuous. She sounds practically murderous. Like she thinks she and Phil would be better off with Xander dead.

"You know what he's like. He's the worst human there is. Selfish, arrogant, manipulative. Oh, and paranoid. He thinks I'm badmouthing him to Phil, which is ridiculous."

While Esther had encouraged Julianne to see Xander as a villain, she never meant to... well, she did mean to, at the time, but she never meant for it to turn out like this. Her eyes flick over to Phil, who's off in his own little world. How often does he have to retreat there, with a mother who's apparently become as self-involved as she's accusing his father of being?

"He really thinks he's God's gift these days," Julianne continues with an eye roll. "He's doing all this international travel. Like this weekend, he was supposed to have Phil and he asked to swap weekends but of course I said no. You would have been so proud of me. I told him, 'You get Phil one designated weekend a month. No more, no less, no exchanges. You're not going to steamroll me.'"

"So Phil won't see him this month?"

"Nope." Julianne sounds pleased. "Xander was practically in tears, saying that if he didn't do this trip, he could lose his job. He begged me to swap. I said no, of course."

Had they been crocodile tears, or had Xander truly been upset that he wouldn't see his son for another month? Julianne doesn't seem to care.

"He's married to his job now, and he's just so full of himself. He's not an IT guy anymore, oh no, he's the right-hand man to the CEO, solving crises all over the world." Julianne rolls her eyes again. "Meanwhile, I'm home trying to raise our son with the proper values. Cry me a river, am I right?"

Julianne launches into a diatribe about all Xander's failings. While Esther had a low opinion of Xander at the time, thinking that he could do great harm to Phil, Esther is shocked at how minor the supposed offenses are. By how petty Julianne's being. Xander forgot to bring Phil's jacket and then didn't buy a new one (when it was 64 degrees outside); Xander doesn't always buy organic vegetables; Xander has brought Phil back with unwashed clothes in his backpack; Xander sometimes lets Phil stay up late so that they can read extra storybooks together.

Are these the crimes of the man that Esther was convinced was a narcissistic sociopath?

Esther always assumed that by wrapping up cases fast, she was preventing her clients from stewing in their aggression long-term. Even a fast high-conflict divorce takes about a year. But other attorneys allow their clients to draw out the process for multiple years in the form of discovery, interrogatories, and depositions, not to mention endless motions. She's always looked down on those attorneys and those divorces, thinking that when it's drawn out, people are keeping their connection to their toxic spouse alive. Hate is a way of staying connected, and Esther was determined that her clients would move on.

But now she's seeing that Julianne is still connected to Xander, that she's deeply invested in confirming everything Esther had pointed out during litigation. Even without the continuing gladiatorial arena of court, Julianne still seems to be in the heat of battle.

It's ugly to watch, but Esther's not here to spectate. She's got to stay on task.

"Do you have reason to believe that Xander might still be holding a grudge against you? Or that it might have intensified recently?" she asks. What she means is, could Xander still be holding a grudge against *her*?

Julianne doesn't really answer the question, though she's a veritable chatterbox. It's clear she loves detailing all her ex's faults and she doesn't seem to realize that she's exposing herself as well. What seems to enrage Julianne the most is that Xander isn't still hanging onto her, that he's moved on to someone new.

"I think it's someone he works with," Julianne says, looking disgusted, "though why would he tell me? I'm only the mother of his child."

Xander might not be a very likely stalking suspect, if he's fully immersed in work, travel, and a new relationship.

"It seems like it might be time for you to move on, too," Esther tells Julianne.

"Like I have time to date. I've got my hands full with this one." Julianne indicates Phil. Until that second, Esther thought that Julianne had forgotten he was there.

"It might be good for you to put your energy into other pursuits." *Get a hobby other than torturing your co-parent.*

"You know how Xander is! I have to put all my energy into stopping him from ruining my son."

Esther is at a loss. This is not her area of expertise. Julianne clearly needs major therapy, and Phil probably does, too.

"I owe everything to you," Julianne says. "You put me in the driver's seat. I'm not afraid to take control anymore. Like with Xander's family. If they want to see Phil, they'll do it on Xander's time, not mine."

Esther recalls that Xander had a loving extended family who seemed to adore Phil. But now Julianne's rejoicing in basically cutting them off?

"I'm all Phil has," Julianne says, "which is why I'm so exhausted all the time." She stands up suddenly. "Could you excuse me for a second? I'll be right back."

Julianne seems to have lost all perspective. She doesn't see any distinction between her feelings about Xander and his parenting skills, and isn't able to differentiate between Xander and the rest of his family. In other words, her capacity to act in her child's best interest is severely compromised. And she has absolutely no idea.

Is Esther the one to tell her? She came here to catch a stalker, not stage an intervention.

Julianne heads down the hall, presumably to the bathroom, and for a second, Esther imagines herself making a run for it. But maybe she can still focus Julianne and get specifics about

Xander's schedule and where he's living. Besides, she can't very well leave Phil alone.

She looks over at him and sees that he's looking back. She offers a shaky smile. She's never been comfortable around kids. It's part of why she makes it clear that parents should never bring them along to appointments. Also, they shouldn't be privy to what's going on in their parents' marriages, and divorces. Lastly, she doesn't want to see the pain that even a well-handled divorce can inflict. That kind of sentimentality would only distract her from what she needs to do.

Esther aches for Phil, but she knows this isn't her fault. The destruction of his family was inevitable, and it likely would have been worse if it hadn't been for Esther keeping the litigation as short as possible.

Phil doesn't smile, he's a somber child, but he does stand up from his little table and walks toward Esther. As he comes close, she finds herself stiffening.

"Can you keep a secret?" he whispers in her ear. Of course she can. "I still love my daddy."

Before Esther can respond, he's run back to his table and by the time his mother reappears, he's coloring again so sedately it's as if Esther imagined the whole exchange.

She wishes she had.

TWENTY-SEVEN

Intellectually, Esther knows she's not to blame for Naomi Emerson's drug addiction or for Phil Tillman feeling like loving his daddy needs to be kept under wraps. If anyone's to blame, it's their parents. They're the ones who supplied the nature and the nurture. They're the permanent fixtures, while Esther was just passing through.

Yet Phil haunts her dreams. All night, she sees him mouthing the words, "Can you keep a secret?"

When she wakes up, she knows what she needs to do. She'll text Wilfred von Holten and invite him out to the restaurant of his choice. Wilfred was the custody evaluator for the Stanton case, among others, and he's written numerous reports that proved favorable to her clients. Specifically, he wrote the report on the Tillmans so hopefully he can both clear Esther's conscience and weigh in on the probability that Xander Tillman is the Sleight stalker. Efficiency at its finest.

Esther sends her first text to Wilfred at 8 a.m., which is a perfectly respectable hour, and the next at 9 on the dot. Then 9:30, then 10:12, then 11:04. She's increasingly annoyed by his lack of response. How many people can be clamoring for his company when he's got the demeanor and sweater vests of Mr. Rogers? (She and Hugh have agreed that Wilfred's affectation can't be mere coincidence, seeing as the resemblance is remarked upon by nearly everyone who comes in contact with him.) By noon, she's pissed. They're colleagues, sort of, and he must have picked up on her sense of urgency.

Finally, just after 2 p.m., he texts: *Dinner at 9? Tony's on College Ave.?*

Yes! See you there!

Tony's is an old-school diner with an early dinner rush so it's largely empty by the time Esther walks in at 8:56. Wilfred's already there in a red vinyl booth. She can tell by his expression that she doesn't look quite like herself, and that it goes deeper than the blowout she completely forgot. But then, as a professional evaluator, he's paid to notice.

She has nothing to hide. Or at least nothing that's relevant to their business here tonight. She intends to be entirely truthful about what she observed at Julianne Tillman's.

"Hello, Esther," Wilfred says, with a gentle yet slightly wary smile. He never asked her the reason for the meeting but his energy suggests that he doesn't entirely trust her intentions. She has no idea why since she's never been anything but civil toward him, even in the rare event that she didn't like his findings.

"Hi, Wilfred," she says. There are already two water glasses on the table along with menus that are lightly crusted with food. Well, she didn't have an appetite anyway.

A buxom server in a throwback polyester uniform with a plastic name tag ("Candy") comes by and Wilfred gestures toward Esther gallantly. "Would you like more time to peruse?"

"I'll have whatever he's having," she tells the server.

"Cheeseburger cooked medium well with a side salad,"

Wilfred says. "No fries." Candy looks at Esther, who nods assent. "I've been trying to figure out what would make you so eager to meet. Is there a case that you expect will be coming my way soon? You're trying to butter me up?" He smiles to show he's kidding, but she's getting the sense he might not have the highest opinion of her. Strange, since Detective Zelnik had made it sound like everyone does.

"No, I'd never do that."

"What is it then?"

"I respect you, Wilfred." She smiles in what she hopes is a disarming manner. "I've recently visited with a few former clients and you worked on one of the cases. I'd love to get your impressions."

"You already have my impressions in the report." Suspicion creases his already lined face.

"But there are always things left on the cutting room floor, am I right? There's one case in particular—"

"This is highly irregular." She can tell that Wilfred doesn't like irregularities. But more than that, he doesn't like her.

"Have I done something to upset you?"

His answer comes back glacially. "I wouldn't say so, no."

"Let's forget my cases, then. What are your impressions of me?" Might as well cut the bullshit.

His eyes dart around the restaurant, as if he thinks he might be on candid camera.

"It's just us here." At least, she hopes it is. She has her phone in a Faraday bag but that's no guarantee of anything. "I can already see what you think of me. It would really help if you'd tell me why."

He's really confused now, and perhaps a touch concerned about her welfare. She must have seemed a little manic earlier, with all those texts.

"Tell the truth. I can take it."

"Sometimes," he says in that gratingly slow way of his, "it seems like you don't know how divorce impacts children."

"Why don't you enlighten me then?" She means it as a retort; she doesn't expect him to actually see it as an educational opportunity.

The lecture commences. He tells her that young children (two to eight) don't really understand what's happening or why, that school-age children (eight to twelve) often blame themselves for the divorce and harbor feelings of shame and guilt that they caused the split, and teenagers are often angry toward one or both parents and distrustful of relationships in general.

"There are often mental health problems, problems in school, behavioral problems and substance abuse, reduced interest in peer relationships and romantic relationships, physical health issues and compromised immune systems. Loyalty conflicts are common, and intensely stressful. Once they grow up, there's a higher likelihood that children of divorce will become divorced adults." He pauses meaningfully. "And that's in a normal divorce, not in one of your divorces." His lip curls almost imperceptibly when he says "your divorces," and she feels her hackles go up. "Watching your parents engage in bloody warfare can make you incredibly aggressive or incredibly meek."

"Or they'll fall somewhere in the middle, like the rest of us," she says sharply. "They figure things out, like we all have to."

He shakes his head sorrowfully. "The kids who've been through high-conflict divorces aren't being taught vital skills. They're not learning how to properly deal with their own emotions or other people's. They're absorbing all the wrong lessons through their role models."

"Then they'll realize that. They'll grow up and choose to do the opposite." Esther saw her parents as lessons in what not to do, and it's served her well.

"You're talking about the rational mind; I'm talking about

the lizard brain. These children are traumatized, Esther. They don't know who to love, or how. And they don't always hate the parent you think they should. But they do learn to be wily. What they can and can't say, and to whom. They have to protect themselves from their own parents. Children can tell when to stay quiet, when the angry parent's opinion has to be the only truth."

Esther flashes uncomfortably on little Phil Tillman.

"Sometimes the safest choice is to denounce the other parent. That way, they don't become targets themselves."

"With my clients, the kids know they'll never lose their mother's love." Esther tries to sound more convinced than she feels at the moment. She hadn't expected to come to this dinner—which she's paying for—and get schooled.

Another head shake. "They saw their father lose her love so they know it can happen. That makes the environment inherently insecure, and it makes love feel frighteningly conditional. They'll likely feel that way their entire lives."

Esther is suddenly aware of just how little she knows about child development or psychology. It's hard for her to mount any sort of counterargument.

"Children often get the message that they need to pick a side. The badmouthing—"

"I tell my clients never to do that," Esther says quickly.

"Some parents explicitly coach their kids to hate the other parent. But usually it's more subtle. They say nasty things where kids can overhear and generally make it clear that Dad should be persona non grata in their lives, regardless of what the court says. Too much is made of how savvy kids are these days when really, they're shockingly suggestible. And when they're terrified of losing one parent's love, they might feel that they have no choice but to sacrifice the other. In other words, in a high-conflict divorce, they're put in an impossible position."

"I'm not doing that to them. The court sets the visitation schedule." But even she can hear how flimsy that sounds.

"You know better than that," he chides gently. "Kids can reject their parents a million and one ways. They might be with the parent physically but they're withdrawn, withholding, disrespectful. Some kids like uniting with one parent in order to have a common enemy. Better to be the bully than the victim."

"My clients are the victims!" Esther protests. Well, except for Peter. In that case, Peter's son is the victim. Left behind with Bianca, who's no prize herself, and as he grows up, he'll learn who his father was. Or maybe his father is already inside, waiting to come out.

"My point is, the world isn't black and white," Wilfred says. "But the kids who grow up in these families don't learn to see gray. They see strong and weak, winners and losers. It alters the course of their lives."

So he's saying that even in cases where Esther thought she'd won—where she soundly defeated the fathers—she still undoubtedly harmed the children.

She can't believe that.

"I've kept kids away from abusive men," she says. "That improves their chances of being healthy."

"You know what's surprising? It actually depends on the degree and kind of abuse. Sometimes what's better is to educate, monitor, and get the parents into therapy so that they're no longer behaving in abusive ways rather than encouraging a total cut-off. Because when parents just disappear, the absence can create a wound that never heals. On one level, the kids might be relieved but on another, deeper level, they feel abandoned. They feel like they weren't important or lovable enough."

"Well, that's just silly." There's no way that keeping abusive parents around is a better course.

"No, it's human. We're all prone to thinking in all-or-nothing terms; we have to be taught to see gray. We have to learn negotiation and problem-solving."

"You're talking in generalities. You're not talking about my clients and their children. You said you don't want to."

He shakes his head yet again, as if she's sadly mischaracterized him. "I prefer not to talk in a public place without access to my files. You asked me to tell you what I know about divorce and what I think about your work, and that's exactly what I'm doing."

"Okay, then. Tell me what you think of my work."

"Your clients are always incredibly well-prepared. Very occasionally they've seemed rehearsed but mostly they're just the perfect combination of self-reflective and vulnerable. They never blame their exes. They're ready and willing to take their share of the responsibility even as the anecdotes they tell implicate their spouses. It's uncanny."

"What's uncanny?" She feels like he's prosecuting a case against her. And winning.

"The similarities in the couples you work with. It's made me wonder if you're replicating some dynamic from your childhood, or rather, you aim to represent clients who'll help you resolve your own childhood trauma. Maybe the husbands are all stand-ins for your father? Though it could be your mother."

"I'm not doing that." Her voice rises. "I'm entirely professional."

"It's easy to think that, seeing as there are no evident improprieties. On the surface, your work is impeccable. That's why so often I've wound up concluding in my reports that the husband is a danger to the child's emotional well-being. But after all your texts, I decided to revisit your cases. Now the pattern seems so clear."

"Their patterns are clear."

"*Your* pattern. I've been at this a very long time, Esther. I've truly seen it all. I thought I couldn't be manipulated but I was wrong. I should have known that everyone can be, especially when it's by someone who's been fooling herself." He gives her a look of pure sympathy. "You've realized it, though, haven't you? The jig is up."

Her heartbeat accelerates. "I don't know what you mean."

"Visiting your former clients. Texting me obsessively."

"It wasn't obsessive. I just wanted to pin down whether lunch or dinner would work better for you." He knows nothing. Who is he to talk about her supposed trauma? "Those husbands are toxic people. They're controlling and selfish and unwilling to compromise. They make rigid boundaries but don't respect other people's. They have no empathy or compassion. No ability to introspect, or to change. They put their needs ahead of anyone else's and always will."

"There are people like that," he agrees, and the way he says it… Does he actually think *she's* one of them? "People have all kinds of flaws. Yet their children love them, and always will, even if they've been erased from the child's life. Do you realize that when there's a child involved, it's not like any other breakup where you can just delete them and move on? That the job of an adult is to manage their feelings and figure out how to communicate in a decent and productive manner even if their co-parent is enormously flawed?"

"And if the other parent isn't decent or productive? You've met some of the husbands of my clients. Xander Tillman, for example." That's it. She needs to get this back on course. Remember the reason she came here.

"Some may be so unwell that they need to be removed from their children's lives, at least temporarily. In some very, very rare cases, permanently. But in all the other cases, they should be taught how to be decent co-parents. The other co-parent can lead by example instead of becoming reactive themselves and escalating the problem. When a toxic person feels that they're being pushed out of their children's lives, they're going to fight back, and they're going to fight dirty."

"Xander Tillman started it." Julianne had to finish it. Esther had to.

"Let's say you're right. A percentage are incapable of co-parenting. Maybe the best scenario is parallel parenting: cutting off all communication and parenting separately, making all their decisions independently. When the tug of war ends, when each parent has to give up control of what's going on at the other person's house, the fixation often ends, too. They're not getting triggered all the time and they can focus on keeping their side of the street clean. Their kids don't have to hear them yelling at each other or complaining about each other." Wilfred regards her. "But I can see by your face what you think about parallel parenting."

He's right, she takes a dim view of it. Because if an ex is so toxic that he can't co-parent, then his children shouldn't be around him at all. It's so obvious. And Wilfred thinks he's so smart.

"I've written parallel-parenting plans before," she says.

"But how often do you suggest them?" She doesn't want to answer, deciding instead to treat it as a rhetorical question. "You're meeting these people at one of the lowest points in their lives. Of course they seem beyond flawed. Some seem downright dangerous. But that's not the whole picture."

"I don't just see them in divorce proceedings. I hear about the marriage, too."

"You hear about the marriage from a wounded spouse. You don't think that colors their memories?"

It's like he's telling her what an idiot she's been, believing the women. But women should be believed.

"I deal with bad men, Wilfred."

"If you're so convinced of that, then why go through the farce of setting up co-parenting arrangements that will inevitably break down? Why waste everyone's time and money?"

"I have to let these men demonstrate who they are. They have to hang themselves."

"Do you really, though?" he asks dubiously.

Just look at him, sitting there acting holier than thou. He spends, what, a few weeks in the company of these people and then writes his little reports? He loves sitting in judgment. Of the clients, and now of Esther.

"You know as well as I do that the courts love co-parenting," she says. "They want everyone to act cooperative and pretend they're all capable of conscious uncoupling like Gwyneth Paltrow. I have to give the judges what they want, and then show them why it won't work."

"You're a brilliant attorney, Esther. Why not get in there right from the beginning and make your arguments for parallel parenting? Persuade the judge and everyone else. Isn't that your job, persuading everyone of what's right?"

He doesn't sound like he's mocking her, but she feels a sudden rush of shame. It's like he's saying that she's been living a lie all along, that she's not one of the good guys after all.

"These people are grieving." His tone is suddenly delicate. "Anger is one of the stages. Your clients stay stuck there throughout the litigation. Some of them don't get past their anger, ever, and their children grow up stewing in it. Why do you think that is?"

"Because I work with high-conflict divorce." She lifts her chin. She will not let him denigrate her, or her work. They're one and the same.

"You instigate high-conflict divorce. Why do you think *that* is?"

There's a long pause while Esther's fury grows. "Are you talking about my family again?" He doesn't answer, which means yes, that's what he was intimating. "Fuck you, Wilfred."

His mouth drops open. She knows that it's not because he hasn't heard an aggressive invective before. He works with the same couples Esther does, and he's probably gotten plenty of angry Sleight messages himself. But from Esther, he'd come to expect measured and moderate, not combative and hostile. But he deserves it. He's hit her below the belt, making it sound like she's screwed up everything she's touched. She's fighting for her life here.

"If you think I'm the villain, you're wrong," she tells him. "You are."

"What could you possibly mean?"

"You wrote the reports that led to the court rulings. If you think mistakes were made, then it's on your head, not mine."

Yes, that's it. Now she's feeling more like herself. How dare he come at her like this? How dare he reference her family dynamics when he knows nothing about them? He's psychoanalyzing her to relieve his guilty conscience and she's not having it. Her past doesn't determine her present or her future.

"Why do you want to sit in your glass house and write reports anyway?" she says. "You can't actually do therapy so instead you sit in judgment of everyone? I don't need this shit."

"You asked for this shit." He looks bewildered rather than angry, as if he doesn't know where it took a right turn. "You wanted my impressions of you."

"I didn't know how off-base they would be. No one works harder than I do."

"It's not about that. It's about trying to resolve your personal trauma through professional means, which can never—"

"You don't even know how much I've done to help those families. But some of them just couldn't be helped. Some were determined to detonate. I wanted those kids to grow up and lead healthy lives. I protect women and children, Wilfred!"

It comes out way too loud and she can see other patrons staring over, amused, as if she's said something funny, as if it's laughable to want to do good in the world. Is that what Wilfred thinks, too?

She leans in, her voice low so that only he can hear. "You want me to doubt myself, just like all the others." Like Peter, and Bianca, and the police, and her Sleight stalker. "You want me to blame myself for everyone else's failings. But I won't."

She gets to her feet and storms out, nearly barreling into Candy, who's holding two plates of medium-well cheeseburgers with salads, no fries. She doesn't apologize.

She never will.

TWENTY-EIGHT

The drive from the diner back to Esther's house takes twenty-seven minutes, and she needs every one of them to dispel Wilfred's wrongheaded ideas and facile armchair diagnoses. How condescending he'd been, suggesting her clients' husbands were stand-ins for her father (or maybe her mother), when he knows absolutely nothing of her personal life.

Maybe he's just never met a principled person before. She pities him, having to psychoanalyze everyone, never being able to turn it off.

Yet little Phil Tillman and Naomi Emerson keep intruding on her thoughts. What she has to remember is that she really had tried to help them, performing the service for which she was hired to the absolute best of her ability. No one works harder than Esther. And no one—including Wilfred—could have predicted or controlled what came next. He recommended to the court that Julianne Tillman get full custody! But now he's acting like Esther's the immoral one? He doesn't get to clean his conscience by kicking dirt on hers.

Esther pushes open her front door and is hit by an overwhelming scent. The air in the foyer is nearly sodden with perfume. It's not Esther's, and it's not Dot's. It's not anyone's she recognizes.

She kicks off her shoes and walks gingerly down the hall, the cloying aroma seeming to loom like a poltergeist. It's suffusing the kitchen, too. Esther's fear is growing. Whose perfume is this? How recently was she here, and how long must she have stayed in order to leave a smell that strong in her wake?

Wait, could she *still* be here?

Esther rushes back out the door, slamming it behind her. She gets in her car and logs into her security system app. Viewing the interior cameras in real time, she sees no one. Then she checks the exterior footage throughout the day. No one's come in or out.

But she hadn't conjured that smell. That much she knows.

She calls the security company to ask if there have been any glitches on their end. Any outages? Times when the cameras to her specific house or neighborhood were disabled or non-functioning, or if any footage could have been tampered with or accidentally deleted? She waits while the employee on the other end of the line does a painstaking review.

"No glitches, ma'am," he concludes.

She grits her teeth at the "ma'am," seeing as it reminds her of the recent interaction with Officer Connors. She's sure the police never bothered to investigate Bianca Tramboni or anyone else. So maybe her Sleight stalker is feeling overconfident.

"Are there any indications that you've been hacked?" Esther asks.

"No, ma'am."

"But it's not impossible." Peter Tramboni's people could have gotten in and out without detection. Maybe Bianca—or Avery—have the same people. "If there was no intruder, then how did that smell get into my house? How can you explain that?"

"I can't," he responds. "But I promise you, our systems are

secure. No glitches, no hacks, no bugs. Based on the camera feeds, no one's been in your home."

"Thanks for your help." Esther hangs up, perturbed. She could check into a hotel, but what about tomorrow and the next night? Also, if her stalker is watching the house, then they'd know they scared her off. They might feel empowered to go even further.

She can't sit outside all night, either, so she steels herself to re-enter her house. In the foyer, she's again assaulted by the smell. This is no olfactory hallucination; she doesn't have a brain tumor or dementia. Someone's found a way in, evading her state-of-the-art security system, in order to stink up the joint. It seems like an awful lot of work for a practical joke.

It might not even have been a woman; it could be someone who wants her to think it's a woman. Someone who sprayed the perfume to mark the territory, so that Esther would know they'd been there. Or had they been lying in wait for her and eventually given up?

Esther turns on every light and goes through every cupboard and drawer. Nothing seems out of place. But they could have just taken photos and left, or uploaded documents to a zip drive. Since she doesn't know who it was, she can't tell what the objective was: whether it was simply to scare her, or to find something and, if so, what that something was.

So much for tumbling right into bed. Now she's wide awake.

She makes herself a cup of tea and pours a generous glug of whiskey into it. Then she sits at her kitchen counter, staring out at the street. This way, at least she can see them coming, if they do decide to come back.

Her breathing is fast and shallow. It's terrifying, thinking that her stalker can get into her home without detection. She has the thought that it could be Peter, from beyond the grave. If anyone could pull off a trick like that, it'd be him.

She knows that's just craziness. But she has no idea what to think. If she did imagine the smell, then that means she literally can't trust her senses. On the other hand, if she does trust her senses, then it follows that she's up against an adversary of such sophistication and means that they can get around any security measure she tries to put in place. It means she's defenseless.

No. She's never been that.

She calls 911. The police will have egg all over their faces now for not believing her sooner. "I need an officer to come to my house right away," she says. "Someone's been here."

"Is anything missing?" the dispatcher asks.

"Not that I can see." Esther answers the series of stock questions, being as polite as possible, then says that she's already made a report to Officer Connors that's in the process of being investigated. "I assume he's off-duty now or I would have called him directly."

"Just to confirm," the dispatcher says, "nothing's missing or out of place, no doors or locks have been jimmied or broken, no—"

"You didn't ask me about any odors. My house reeks of perfume."

"Whose perfume?"

"I don't know." She tamps down her exasperation. "I can't identify the perfume or the person who was here. That's why I want an officer out here to collect evidence."

There's a long pause.

"Hello?" Esther says. "Are you sending someone?"

"I will, but it might take a while."

Because the dispatcher thinks that Esther's some sort of quack. Did Officer Connors flag her in some way? Or maybe it's the fact that it's Friday night and there are five carjackings, three muggings, and a drive-by shooting ahead of Esther in the queue. That's the wildest part of paying the exorbitant prices to live in the Bay Area. Safety is most decidedly not guaranteed.

"They need to hurry," Esther says. "If they don't, the smell will be gone."

"We'll do our best, ma'am," the dispatcher says.

After Esther's hung up, she debates what to do next. Should she call Dot to come over? No, Dot would be too freaked out and then Esther would wind up having to comfort her. That's why Esther already made the decision not to say anything about the Sleight messages.

Could she call Hugh?

No, because if he's not the stalker, she doesn't want him to see her like this. And if he is the stalker, she doesn't want him to see her like this.

She walks outside and comes back in once, twice, thrice. Each time, it's confirmed. The smell is real. Esther's perimeter has been breached, her sanctuary violated. Someone wants her to know they can get to her any time they want.

Two and a half nerve-wracking hours later, a squad car pulls up in front of Esther's house. It's a man and a woman in uniform. He's tall and thin, she's short and large. Jack Sprat and His Wife, is how Esther thinks of them.

Officer Sprat asks what seems to be the trouble. Esther tells him, and he and His Wife walk around, sniffing. It would be funny if it weren't so infuriating.

"I can't smell anything," Officer Sprat says.

"I can't either," His Wife adds.

"That's because you took so long to get here," Esther says, trying to sound reasonable rather than antagonistic. "I understand I'm not the only victim of a crime tonight, but I let the dispatcher know that time was of the essence."

"So there are no signs of forced entry?" Sprat queries, looking at the front door and then at the windows.

"No."

"Nothing's been stolen, or disturbed?" His Wife says. Are they really going to run through all the same questions the dispatcher did?

"The only sign was the smell, and now it's gone. Would you be able to do some sort of forensics? Check for atomized particles in the air, or for shoe tread, or take fingerprints from various surfaces, for example?"

"That's not what we do," His Wife says with a disapproving expression, as if Esther has overstepped her bounds by deigning to ask for actual assistance.

"Can you at least let Officer Connors know about this?" Esther says. Maybe it'll light a fire under his ass. He told her he needed more incidents to make a pattern, and voila.

"Sure." But Sprat isn't a very good liar. He's examining the security panel near her door. "You've got a pretty fancy alarm system here. It didn't go off?"

"No, it didn't."

"And you don't have anyone recorded on your security cameras?" asks His Wife.

"No, I don't."

Sprat and His Wife exchange a look. They think Esther's a paranoiac who wasted their time. Now word will surely get back to Officer Connors, and he'll take her even less seriously (if that's even possible).

What about Detective Zelnik? If he hears about this, will he think she's more or less likely to have murdered Peter Tramboni?

"Nine-one-one is for emergencies," His Wife says primly. "You're welcome to follow up with Officer Connors during business hours."

"I'll do that," Esther says. She wants them out of her house, pronto.

Since they had no interest in being there in the first place, it doesn't take long for that to happen. Once she's left alone, she triple-bolts the door and goes upstairs. She normally takes a shower before bed but she needs to stay vigilant. Instead of pajamas, she puts on fresh but comfortable clothes, in case she needs to run out into the night. Then she goes downstairs to the living room couch. That way, if anyone comes in through the back door, she has a clear path to the front; if they come in through the front, she can get to the back. While, theoretically, it's unlikely that someone would break in twice in a night, she can't take anything for granted.

But what's she going to do tomorrow, and the next night, and the night after that? At some point, she'll need to sleep again. She can't live her entire life standing sentinel. She'll go crazy.

Unless she's already there... because she finds herself thinking that if she *is* the subject of a haunting, there are two suspects: Dale and Peter. Peter would have no reason, really, since why would he hold a grudge? Esther had been his soldier. She was his puppet. But Dot's ex-husband, Dale, is another story.

An errant tree branch rustles up against the house and Esther jumps a foot in the air. She needs to get a grip.

There has to be a rational explanation for that perfume, and the lack of video footage. Esther might not be able to figure it out tonight but it's there, waiting to be discovered. Facts exist. Truth exists. Ghosts do not.

Esther doesn't know what she thinks about karma but she knows that she has genuinely tried to make the world a better and safer place. Has she made mistakes? Of course. She's never claimed to be perfect. She might not have been 100 percent accurate in her assessment of every client's husband, but generally speaking, children do benefit when a bad man is marginalized or, better yet, excised entirely.

This belief had been shored up just a few days ago when Esther called another former client to see if the ex might be nursing a grudge. In Esther's estimation, he had been superficially charming but incredibly dangerous. He'd fought his wife tooth and nail, seeking full custody. But the judge saw through him and he was instead awarded 20 percent visitation. He paid his child support on time every month and never again saw or called his child. His wife had always contended that he was only interested in torturing her and was using their daughter to do it. Obviously, she'd been right. Esther had been right. Esther called that one from the start.

She wishes that the mother had stopped there but the story went on. The mother said that, despite everything, it was his absence that had caused the most harm. Night after night, that little girl cried for her father and said how much she missed him. His disappearance—his rejection—was proof that she was unlovable.

Just like Wilfred said.

But Esther's not about to take Wilfred von Holten seriously. He can get in line behind all the others who've misunderstood or impugned her. She might be under attack by people both dead and alive, but she will not be driven mad. She will not start doubting her judgment or sanity because that's what they want. She's stronger than all of them, and she will not break. In fact, she's about to double down. Esther knows she can work harder than anyone. Can fight harder than anyone. That's what she'll continue to do.

She's going to fuck up anyone who gets in her way, just as she always has.

TWENTY-NINE

Esther is sitting in one of her favorite places on earth, the Berkeley Rose Garden. She's on a bench, surrounded by tiers and tiers of roses. The air is redolent and, normally, she loves the scent, but tonight it reminds her of another heavy odor, the one that pervaded her home last night. Because someone invaded her home.

But she's not going to think about that. She's certainly not going to talk to Dot about it.

Maybe she'll talk to Wilfred. He's sent a few texts, apologizing for upsetting her, saying that he hopes she gets some relief from all the stress she's clearly under.

Ha. She's never going to talk to Wilfred again. But she thanked him for his concern and said she'd appreciate his discretion—meaning, *don't you dare try to mess with my reputation*. He won't, if he knows what's good for him.

"So how's work?" Dot asks. Esther can tell from the ambient noise that Dot is driving somewhere.

"Really good," Esther says emphatically, holding the phone closer while casting a furtive look around. It's the Saturday tourist crew, and no one's paying her a bit of attention. "But you know what I've been thinking about? Who I've been thinking about? Dale."

Dot goes silent for so long that Esther thinks maybe they've lost reception. "You never think about Dale," she finally says.

Esther tries not to. But could Dale be thinking about her? "We're probably coming up on the anniversary of his death, aren't we?"

"We are." Dot is being uncharacteristically taciturn. She's probably just thrown because Esther doesn't ordinarily bring up Dale.

"I've been thinking about how something can be sad—tragic even—but that doesn't mean it's anyone's fault. It also doesn't mean that the person who suffered the tragedy was blameless. Do you know what I'm saying?"

"No."

Esther tries again. "I'd imagine that sometimes you still miss Dale, despite everything. I respect that, I do, but even though he wasn't actively malevolent, he was parasitic. Don't you think? I mean, with the benefit of hindsight?"

Dot hesitates before saying, "Um, maybe?"

"Not maybe! Definitely! You did absolutely everything for him, and he made it so that you had to do absolutely everything for the kids, and then he blindsided you by asking for a divorce."

In Esther's opinion, men are just constitutionally weaker than women, and the ones who pretend to be strongest are often the weakest, like her dad or Peter Tramboni. Then there are the ones like Dale who pretend that their weakness qualifies as vulnerability and that by expressing it, they're strong. They're evolved.

Dale had irritated Esther from the second she met him. He proudly declared himself a feminist and proclaimed that everything in his relationship with Dot should be equal; he pledged to always do his share. To hear him tell it, he was putting Dot up on a pedestal by admitting that she was "simply better" than him at so many things, like household organization and DIY projects. He was man enough to step aside and let her unclog a garbage disposal. What a gentleman. What a catch.

Dot thought he truly was. One of the only times she ever vociferously disagreed with her sister was after Esther first met Dale. Esther said, "There's something off about that guy," and Dot said, "No." That was it, just no. Stop. Go no further.

Dale proposed after six months of dating and Dot was over the moon. Esther privately thought that of course Dale had moved fast; he didn't want to give Dot a chance to come to her senses and get away. They eloped to Vegas at seven months. Dot hadn't wanted a real wedding, not if it meant having their father pay for it and attend.

Esther wished she could have seen Dale's charms. It would have made life so much easier. Instead, Esther spoke to him and about him as little as possible. Dot never took the cue, though. She would wax rhapsodic about him at every opportunity, trying to change Esther's mind. But every anecdote just furthered Esther's initial impression: Dale was a weak, dependent man, destined to suck her sister dry.

"Where is this coming from, Esther?" Dot's voice sounds not exactly cold, but not entirely warm either.

"I just realized we haven't talked about him in a long time and that with the anniversary coming up, you might be having certain feelings. But he made the right call for you and the kids. That life insurance policy was the best thing he ever did."

There's some sort of commotion coming through the line. "Stop it, both of you!" Dot says.

Esther is floored. She knew Dot was driving and had assumed she was on speaker, but Dot had given no indication the kids were in the car. "Have July and Tyson been listening this whole time?"

"Hi, Aunt E!" they chorus.

"I'm sorry," Esther sputters. She's unwittingly broken her

cardinal rule about badmouthing the father. "I'll let you all go. I didn't realize..."

"No, you don't need to," Dot says. "We're just on our way to an early dinner." It's as if she thinks this has been a totally ordinary and unrevealing conversation when, actually, Esther's invoked (and insulted) the kids' dead father. How can Dot sound so blasé?

"I'll call you tomorrow, okay? Love you." Esther hurriedly disconnects, trying to replay everything she just said and how it might be impacting July and Tyson. She's angry with Dot, which she almost never is. She can't believe Dot's judgment in allowing the kids to overhear something so inappropriate. It makes Esther wonder what else July and Tyson might have been privy to over the years.

A text comes in from Avery. It's breezy and friendly and insistent and sinister, like they're a couple of girlfriends even without Esther's consent. There's something diabolical about willfully ignoring another person's wishes with such casual aplomb.

Check out the NY Times tomorrow, kay

Given her usual lack of punctuation, it reads less like a question and more like a command.

Peter's dead but it's possible that Avery knows Esther's secret, either because Peter told her or because Avery put her own substantial resources toward discovery. What was it that Avery said?

Since I was five years old, I've wanted to run shit.

Meet the new boss, same as the old boss?

THIRTY

"What is that?" Hugh jokes, leaning toward his plate. "I think I can make out a potato."

"It is dark," Esther admits. "Darker than I remembered."

The truth is, Esther doesn't get out much. In her memory, this restaurant was romantic—i.e. dim enough to provide cover for her acting deficits while still bright enough for her to study Hugh's non-verbals. In reality, it's like an underground cave, with drapery and tapestries that emit no light at all. There's not so much as a votive candle on the table to see by. Hugh is thoroughly camouflaged.

"I appreciate your effort," he says. She doesn't think he's being sarcastic, but even when she squints, she can't be quite sure.

"I listened to what you said," she tells him. "About not wanting to feel like a secret."

It's the first reference either of them have made to the last time they saw each other. They haven't touched on it by text either. She's been debating whether to apologize for essentially kicking him out but once she says it was just stress affecting her, he'll want to talk about the stress. About Peter Tramboni, the investigation, Detective Zelnik, the whole nine. And she obviously can't tell him about the stalker when she's still trying to figure out if he *is* the stalker.

"How is everything?" Their server pops by.

"Fine," Hugh says gruffly.

"It's good," Esther adds. "I'm really enjoying my scallops." Their painful date is not this young woman's fault.

"Can I get you anything else?" she asks, looking between them with what Esther thinks is a note of sympathy. "Wine or a cocktail?"

"How about a flashlight?" Hugh says.

"A glass of wine," Esther says. "Whatever you think pairs well with the scallops."

"I'll have wine, too. Whatever pairs well with steak." Hugh's tone sounds borderline competitive. She realizes how long it's been since they played tennis. She misses that staple activity. She misses the way they used to be. It had been so easy for a while there.

The server leaves them alone, and Esther has to ask. "When did you start drinking again?"

"It's a recent development. No big deal, it's just social."

Hugh's not social. As far as she knows, he doesn't have many friends, and his closest are those from AA. "Do you still go to meetings?"

"I've got client meetings every day, just like you." She thinks his mouth is twisting as if in jest, but she can feel the edge. He doesn't like being questioned, not about this.

She realizes how little she knows about his alcohol abuse issues (that's what he called them, never saying the word "alcoholic"). He also hasn't said outright that he'd never have another drink in his life, but she'd assumed, since that's the AA credo and because she never saw him drinking. But maybe he's been "just social" this whole time, same as he's been carrying a gun.

How well does she really know Hugh Warshaw?

They eat in silence for a bit, and then after their glasses of wine arrive, they drink in silence. It's broken only by the ping of a Sleight message.

"You're not going to check that?" he asks.

"No need." She tries to keep her voice level though her antenna's gone up.

"Since when? You always check your incoming texts."

She thinks he might be raising an eyebrow slightly in a manner that's meant to be disarming, to tell her to *relax, we're all friends here*. But are they really? The fact that he's sitting across from her when a Sleight message came in doesn't mean it's not from him. The app has a feature where messages can be scheduled and sent later. Hugh could have intentionally scheduled this one to make himself look innocent.

He sighs. "I just don't know what we're doing anymore."

"We're going public, like you wanted."

"This is public? My own mother couldn't recognize me from five feet away." He shakes his head. "Come on, Esther."

"Come on what?"

"Tell me what you really want. Tell me what's really going on."

Hugh's no idiot. He must know she's been hiding things for months. Esther can't tell him the truth, though, when he might have been doing the same. He looks so trustworthy right now but that doesn't mean anything. They're in the dark.

She does know this much: She doesn't want to end the relationship. Not yet.

Part of her would love to vilify him because that's familiar, and because it would simplify things. She'd have a clear path forward, and she wouldn't have to keep living in purgatory. But she does care for him, for better or worse, and it's entirely possible that he cares about her more than any man ever has.

Her feelings and motivations are a moving target. In one moment, she's keeping him around for protection; in the next, she thinks she might need protection from him. It could be that she's keeping her enemies closer, like Avery said.

Speaking of Avery, Esther did check out that *New York Times* article. Titled "Sorry Not Sorry," it was a joint interview with Avery and Bianca Tramboni that seemed to contain little to no fact-checking. It was almost like a transcript with just a few asides about their hair, makeup, and the occasional tension and cattiness that reared its head between the two women. It was apparent that they're not actually friends though their interests have temporarily converged. They both want to out Peter Tramboni for the brute that he was.

They did it in somewhat veiled terms, not yet willing to give specifics but alluding to a future in which they would. The article was like a teaser, a preview of what's to come. While they made no direct mention of Esther, Bianca spoke about how much Peter loved forcing women to do his dirty work, attaching a female face to his misdeeds. She called it "wombwashing" instead of whitewashing, and said that it had happened recently in their custody battle.

Avery and Bianca expressed mutual outrage at the way women have always been either silenced or urged to sing the praises of abusive monsters who've died. They're not willing to play that game anymore, not willing to be tasteful and demure. They're inviting all the women who've been mistreated by Peter to come forward and share their stories.

This seems to fly in the face of what Avery told Esther about not being an activist or a victim, not wanting to be defined by what happened with Peter. Now all of a sudden, Avery is not only coming forward but palling around with Bianca? Is WAPT (Women Against Peter Tramboni) for real, and Avery and Bianca are the co-founders? Esther wonders if she'd been Avery's first choice, and Avery had to settle for Bianca.

There's no mention of WAPT in the article, no mention of any protective infrastructure being put in place for women who do choose to speak out against Peter. Esther would be surprised if the floodgates open.

It might be that neither Avery nor Bianca are interested in a #MeToo reckoning, that what they really have in common is a need to save their own asses. They're probably both suspects in Peter's murder and this could be their way of getting out in front of the story, of making Detective Zelnik's job harder. After this article, arresting one of them would be a PR nightmare. They might already be preparing their defense, branding themselves as feminist heroines.

Esther has no idea what this means for her own fate. Does this make Avery or Bianca more or less likely to be her stalker? She hasn't a clue. Actually, there are too many clues, which can be worse than too few. Her head is starting to ache.

Meanwhile, Hugh is staring at her, waiting for an answer to his questions. Realizing nothing is forthcoming, he drains his wine. "So, okay, you're not prepared to tell me what's going on or what you want. Or maybe you don't know what you want. So I'll tell you what I want. I want to stop getting surprise visits at my office about you."

"Who are you talking about?"

"First it's a homicide detective, and then it's the widow of a murdered billionaire." Avery and Bianca join forces, and now Bianca's showing up at Hugh's office?

"She's not the widow. The divorce had already been finalized."

"Semantics are beneath you, Esther. The point is, I'm sitting in my office and in walks this woman who's done up like it's, I don't know, Easter. She's wearing this hat and gloves—"

"She used to be a fashion designer."

"Semantics." Hugh is losing his patience.

She can see he's genuinely upset, though she's not entirely sure why. A run-in with Bianca might be awkward or uncomfortable for him but it's a whole different order of magnitude for Esther. None of this really has anything to do with him.

Does it?

"None of this has anything to do with you," she says, waiting to see if he'll refute her. If he'll be the one to come clean.

"Of course it does! These people are showing up at my office and disrupting my day and I don't know why. I don't know who's next."

Avery Brengle, perhaps? "I didn't send them, Hugh."

"But I have to deal with them. First I had to lie to a detective—"

"I never told you to do that."

Hugh stares at her in amazement. "What was I going to do, feed you to him? I fucking love you, Esther!"

It lingers there between them like a rotting fish.

Hugh resumes his rant. "Then it's Bianca Tramboni, inquiring about my services. She wants to sue you for defamation and slander."

"What did you tell her?"

"That I don't do that kind of work."

"But you do." He doesn't specialize, considering himself more of a jack-of-all-trades. It's another reason she didn't have much respect for him when they first came across one another professionally. Another reason she'd once thought of him as a bottom feeder.

"Should I have said, 'I can't help you because I'm sleeping with the woman you want to sue'?"

"She already knew that. Why else would she have come to you?"

"I still wasn't going to confirm it. The real question is, why was she there? What are you caught up in?"

From what she can make out, it looks like he doesn't know

what to believe about her anymore. But he still wants to believe in her. After all, he loves her.

Oh Lord.

Esther does not know how to process that declaration. She certainly doesn't have the bandwidth to decide how deep her feelings for Hugh go.

But there's something about that stare of his, intense enough to cut through the darkness. Is it possible he thinks she actually is the murderer and that he's been covering for her?

"I didn't kill Peter," she says. She waits for him to respond with something like, "Of course you didn't."

And waits.

And waits.

"Do you think I killed Peter?" she demands.

"I didn't say that. But it's getting very strange around here. First the detective, and now Bianca Tramboni. It seems like you haven't been doing a great job keeping our relationship on the down-low."

"*I* haven't been doing a great job?" So now he's mad that she's exposed him when before he was mad at being treated like a dirty secret? Pick a lane, buster.

Hugh is onto something, though. The visits from Detective Zelnik and Bianca Tramboni could be related. If Bianca was the one who had Esther surveilled, then she would have known about Hugh and could have given that tip to the detective. Feeding him information about Esther could be a great way to keep the heat off her. Bianca should, by rights, be the prime suspect. She had the most to gain by Peter's death. Esther wouldn't blame her one bit for wanting to excise Peter from her son's life, permanently.

Then there's Avery Brengle. Is she in the mix, too? She was all girl power in that article but that's a public persona. In private, Avery could be behind this, encouraging Bianca to sue Esther. For what end, though? Is it to force Esther to fall in line and join their coalition or do they have some other terms that they haven't yet presented to her? Avery knows what it feels like to be blackmailed but that doesn't mean she wouldn't turn around and do it to someone else. After all, she'd been harassed by Peter and then created an app to make stalking more user-friendly. There's nothing these fuckers won't optimize.

"You look like you're going to throw up," Hugh says. "Listen, I know these months have been hard for you. First being Peter's bitch, and now his suspect."

"What do you mean, being Peter's bitch?"

"It's just a figure of speech. Everyone who works for Peter is his bitch, men included. It's how he likes it." Hugh seems as if he's about to reach across the table and then thinks better of it. "I'm sorry."

"For what?"

"For not knowing how to support you. I'm trying my best here. Like I said, I didn't tell the detective anything, and I turned Bianca down."

Like Bianca must have known he would. Was the intent for Hugh to tell Esther that Bianca's coming for her, heightening Esther's paranoia? Or does Hugh's reputation suggest that he's the kind of lowlife who'd take the case for the notoriety, despite the conflict of interest?

Esther can't tell what's a warning shot anymore, or if someone's going to shoot to kill.

THIRTY-ONE

Stylist is humming while she works. Esther finds it slightly ostentatious, exhibitionistic even, but since it's never happened before, she's willing to let it slide.

Esther's in a foul mood herself. She hasn't felt comfortable at home ever since the perfume invasion; she's still aggravated with Dot for letting her talk about Dale on speaker with Tyson and July right there; she's not sure if she needs to say something to her niece and nephew though what can she say when she meant every word? Not to mention the Sleight messages have continued and she still has no concrete evidence of who the author is. She remains conflicted about Hugh and uneasy about what Avery and Bianca are up to. Meanwhile, the police are either too interested in her (Detective Zelnik) or too disinterested (Officer Connors, Sprat and His Wife).

At least she has her work, and no one can stop her from doing it. She can still help those far more vulnerable than herself.

"Ow," she says, when Stylist pulls too hard on the roller brush.

"Sorry," Stylist says. "I'm just overly excited today."

Esther realizes she's supposed to ask why but she's not about to encourage such unprofessional behavior. This moment is what boundaries were invented for.

She returns to her open laptop. Kiersten and Miles's relationship has degraded (predictably) and they're now communicating exclusively in written form, via the co-parenting app Esther suggests to all her clients. While ordinary texts can be deleted, the co-parenting app saves and authenticates all messages so that they're admissible in court. Also, Kiersten has given permission for Esther to view all exchanges, which is what she's doing now. It's tedious work. Most messages are mundane: pick-ups, drop-offs, what the kids ate, what the preschool teacher said, blah blah. Esther has coached Kiersten to be all information, no emotion, and Miles seems to have received the same advice. In the app, he's on his best behavior. He confines his digs and insinuations to in-person contact with Kiersten so it'll become a he said/she said. Kiersten documents every one of his comments. A dated and detailed log looks a lot less like hearsay to a judge.

Meanwhile, Esther's been praying for a slip-up from Miles in the co-parenting app, and there it is, a perfect pearl: I get what you're doing. I'm not blind.

It's sandwiched between minutiae so maybe he thought Esther wouldn't even notice it or that it would come off as innocuous. But it's everything. Well, it'll become everything when Esther's through with him.

Kiersten's lost even more weight since the case began because she can't keep any food down. Frail, nervous, prone to anxious crying jags, and delicately pretty, she's just the kind of woman that men like to protect, and the vast majority of judges are men.

Kiersten's had a few sessions with the therapist Esther recommended. She's a great documentarian herself, a master of the telling detail. Esther initially fobbed off Kiersten on the therapist because Kiersten was too high-maintenance, but now it'll become part of the strategy. Kiersten's distress can be a feature, not a bug. Esther will use Kiersten's fragility to prove that Miles has been intentionally trying to destroy her.

Esther has a lot of lemons in her personal life right now. It would be so satisfying to make some professional lemonade. To really squeeze a bastard like Miles.

"Looks like you're in a good mood, too," Stylist says.

"Hmm?" Esther looks up from her typing in absent-minded irritation. If this continues, she's going to need to find someone new to do her blowouts.

"You're smiling."

"Am I? I hadn't noticed." But it's true, her mood is much improved. She does love when a plan comes together. Justice will be served.

THIRTY-TWO

Look around. You're never really alone.

The voice is smooth and calm, a male version of Siri's, emerging from Esther's phone.

She spins around, mace in one hand, alarm in the other. Even before the Sleight stalker, she was vigilant while walking through the parking lot beneath her office building. Now, every time she comes and goes, she's tensed and ready, a coiled spring.

The talking feature is one of Sleight's most controversial, with good reason. Unless a person has the sound turned off, Sleight is able to basically hijack the victim's phone. The victim experiences fear and mortification (including the fear of future mortification), and often has to change their behavior to avoid it. For example, they might start turning the sound off, which could mean missing important messages and alerts. They're forced to live in a state of hypervigilance.

No wonder Avery came up with the idea for her app while working for Peter. No wonder he sued for intellectual property. After all, he was the inspiration. The bullied becomes the bully. Avery's basically bullying millions of people by proxy, through her tech. So why would she have any compunction about doing it to Esther?

It's late at night; Esther has outlasted the building's other occupants. She doesn't see anyone but that doesn't mean they're not there. They could be hiding, or someone could be using some sort of distant surveillance tool and then feeding the data back to her stalker. Avery's funds must be limitless, like Peter's. Bianca has plenty of dough, too. Some of Esther's clients and their exes are in decent financial shape as well. And then there's Hugh. He could afford to pay for an island resort that normally caters to the multi-millionaire set. He has his own secrets, that much seems clear.

Or no one's watching, and Esther's all alone with her paranoia. The timing of the message could have been a coincidence, or possibly connected to another Sleight feature. Esther wouldn't put it past Avery or her engineers to have created a geotracking function where a message gets sent once the recipient is in a particularly vulnerable location.

Like now. Esther can't wait to make it to her car.

She's trying to be brave but she can't help looking over her shoulder constantly. At work, she locks the door behind her and has to fight to concentrate. At home, she closes all blinds and drapes and stays awake for hours, running scenarios. Whether she's in her office, her house, at the courthouse, walking down the street—there's not one moment of true safety and security.

The terrorists are winning.

Should she hire a bodyguard, or her own team? They could do countersurveillance, follow her in order to figure out who's on her tail.

No, the last thing she wants is more people watching her, on her own dime.

Peter must be laughing in his grave.

She remembers an exchange they had. It was late in the custody battle after Esther had delivered a devastating series of body blows to Bianca. She'd also helped Peter bob and weave so that Bianca's lawyers never landed a direct hit on him. It was masterful, and during a conversation with Peter, he must have sensed that she was feeling some small measure of pride. Being Peter, he couldn't let that stand.

He instantly scoffed at her, pointing out what he thought was a mistake, or rather, a missed opportunity. Then he said, "I've done everything for you. I've made this case idiot-proof. A chimpanzee could win."

For the previous four months, Esther had been the picture of restraint. She didn't register offense; she didn't let on when her blood felt like it was literally boiling. But she finally had to release a bit of steam.

"You should have hired a chimp," she said. "I never wanted to work with you. You knew that." *You must know that I despise you and everything you represent. That in my deepest soul, I wish people like you dead.*

"You're your own worst enemy, Esther. I knew you'd turn me down but I'm doing you a favor. You suck at gratitude, I get it, I suck at that, too. But I made Greg Stanton a starchitect and now I'm making you a... what should I call it, a star-torney?" He smiled.

"Greg made himself. He's incredibly talented." Esther couldn't believe it had come to this, her defending Greg Stanton when she'd worked so hard to get her client Madeline to see him for what he was.

But was he really what Esther thought? How many of them actually are?

Peter, however, proved to be exactly what she thought. He was a real live supervillain. And there he'd stood before her, smirking, intent on getting a reaction, and after months, she'd broken down and given him one.

"I've never needed you—or any man—to make me anything," she said. "I know exactly who I am."

"You like who you are? You like everything you've done?" She said nothing. "I'm here to help you. I'm setting you free. You've built your world on a foundation of lies. Esther Kahn, protector of innocent women and children! Now that you've represented me, you can stop all the bullshit. You can just be the great attorney that you are, working for the highest bidder."

"You mean I can dispense with the burden of integrity?"

"Yes," he said, with the most sincerity she'd ever heard from him.

Her eyes nearly bulged. Did he really see himself as some kind of savior? It's mind-boggling to think he might have been that misguided. Meanwhile, his delusions were destroying people's lives.

But she would not let him destroy her.

"Oh, Esther." Peter's tone was pitying. "You think you're so smart but you really don't know anything at all. Let me guess. You actually believe I've been telling you all my secrets. Do you think I'd tell an *attorney* the whole truth?" He made a face of bald contempt.

He'd told her many terrible things that he'd done, to Avery Brengle among others. How much more could there be?

"I spend money to surveil people," he said.

"Yes, I know. You've employed entire teams just to find out my dirt—"

"Not my A teams. Sure, I've got private spy firms looking into people like you but that's chump change. You think I'm going to pay Black Cube for a dossier on you?" He shook his head at her idiocy. "I don't pay Black Cube to find out other people's secrets; I pay to protect mine. You think they're digging up dirt but it's the opposite. Six feet under isn't good enough; my stuff's at the bottom of the ocean. No one can ever touch me, Esther. Least of all you."

"Believe me, I'm not trying to touch you."

He roared with laughter. "You're a card, Esther. I've enjoyed knowing you."

"Too bad it's coming to an end. With what happened in court today, I'm sure Bianca's attorneys are advising her to settle." That's why the recent win had been so satisfying. Esther's escape was imminent.

Peter smiled at her with something akin to affection. "Haven't you figured it out by now? I don't end. I go on and on."

THIRTY-THREE

It's twilight, and Dot and Esther are in side-by-side recliners in Dot's yard, which is unkempt and overgrown and not in a fairy-tale way either. In the past, Esther's reminded Dot that she has the money for a landscaping service, given the insurance payout, but Esther's disinclined to call attention to that fact anymore. She's not about to bring up Dale again.

She lets out an involuntary and world-weary sigh. It's been the very longest week.

"Anything I can do?" Dot asks.

Esther shakes her head. She's been trying to buoy herself—writing the motion about Miles provided a brief respite—but paranoia is exhausting. Uncertainty is exhausting. Esther trusts no one, except Dot. Trusting Dot's intentions is different from trusting her judgment, though.

Esther's no closer to figuring out the identity of her stalker. Hugh, Avery, and Bianca remain at the top of the suspect list but she's not sure about the next steps in the investigation. Should she be seeking out more former clients, and their husbands? She still hasn't met with Xander Tillman.

She's been following him anonymously on social media,

using her dummy account (which is her only account), and he appears to still be out of town. His posts are all inspo porn with pictures of exotic locations, accompanied by humblebrags about getting to travel there for work. He never says where he is, using cagy captions, exhorting people to guess and then never telling them whether they're right. There's nothing in his feed about little Phil, which could mean that Xander is a completely disengaged father or that he's safeguarding his child's privacy.

Esther's not trying to gauge his fitness as a parent; the court has already done that. Her job is to recognize threats, and it's hard to imagine that Xander is one, seeing as he's off living his best life.

"There's a lot you're not telling me." Dot sits up and turns toward Esther. "Why?"

Esther can't say the true answer, which is that she doesn't want Dot to worry, because that would surely make Dot worry.

"I just feel like we haven't been on the same page lately," Esther says. It's not untrue.

"What do you mean?"

"Like when we talked about Dad." And about Dale. But Esther will be damned if she'll go down that road.

"Why does it matter whether we see our childhood in exactly the same way? You're not making sense."

Esther probably isn't. But it matters to her anyway. "Okay, here's an example. Something you never knew. Remember when you were maybe ten years old and you had a dance recital and Dad didn't make it? He said he had a flat tire—"

"He said he had two flat tires." Dot still sounds grumpy about it, after all these years.

"You thought it was a lie and that he just didn't care enough to be there. And it was okay because if he had been there, he would have acted really nice afterwards and given you lots of compliments and hugs and then a day or a week or a month later, when he got mad about something that wasn't your fault at all, when he just needed to blow off steam, he would have told you how embarrassing you were. He'd say that you'd been the worst dancer up there."

"He probably would have."

"That's why I skipped school and took two buses so I could puncture his tires. I was looking out for you, as always." Just like Esther's spent her life looking out for women and children. She glances over, expecting gratitude but, instead, Dot is looking at her askance. "You're welcome."

"How could you do something like that?"

"I wouldn't have had to if he wasn't such a monster." If they weren't all such monsters. Wasn't Dot the one saying that, given the chance, Dad would have been just like Peter Tramboni?

Dot goes quiet, then she starts to shake her head, almost imperceptibly. "Dad was nice sometimes," she says finally.

"He would have started out that way and then turned on you. That's why you needed to reject him even when he was 'being nice.'" Esther finds herself doing air quotes, even though she hates air quotes.

Another long silence.

"I rejected him because you told me to," Dot says.

"And I was right. I'm always right, you know that."

"Maybe." Dot's voice sounds faint. "I mean, yeah, you were. You are. This is probably stupid but I really would have liked to have had him there. At the recital. Just because he was my dad. I kept looking around and seeing all the other girls with their fathers and wishing..."

"We weren't like other girls! We had each other."

"True." Dot pauses and then says quietly, "You said he wasn't violent."

"What?"

"The last time we talked about Dad. You were acting like words don't hurt, as if I was making a big deal out of nothing. I should have just let it roll off my back like you did. But now he's a monster?"

"I never said words don't hurt. I think I said—"

"The last time we talked about Dad, when I was hard on him," Dot cuts in, "you were basically defending him, saying he's not really that bad. How come you couldn't agree with me then? Does everything have to be your idea?"

Dot's never this accusatory, and it's at a moment when Esther feels least capable of withstanding an onslaught. She thought she had at least one person who would always be on her side.

"Sorry," Dot says. "I know you're going through something, and I don't mean to make things worse for you."

"Don't worry about it."

The sisters are sitting in a silence that's neither combative nor companionable when July comes out through the screen door. She's barefoot, holding something that Esther can't quite make out, as she crosses the lawn.

"Hi, Aunt E!" she sings.

"Hi, July. What have you got there?" Esther is relieved for the interruption. She's also relieved that July is so mercurial, so very teenaged, because if she did experience any negative feelings about overhearing Esther the other day, they appear to have been forgotten.

"It's a present. I made it with my 3D printer." July arrives at Esther's lounger and sits on the edge. She passes it to Esther, who looks down in amazement. It's a small statue made of some sort of ceramic or polymer, a fairy-tale figure in a long cape.

"This is incredible!" Esther says.

"You're lost in the wood but you're going to find your way out," July says.

"It's me?" Tears spring to Esther's eyes. "I absolutely love it. And you said that you *printed* it? How?"

"I'll have to show you sometime."

"My genius daughter," Dot says, beaming. "She's going to change the world."

"She really is." Esther reaches and clutches July to her in a hug.

July's body tightens, and then she yields entirely to the embrace. Melts into it, like it's something she hasn't even known to hope for yet has needed for a long time.

Esther's eyes flick over to Dot. She thought Dot would be smiling at the moment between aunt and niece. But Dot seems troubled.

"Thank you," Esther says.

"You're welcome." July stands up and looks toward Dot. "Is Aunt E staying for dinner?"

"I don't think so," Dot says, though she hadn't actually asked Esther. Once July has gone back inside, Dot turns to Esther. "So where were we?"

"Nowhere. I should be heading home."

"You're sure you don't want to stay for dinner?"

Esther had the impression that Dot didn't want her to stay but that might be all in her head. "I'm not the best company right now."

"You don't have to be good company. We're family."

Esther shakes her head, and takes her leave. Driving home, she plays classical music at a volume that's ear splitting and thought stopping. She holds her mace as she approaches her porch. There's a massive bouquet of flowers, an absolute riot of color, and she lifts the card like it might be a bomb, or at least a bomb threat.

All it says is "WAPT."

Women Against Peter Tramboni.

So they're from Avery Brengle. Or could they possibly be from Bianca Tramboni, based on that joint interview? From Bianca *and* Avery?

Esther doesn't understand why Avery is so persistent. In

that interview, Avery and Bianca made it clear that they believe there are many victims out there. So why focus so much attention on Esther, who clearly doesn't want it? Is Avery being tongue-in-cheek about WAPT or is she really trying to recruit Esther to what's either a support group or vigilante society or both? Esther wants to move on and forget Peter Tramboni ever existed. For some reason, Avery won't let her.

Esther thinks of Avery's lipstick and vape pen that were really spy technology. She eyeballs the enormous bouquet. Anything could be embedded in there. So Esther takes the card out and stuffs it into the trash can of one neighbor before depositing the flowers on the front steps of another neighbor (who she's never liked).

Then she looks up and down the silent street, wondering who's coming for her next. Her stalker? Detective Zelnik? He could be out gathering more evidence, making sure his case is sewn tight before the next round of questioning. That's what she would do, if she were him. He might already know her secret, and that Peter Tramboni did, too.

If it gets out, it won't only destroy Esther; it'll also destroy Dot and the kids. So Esther might have to do things she doesn't want to do.

Again.

THIRTY-FOUR

Did you read the article You never said

Did you get my flowers

Do you hate Gloriosa lilies is that the problem

Have you blocked me is that the problem

Esther never blocks anyone because she wants to know what they're thinking. The real problem is that she can't tell what Avery is thinking, no matter what she says. Esther could really use a decoder ring.

Esther sends back, *You're not blocked. Thank you for the flowers.*

Are you a bot, or is this the real Esther

The reply has come back so quickly that Esther wonders if it could be a bot. That's why Avery is so unnerving. She provides too much data—some of it inconsistent—to get a real beat on her.

This is Esther, and it's time you left me alone.

Aw, that sounds so boring And so lonely

Is this a game to you?

Esther's had it. She'd give Avery a piece of her mind but she worries she could never get it back.

I'm incredibly serious let's meet again and i'll explain

No. Whatever you're up to, leave me out of it.

Whatever Avery and Bianca Tramboni are up to, that is.

Avery sends a disappointed face emoji followed by a blowing kiss and—is that some sort of melon? What is wrong with this woman?

So Peter Tramboni wasn't the only billionaire to find consent to be an irrelevance and an inconvenience. If Avery's a sociopath, too, she might have killed Peter not because he was bothering her but for the adventure. She'd already conquered the world so she needed a new challenge. Why not try to get away with murder?

It might be time to block Avery, though that's hardly the same as stopping her.

Avery's made it clear that she'll just keep on coming, and there's nothing Esther can do about it.

This is the very same feeling of powerlessness she had with Peter.

Someone took care of him, but Esther can't imagine she'll get that lucky this time around.

THIRTY-FIVE

"I'm at the end of my rope with this," Esther fumes. She veers *just slightly* into the next lane and is rebuked by a loud horn. "Everyone's so on edge lately. It's the whole Bay Area, isn't it? It's not just me."

"It's not just you," Dot says, her voice reassuring through the speaker phone. Esther started this conversation by confirming that Dot is, in fact, alone and no one else is within earshot. "Just to clarify, you're at the end of your rope because Avery Brengle won't stop trying to be your friend? Avery Brengle, the icon and idol of millions, including July?"

This is why it's so unsatisfying to vent to someone who can only know half the story. "You're not getting it," Esther says. But then, how could she?

"I guess I can't relate. No celebrity billionaires have ever desperately wanted to hang out with me. If only I could breathe your rarefied air!" Dot says it jokingly but Esther thinks there might actually be an undercurrent of envy.

Dot seems to have completely forgotten the circumstances by which this has come about. That Esther first met Avery at the divorce party of a blackmailer, and then saw her again at the funeral after said blackmailer had been murdered. Esther's life is about as far from enviable as it gets.

"Maybe you could get together with Avery just once," Dot suggests. "And July could come along?"

Esther takes a left turn wildly and almost goes into the median. She tries to calm down, reminding herself that Dot doesn't know about the Sleight stalker, who might very well be Avery.

"Is everything okay?" Dot asks.

"I didn't crash my car so that's a bright spot."

"Yes, that sure beats the alternative. I was just thinking that meeting Avery would make July's whole year. It would make her whole life, is what she'd say. But there's no pressure."

"I think you're missing the point. I've told Avery no, in clear and certain terms, and she keeps coming for me."

"Coming for you? She wants to take you to lunch. It sounds like she finds you fascinating."

"Which is flattering, I get it." Esther decides to try to let Dot in, just a little. "You keep thinking it's about me. It's not. It's about our shared connection to Peter."

"Don't sell yourself short, Esther."

"She came to my office uninvited to tell me all the terrible things he did to her. She assumes he must have done terrible things to me and she wants to hear all about them. You know, trauma as currency." Esther pulls into the underground courthouse parking lot and starts circling.

"Maybe it would be good for you to swap stories with someone who can understand," Dot says, "since I don't seem to be able to. Did Peter also blackmail Avery?" Dot knows there was blackmail but she doesn't know what it was truly about. Esther said that it had to do with a random case from way back when: one error in judgment that was grievous enough to potentially lead to disbarment. Dot's so trusting that she didn't even ask for the details.

It suddenly hits Esther: Someone could be listening in, and Dot basically just said that Esther was blackmailed by Peter. Even though they were talking via WhatsApp and the technology is supposed to be secure, nothing's necessarily secure with the likes of Peter Tramboni and Avery Brengle. Esther's gotten sloppy, and it could cost her.

"I've got to go," she says, trying not to let on how unsettled she is. "I'm due in court."

"Call me later, okay? I love you."

"Love you, too." It's said hurriedly, in a state of rising panic.

Esther ascends the courthouse's stone steps. Kiersten is at the top, pacing and smoking, looking entirely wrung out. It reminds Esther uncomfortably of the last time she was accosted in almost this exact same spot by Bianca Tramboni.

"Good morning," she says.

Kiersten stubs out the cigarette under her sensible flats. She's wearing the muted clothes and makeup that Esther advised and, hopefully, the judge will think that her blanched appearance is evidence of what Miles has been doing to her and to their kids.

"I thought you'd be here earlier," Kiersten says, unsmiling. "I'm about to have a heart attack." That'll work well with the motion Esther filed, pushing the narrative that Miles is intentionally trying to cause Kiersten to break down.

"Some anxiety is normal for your first time in court. But as I've told you, it won't be your last." Esther is speaking rapidly. She's in no mood to linger on a speech she's given a thousand times. "This is a marathon, not a sprint."

"I picked you so it would be fast."

"Faster," Esther corrects. "Nothing's fast in the court system. You didn't tell me you smoked." That doesn't align with the image Esther wants to present. "Do you smoke around your kids?"

"Never."

"Don't do it on the courthouse steps again, do you understand?"

Kiersten narrows her eyes. Again, this doesn't fit the picture Esther needs to paint. Kiersten better get into character quick.

"We're supposed to be partners," Kiersten says. "But you didn't tell me what you were going to put in that motion. You should have run it by me."

"We're a team. I'm the quarterback." Esther doesn't have much patience for anything, let alone second-guessing.

"I don't like my anxiety being brought out in court. What if it backfires and the judge thinks I'm some sort of mental case, that I'm not able to take care of my kids? Couldn't Miles's attorney argue that?"

"I've got this, all right?" It comes out snappish. "While there's a slight possibility that we won't win today's motion, that doesn't mean it was the wrong strategy. We're laying the groundwork. We're testing the waters." Esther is basically just stringing clichés together.

"We might not win today?" Kiersten's voice goes up an octave, and she grows even paler.

"Victory is never assured." And even victory isn't winning, as Esther's recently discovered with the Emersons and the Tillmans. How many others? She can't know. She doesn't want to know. "But I'm the best."

Kiersten looks unconvinced.

"Look, this is a great opening move," Esther says. "It's paradoxical. We're weaponizing your vulnerability. It establishes at the outset that he's a bully who'll be under the microscope going forward. Most importantly, it's true. Miles is breaking you down mentally."

"I might be stronger than you think."

"I hope you are. I'm talking about his intention. Maybe you can't see what he's doing because you've been living this way too long. Fish can't see the water they're swimming in."

"Maybe." Still unconvinced. Still partially under Miles's spell, no doubt.

When women delude themselves, it's not only out of fear; it's also out of ego. They don't want to feel like they've chosen the wrong husband for themselves, and the wrong father for their kids. They're desperate to preserve a sense of trust in their own judgment. Ego can also make them stay too long and defend their partners too vigorously to friends and family. They want to sell the lie that they've already bought into.

Could Hugh have been tricking Esther all this time by using her sizable ego against her? Even that supposedly offhanded confession of love at dinner might have been a manipulation. But what would his motive be?

It's not money, as he's never shown the slightest interest in hers. Could it be as base and simple as power, that he wants to subjugate Esther like Peter Tramboni did? Avery said what Peter really enjoyed was bringing a strong woman to her knees. Deep down, is that what all men really want?

Esther doesn't want to think that she could be as bad a judge of character as her clients. Like them, though, she finds herself making excuses for Hugh, seeing the best in him. She wants to believe in him, because really, it's the same as believing in herself.

"Let's go inside," Esther says.

Esther needs to focus on the matter at hand, which is Kiersten's motion. Kiersten's been doing her part, providing careful documentation, and that motion is bold but sound. Esther has to seem cool and collected. She reminds herself that this is her battlefield, and she's an amazing general. The judges love her. Her reputation is sterling; even Detective Zelnik has verified that.

Don't think about detectives. Or murder. Or stalkers. Or...

"Are you all right?" Kiersten asks. They're at the metal detector, and Esther had stopped dead still, holding up the line.

"Yes, sorry." She should have had her keys out and ready for the bowl, should have made this as smooth as possible given Kiersten's neuroticism. She's behaving like a rank amateur. The security guard shoots her a surprised look. Esther is always prepared, if never exactly friendly.

She feels off-kilter, and Kiersten must be sensing that. Their anxiety is commingling in an escalating feedback loop. Esther needs to get it together. She has to be the adult in the room, the voice of reason, the paragon of confidence. Her entire practice is predicated on her unflappable demeanor. She is eminently trustworthy, and every judge knows it.

She and Kiersten are through security and headed for the courtroom. Esther turns and sees that Miles and his attorney are now being screened. She reminds herself that half of her is worth two of any other attorney, and the motion should hold up. The first motion sets the tone for all that'll follow. It's when Esther wows and cows: wows the judge, cows the opposition. Like she told Kiersten, she's got this.

She's seated at her table with Kiersten, and Miles is seated at the table with his attorney. About five feet separates them but Esther knows the gulf is much greater. She has the experience. She has the skills. While she may not be bringing her absolute A game, she's still Esther Kahn.

She feels steadier as she reaches into her briefcase and takes out a copy of her motion. Rereading it is a balm. Her prose has the familiar persuasive snap. She's definitely got this.

You've done bad bad things Esther

Holy shit. She can't believe she forgot to turn down the sound, and Sleight just read an incoming stalker text out loud, for the entire courtroom to hear. She fumbles for the phone and turns it off, her face crimson. She doesn't even look over at opposing counsel, doesn't want to see the exchange of glances that must be occurring between Miles and his attorney. She knows what it's like to suddenly smell blood in the water. Normally, she's the one doing the smelling.

She can't look at Kiersten either, who's already an anxious mess.

Esther feels like she's been set on fire. She's suddenly thinking of bad things, of Dale and the Tillmans and the Emersons. Of how many others there might be.

No, no, no.

That's exactly what her Sleight stalker wants, to throw her off her game and make her doubt herself. She has no reason to. Wilfred was spewing nonsense. The Emersons and the Tillmans are just one-offs. Well, two-offs.

The bailiff has everyone stand up as the judge takes the bench. Esther has appeared often in front of this particular judge and he almost always rules in her favor.

"I've reviewed the brief," he says, "and I have to say, what I'm seeing here doesn't justify an emergency motion." He looks sternly at Esther. "Ms. Kahn, you know my feeling about attorneys abusing ex parte motions. I don't appreciate people trying to jump the queue."

Esther is astonished. She thought she'd at least have the chance to argue her motion, which has clear merit. But the judge is saying she thought wrong. She can feel Kiersten staring at her. Or maybe glaring. Esther won't turn to find out. She keeps her gaze locked on the judge as she gets to her feet.

"Your Honor, you know me. I wouldn't bring an ex parte motion unless I was seeing a strong early pattern that requires a strong early response." She's not at her most eloquent but she is starting to warm to her argument. Esther knows men like Miles very well.

Doesn't she?

Miles's attorney leaps to his feet, and into the fray. He'd like to present his counterargument, all the problematic behavior that the children's mother has been exhibiting, a sort of low-level gatekeeping. What he starts spelling out makes it sound like Kiersten is the manipulative one, always playing the victim, and that this predates their relationship and extends beyond it.

He's convincing, actually. Esther realizes that she hadn't been as careful in vetting Kiersten as she would normally be. She'd been too preoccupied with Peter Tramboni, and too eager to have a go at Miles. What if Esther can't trust her radar anymore, with her clients or their husbands?

Kiersten is looking at her; she can feel it. Now the judge is looking at her. Obviously, she's supposed to defend her client. To represent her client, that's the mandate. But no words are springing to mind.

In contentious divorce cases (and nearly all Esther's cases fit this bill, because she cherry picks for that very feature), it's about showcasing injustice, painting people in the worst possible light. It's all about excess. She sets out to prove that the other parent is the absolute worst: the most abusive, irresponsible, inconsiderate, immoral, controlling, inadequate, uninvolved. Esther's trick is presenting an extreme picture while sounding like the voice of moderation in an increasingly immoderate world.

Has it all just been smoke and mirrors? She doesn't know what's true anymore.

But she needs to perform. Now. Or this is quickly going to get away from her, and Miles's attorney will have momentum on his side.

Throughout her career—throughout her life—Esther has projected an aura of implacable strength, and she's been rewarded for it, handsomely. She's believed herself to be strong since she could do such brutal work with so little feeling.

Wilfred would say she's been doing it to avoid feeling. That she's been trying to resolve her past through her clients' present, which never works. It only delays the inevitable reckoning.

"I have nothing further, Your Honor," she says, sitting down, her eyes downcast.

She's never suffered from imposter syndrome. If anything, she's suffered from the opposite affliction.

Esther's starting to feel like she's the one on trial. But who's going to render the judgment?

THIRTY-SIX

"I'm glad you called," Hugh says. He's standing uncertainly on her doorstep, racquet bag on his shoulder, spine unnaturally straight like a caricature of an upright citizen.

She wants to think he's just nervous to see her and while that may be true, she suspects that he's also nervous because he's been drinking and driving. He knows how Esther feels about that, and he must realize that their relationship is already hanging by a thread.

This is the last thing she needs. She was hoping for a night where he proved his trustworthiness.

Despite her poor performance in court this morning, the judge still ruled in her favor. Miles's attorney had looked dumbfounded, and Miles himself incensed. The judge explained that the written motion had been persuasive, and he warned Miles to "avoid any type of psychological escalation or retaliation." She should feel triumphant but instead, she's humiliated, having had to coast on her reputation. She'd been second best, and everyone there knew it.

At her office afterwards, she was so mired in self-doubt that she couldn't even work. That's why she knocked off by five, came home, and texted Hugh for a tennis match. She needs to kick someone's ass and his is the most socially acceptable.

"It's still light outside," she says, with more dismay than disgust. "What time did you start drinking?"

"I haven't had anything to drink. You can smell my breath."

"Hard pass." He was either drinking vodka or has just eaten a mint. Whatever his game is, she doesn't want to play. She wants to play tennis.

He buckles immediately under her stare. "I'm sorry," he says. "I did stop for a drink on the way here. It's been so strained between us that I didn't know what I might be walking into."

She has been erratic, but that's no excuse. She's made it clear since the beginning that she doesn't want to be with an overgrown frat boy. He needs to be able to handle his alcohol, or have the self-control to abstain.

"If you want to drink, then drink," she says. "But you don't drive, and you don't lie."

He looks like he might actually start crying. "I don't know what to do anymore. I need this to work." What does he mean, he needs it? Is that a clue?

"All I wanted was to play tennis," she says.

"I know I'm screwing up. I'm not giving you what you need. I feel guilty all the time."

"What I need right now is to take a walk." Esther grabs her racquet bag, putting it over her shoulder. "I'm going to hit some balls against the backboard. You can hang out here and sober up."

"It was one drink, Esther."

She doesn't know if she believes him. She doesn't even care right now. He can hold down the fort and if someone tries to break in, she'll finally have independent confirmation that her stalker is real (and that it's not Hugh). Also, she can watch what he does. All the internal cameras are turned on.

"See you later!" she says, pushing past him and striding down the street.

There are groups clustered, waiting for a tennis court, laughing and jostling each other, but Esther has the backboard all to herself. She tries to drown out the revelry around her and focus on her goal of a hundred controlled forehands. Every time she screws up, she has to start again from one. It's entirely absorbing, so much so that she doesn't notice the turnover around her, that the courts are starting to clear out.

"Hi, Esther."

She spins around, racquet held up high like a weapon, and sees Detective Zelnik. She's breathing hard not only from the exertion but from the adrenaline. "How long have you been watching me?" she asks.

"I just got here. I went to your house and saw your boyfriend."

"I'm a fifty-one-year-old woman. I don't have boyfriends."

Detective Zelnik smiles. He really is a painfully nondescript man. "Hugh Warshaw answered your door and told me you were here. I just have a few more questions about the Peter Tramboni case."

Esther's eyes flit toward the nearby court. There's one doubles match still in progress and no one is paying Esther any mind. She moves a little closer to the detective so they can't be overheard but she doesn't intend to find a bench. Unless he has a warrant, this better be quick.

"I'll get right to it," he says. "I know you were blackmailed into taking Mr. Tramboni's case."

Does he know that because of Dot, because he listened in to their WhatsApp call?

"Can you confirm that?" he tries again.

"I already told you why I took Peter's case."

"So you're denying you were blackmailed?"

"I didn't kill Peter Tramboni," she says. "All the time you're spending investigating me would be better spent on legitimate suspects. There must be many."

"Why's that?"

"Because Peter made enemies. That's no secret. I just didn't happen to be one of them. I represented him in a custody case that was over at the time of his murder. We had no outside relationship." Esther would prefer if she didn't have to spell it out for Detective Zelnik but he's left her no choice.

"So you weren't blackmailed by Peter Tramboni?"

"Who told you I was?" He's silent. "Oh, right, you ask the questions around here. I'd like to know who's telling such outrageous lies about me. I'm sure you can understand that." Still nothing. "And what was Peter's supposed leverage?"

"I can't say." Because he doesn't know? "I'm trying to help you."

"I don't doubt that." Of course she does. She doubts everything.

"I'm giving you the chance to come clean right now. It'll save me time, and if you didn't kill Peter, it'll save you, too."

"I've already told you what I know." He gives her a dubious look. "Everything that's not protected by attorney-client privilege. Unfortunately, that doesn't leave much."

He's staring her down, turning the screws. She's not sure how much longer she'll be able to hold him off.

"If you change your mind," he says, "you know where to find me."

"I do." She forces herself to smile. "Have a good night, Detective."

After he's walked away, she checks her phone. Was it turned on? Could someone have been eavesdropping on their conversation?

She sees that Hugh texted her a heads up earlier to say that Detective Zelnik was on his way: *I thought of telling him I didn't know where you were but you said no more lies.*

Picking up her racquet, she heads back toward the wall with a murderous expression on her face. She starts hitting the ball as hard as she can, enjoying how every time it ricochets back harder.

THIRTY-SEVEN

"Don't come in!" Hugh calls from the kitchen. "I'm making dinner, it's a surprise!"

As if the island resort hadn't been enough of a bust. Will he never learn?

She drops her racquet bag in the foyer, noticing that's where Hugh has left his. She inches toward it as she calls back, "I'm not coming in!"

She can hear him bustling around two rooms away, stirring and slamming with vigor, and figures the coast is clear. She unzips his bag and begins methodically working her way through each and every compartment.

As expected, the organization is haphazard. There's a towel, sunscreen, three visors, overgrip, a massage roller, deodorant, a first-aid kit, extra jock straps, t-shirts, shorts, and socks. She feels along the inside of every pocket. There it is. Not a gun, fortunately, but a flask. Half-full.

She carefully replaces all the items, her disappointment swelling. She knew he was lying earlier about stopping off for one drink. He couldn't even wait to get to her house so they could have a whiskey together like a couple of legitimately stressed out, responsible adults. That's because at dinner the other night, he'd been telling another lie. He doesn't want to drink socially; he wants to drink antisocially. That way, no one can keep tabs on his quantities.

What other secrets is he keeping?

She thinks of what he said when he arrived. *I need this to work... I feel guilty all the time...* What did he really mean?

"I'm going to take a quick shower!" she shouts. She's glad she doesn't have to walk into the kitchen and put on a little show about how good it smells, how sweet he is, etc.

She heads upstairs to the master bedroom and strips off her clothes. In the en suite bathroom, she turns on the shower spray, waiting for the water to heat up. Once she steps inside, shutting the glass door behind her, she feels a flutter of anxiety. She doesn't know what she'll do if he comes in to join her. They haven't spent a night together since Gaia, haven't even kissed.

Maybe this is it, their swan song. They'll share one final meal together and have an amicable parting. "I really tried," she'll say, "but I'm not cut out for relationships."

She rinses the shampoo from her hair and decides to skip the conditioner. As she hastily soaps up her body, she realizes that she's a little bit afraid to break up with him. If he's her stalker, she'll be inciting even more anger; if he's not, she'd be losing a valuable protector.

She turns off the shower, towels off, and dons a loose-fitting top and yoga pants. No makeup. No need to impress.

He smiles when she enters the kitchen. "You look beautiful," he says.

She waves a hand dismissively. She's had enough lies, whether in the name of romance or something else.

"It smells good," she says, which is true.

"French toast." He gestures toward a plate where the

completed slices are piled high with a plaid tea towel draped over the top to keep them warm. "I know you love it."

She can see how he would think that since it's one of the only dishes she cooks. She seats herself at the island and watches him pirouette around the kitchen. He doesn't seem inebriated, just light on his feet. Happy.

That's until he glances out the window, his brows knitting together. He returns his attention to the stove.

"What?" she demands.

"I didn't want to say anything but..." He looks uncomfortable before plunging ahead. "Every so often, I catch sight of a drone. It's probably nothing. Just some kid playing around."

"You think it's circling the house? Spying?"

He hesitates. "It might be."

She runs to the front door and yanks it open. She steps outside and sure enough, there it is, hovering near the house, a small hunk of metal with two tiny propellers and a camera that seems to be trained on her.

She slams the door and dashes back into the kitchen, closing all the blinds that Hugh had opened.

"It's probably nothing," he says unconvincingly. "Just a kid playing around."

"You already said that. It looks really sophisticated." Not that she has any actual knowledge. "I bet it can see through walls. It's looking at us right now." That's the level of technology that Peter would have had, and that Avery probably does.

"I'm no drone expert but that sounds pretty much impossible. We're inside. We're safe now."

But Esther knows better. She's not safe anywhere. That's what the Sleight messages, the perfume, the flowers, and the drone are all telling her.

She feels a small measure of relief because her stalker is

now unlikely to be Hugh, followed by a major uptick in fear since it's probably someone far more powerful. As that awareness sinks in, she starts to crumple to the floor, and Hugh immediately comes to take her in his arms. It seems so easy for him to love her in one of her weakest moments and, in turn, she abandons herself to his embrace in a way she's never done with any romantic partner.

A partner. Maybe that's really what he is. Sure, he's told a few lies and he probably needs to go back to AA meetings but no one's perfect, right? She certainly isn't.

She's afraid, yes, but she's not alone. She murmurs with a peculiar ecstasy, "It's not you!"

He pulls his head back to look into her face. "It's not me?" he asks, confused. Worried.

She laughs. "No, I mean... it is you. You're my person. But you're not my stalker. Which is great. It's amazing." She's not used to rambling and she hopes he'll laugh with her.

Instead, his face is suffused with a complicated mixture of emotions. "You thought I was a stalker until just now?"

"I'm sorry for suspecting you. But now I know I can trust you completely."

One single emotion crystallizes across his features, and it's unmistakable. It's guilt.

She thuds back to earth, pulling free. "What have you done, Hugh?"

"Nothing," he says, sounding like a very bad actor, in more ways than one.

"There's something. Tell me now." She sounds accusing but that's just a front. She wants him to exonerate himself. She needs him to be innocent of... whatever it is. It's probably not stalking—though, come to think of it, he could have an accomplice who's operating the drone. He was the one who noticed it first and then pointed it out to her. "This is your chance to come clean." She realizes she's paraphrasing Detective Zelnik from earlier.

She stares at him and sees him wavering. Then he doubles down. "There's nothing, Esther."

"I don't believe you," she says sorrowfully. When he takes a step toward her, she takes a step back.

"I love you. That's the God's honest truth." He looks so sincere. She wants him to be innocent but she can feel that he's not. He's lying about something and she won't spend any more nights trying to suss it out. "I'm not a stalker, Esther!"

"But what are you? Who are you?"

"You know who I am. And I know who you are." Is it her imagination, or did he go from plaintive to just the tiniest bit menacing?

"I need you to leave. This is over."

It's not like she's never pictured herself saying those words. Really, when she and Hugh started out, it seemed inevitable. Everything ends, and why would their relationship be the exception? But she didn't know it would burn like this, and she hadn't imagined the devastation on Hugh's face. This is by far the most vulnerable she's ever been with him, the most vulnerable she's ever been with anyone.

"You don't want to do this," he says.

"I have to."

"Come and eat dinner with me. You can't make a decision like this on an empty stomach." He gives her a crooked smile.

"It's decided."

His smile disappears. "You haven't been yourself lately, Esther. Why don't we just take a little time off and you can see a therapist and talk it over?"

She should tell him to go fuck himself. She's not crazy; she's not about to let a man gaslight her. But she has felt a little crazy lately, hasn't she?

"Please reconsider," he says. "I'm begging you. I'll do whatever you want." He knows better than to move closer but she can see how hard he's fighting himself not to. How much he wants to be with her.

"Go now," she says. While unbearably painful, it also feels like the last vestige of control she has.

THIRTY-EIGHT

Worst. Night. Ever.

In the morning, Esther can barely drag herself to work. She sits at her desk where she's capable of nothing. For the first time since she opened her practice, she has zero billable hours. She refuses to take any client phone calls, telling her assistant to leave her alone unless something's on fire. Literally.

Kiersten's called four times already. On Esther's best day, she's not one for hand holding. She's already referred Kiersten to a therapist and doesn't appreciate this entitled bullshit. Does Kiersten think she's Esther's only client?

Esther calls Dot, hoping her sister will draw the story out of her (though of course Esther will have to omit some of the finer details), but Dot is in a frenzy of her own. She made a mistake that's proven costly for the VP she supports, and now she's in fear of losing her job. Dot always gets that way after a mistake, and Esther reminds her of that, a touch impatiently, and also of the fact that Dot's VP adores her. When they get off the phone, Dot seems somewhat placated while Esther's just as miserable.

She starts searching for escapist Netflix shows she can binge-watch, discovering that anything that isn't a kids show or a romcom seems to feature stalking, abuse, assault, accidental death, or murder. When did thrillers take over the world? If she wanted to be immersed in darkness, she'd read the news and scroll social media. Or she could just think about her own life.

There's a knock on the door. "Sorry to bother you." Esther's assistant sounds hesitant. "But Kiersten's on the phone again, and it's kind of an emergency. She's threatening to fire you."

Esther laughs. "Is she now?" Maybe Kiersten and Miles deserve each other. "Please tell her to make good on her threat."

"Are you sure?"

"I'll be happy to refund the unused portion of the retainer and have her file delivered to her new attorney. Godspeed."

"Okay, I'll let her know." A few minutes pass and then there's another knock. "Kiersten asked me to tell you, um"—a long pause—"that your motion was fucked up, and you did a shitty job in court, and she doesn't trust you as far as she can throw you. She says you're a fraud and a phony and she's not the only one that thinks so."

"Well, that's a mouthful!" Esther feels like she's had her first stroke of luck in quite some time. She's clearly dodged a bullet.

It's time to pull herself together, and get back to work. Back to sleuthing, that is.

Most likely, Hugh's not her stalker, which means she still has a mystery to solve. She doesn't have time to sit around moping and grieving. That drone was a clue, though it seemed to be one that the stalker wanted her to see. It was in-your-face, which is Avery's calling card. Esther hasn't had any texts from her in a while. Is that because Avery has gotten bored with Esther, or because she's plotting her next move?

Detective Zelnik is on Esther's tail, and so's her stalker. Esther can't afford passivity; she has to consider all leads.

She hasn't yet adequately investigated Xander Tillman. She's been looking at his social media, which is what he wants the world to see. She needs to figure out what he could be concealing.

It occurs to her that she doesn't even know where he's working. Despite the many allusions to his Big Important Job on Instagram, he never names the company. So Esther decides to start with his LinkedIn page, where she makes a shocking discovery. During the divorce proceedings, Xander had been an incredibly expensive IT contractor, selling himself to the highest bidder. Now she sees that one of his biggest clients had been Nimbus and two years ago, he was hired at Sleight where he's had a meteoric rise, going through three titles in less than two years. He's currently listed as "chief crisis engineer." What had Julianne called him? The right-hand man to a CEO. That CEO is Avery Brengle.

So Avery had poached Xander. That's how Peter would have seen it anyway. He may even have been suing Xander at the time of his death, seeing as Peter's left behind more lawsuits than heirs.

Esther feels a twinge of excitement. Xander's the first person who's independently connected to herself, Peter, and Avery. Esther doesn't know what that means, but she's going to find out.

She has to proceed with some degree of caution; you can't just roll up to the office of a potential stalker/murderer. And as far as she can tell from Xander's Instagram, he's still out of the country, incessantly posting photos of his very charmed and jet-setting life. He's undoubtedly a douche, but is he also a sociopath?

Esther's sifting through possible plans of attack when she hears a commotion from the reception area. A man is giving her assistant a hard time. He's belligerent, insisting he needs to see Esther and he won't take no for an answer. He doesn't care if she's not available right now; hell, he can wait all day! He'll just be sitting in that chair over there! When Esther's assistant asks politely that he leave a message rather than camping out, he retorts, "It's called a waiting area for a reason, right?" Oh, he's a clever one.

Esther's lip curls. She can't quite place the voice. Her assistant shouldn't have to put up with that kind of bullying. She shouldn't have to go about her business with a guy like that less than ten feet away.

Esther considers texting to empower her assistant: *Tell him he needs to leave or you'll call the police.* But for a certain kind of man, them's fighting words. Also, this is Oakland. Everyone knows it'll be hours before the police arrive, if they ever do.

Esther's going to have to take care of this herself.

Getting to her feet, she goes into her shadowboxing routine. She's feeling more like herself by the second, and that charmer out there is going to get what's coming to him.

She opens the door to see Miles lounging in a chair in the reception area, holding a copy of *Architectural Digest*.

At the sight of her, he breaks into a broad smile. "Well, someone sure had a rough night!" he says, his smile growing meaner.

She knows she's less polished than usual, that her hair isn't blown out and is instead exhibiting its natural waves but she did pull a brush through it. She's in a sharp pair of trousers and a sweater, not disheveled at all, and she's not going to let Miles score any cheap points. She holds her chin up higher as she approaches him, standing closer to him than he probably expected.

He gets to his feet. He's a large man, but she won't be intimidated. "What can I do for you?" she says.

"You can't do anything anymore!" He turns gloating. "Because you got fired!"

"I'm not at liberty to discuss—"

"Kiersten told me herself. She said that she never consented to that motion, that you took things she told you completely out of context. You called me"—he lowers his voice, which means he is at least capable of some shame—"a wifebeater."

"I don't use that kind of language." Esther is keeping her tone neutral and her face expressionless but inside, she's feeling some anger. Kiersten hung her out to dry.

"I never hit my wife."

It's possible Kiersten had been lying, though in Esther's experience, only an infinitesimally small number of women claim to be victims when they're not. It's far more likely that they'll deny it when they are.

"You have no business here," Esther says. "You need to leave."

His voice is still low, but now it's more of a growl. "Do you really think I beat women and make them go crazy? Well, then maybe you're my next victim."

"Do you know how it'll boost Kiersten's case if I file a police report for harassment? I'll also be more than happy to reach out to her next attorney. I've always wanted to be the star witness against a real peach of a guy like you." She lets a smile graze her lips.

He's visibly angry but clamps his lips shut. He knows he still has a lot to lose.

"You've got one minute to leave or I'm making the call." She pivots on her heel and heads into her office. She won't look back or look to her assistant but she can sense that his wheels are spinning, wondering if there's some parting shot he can get in before she shuts her door. Spoiler alert: He can't.

While Miles and his ilk might not be as bad as Peter, they all reside along the same spectrum. Peter was the most extreme because he had the most power. Or had he made sure to amass the most power because he was already the most extreme?

"He's gone!" Esther's assistant calls through the door. "Thank you, that was awesome!"

"My pleasure," Esther calls back.

She begins reviewing her potential suspects and doing additional reconnaissance on Xander. At exactly 5 p.m., the Sleight messages begin:

Quitting time Esther

someone's waiting

to string you up

to make you bleed

to rip out your innards

and your heart

wait you don't have one of those

you think you're better than everyone

so maybe you should be nailed to the cross until the streets run red and you can't hurt anyone

ever again

It's so different from the others. It's a sort of poem, as if the stalker is taking artistic pleasure in the gruesome images. Even Officer Connors would be able to see the threat, but the messages have disappeared as quickly as they came, impossible to screenshot.

Could it have been Miles? Or Kiersten?

Avery, with Xander by her side?

Bianca?

What about Hugh, a man scorned?

Could it be all of them?

Not working together, of course. Even Esther's not that paranoid. But perhaps they've all independently decided to take a swing at her. Sleight makes it so convenient and risk-free that anyone can be a stalker.

Esther had heard that stalking's gone up 5000 percent since the app's debut, and that's a conservative estimate. Avery says that some people misuse her app but that happens with all technology, and Sleight is intended for legitimate purposes, to facilitate connection between people. It's a thin defense, like the disclaimer on the Q-tip box that says they're not supposed to go in ears.

But what can anyone really do about Avery? She's too rich and too pretty and too charming and too in-your-face and two steps ahead. She's Peter Tramboni 2.0.

So if it is her, if she's the one, or one of the ones, who's got Esther in her sights... then Esther could be well and truly fucked.

THIRTY-NINE

Esther's sitting in her car outside Dot's house, debating whether to knock. She doesn't want to bring her problems to her sister's doorstep but she's not sure she can be alone.

The joyful and grisly vitriol of that Sleight poem really has her rattled. Someone's reveling in their hatred. Assuming they'd already been engaging in mental torture, will it soon progress to the physical? How much danger is she truly in?

The police have made it clear that they don't care. Sprat and His Wife took hours to get to her house and were then offended that she wasted their time, and though she contacted Officer Connors the next day to follow up, he's never called back. She can only imagine what Sprat and His Wife said to Officer Connors, the laugh they had at her expense.

But she hasn't tried every cop she knows, has she?

Before she can stop herself from what might very well be a terrible idea, she's gone through her purse, found the business card, and dialed the number. He probably won't even answer.

"Detective Zelnik," he says.

"This is Esther Kahn. I have information that could be relevant to your investigation." There's a quaver in her voice but she doesn't sound unhinged.

"Go on."

"The problem is, it's not verifiable. You know Sleight messages vanish, and they can't be screenshot. So I have no proof. You'd have to take me at my word."

"What's the information, Esther?" He sounds gentle. Is he handling her with kid gloves because she *does* sound unhinged?

"For weeks now, I've been receiving anonymous messages through the Sleight app. They started soon after Peter's murder. While I couldn't save them, I did document every one, immediately writing them down in my Notes app." She fumbles with her phone. "The first was, 'You think no one knows who you really are?', followed by, 'You think no one knows what you've done?'" Esther's heart is beginning to race. "Should I continue?"

"Absolutely." Is he intrigued because he thinks this could be a clue as to who the murderer is, or because he thinks it's confirmation that Esther is the murderer? This is a huge gamble. But she's running out of options.

"Mostly the messages are vague. My theory is that the author doesn't actually know anything about me but assumes that, like everyone else, I have skeletons in my closet. They're assuming I'll drive myself mad. Sometimes the messages are mocking in tone, sometimes they're—"

"Could you please read the rest?"

Esther probably never should have started this but now that she has, she needs to finish it. She reads them all aloud, in order, and when she gets to the poem, she can't help it, her voice breaks. The messages might not be specific but the malevolence is targeted. People despise her. Not only that, they think she's the one who's evil.

"Thank you for sharing those," the detective says. Is he mocking her, too? No, he sounds kind. Sympathetic, even.

It's almost like he believes her.

She's overcome by an intense rush of relief and gratitude. Maybe this call was the best thing she's done. It could hold the key not only to her exoneration but to the actual perpetrator(s) being held accountable. It's possible the stalker and Peter's murderer are one and the same. But if they're not, Detective Zelnik speaks cop. He can convince Officer Connors to finally do his job.

"I've made some enemies in my work," Esther says. "I can't name my former clients but I'm looking into their former husbands. Bianca Tramboni was clearly very angry with me. She accosted me twice: once at Peter's funeral, the other time on the Oakland courthouse steps. Avery Brengle has sent me texts repeatedly and even visited my office unannounced, insisting on girl talk about Peter, even though I told her that I'm not interested."

"You think Avery Brengle might be your stalker?" It seems like there might be a hint of incredulity in his tone. But Esther can't afford to hold that against him, when he's virtually all she has.

"I know, it sounds crazy. The Sleight founder using her own app to stalk a middle-aged attorney. But she's told me repeatedly that she's intrigued by me, that she thinks—" Esther stops herself. If she says that Avery feels like she and Esther have something in common, that they were both traumatized by Peter, then she's not just giving Avery a motive for his murder; she's giving herself one, too. It would also contradict the story Esther's told Detective Zelnik about how Peter was a client, nothing more.

The detective claimed to already know about the blackmail but that doesn't mean he knows what Esther actually did. He could have just been floating a theory, seeing if she'd bite.

Until this moment, she hasn't bit. She's fully kept her own (and Peter's) counsel. But during the course of this phone call, she's placed an enormous degree of faith and trust in Detective

Zelnik, without any real evidence that it's warranted. What if he's been stringing her along, feigning compassion?

He didn't crack her; he let her crack herself.

"Finish your sentence," he says. "Avery Brengle thinks what?"

"I'm not sure. I barely know her, but for some reason, she seems to want to know me. For example, she texted me that I should read that *New York Times* interview she gave with Bianca Tramboni." Time to throw aspersions back on Avery and Bianca. "You must have seen that, right?"

"Let's review the suspects. You think your stalker could be Bianca Tramboni or Avery Brengle. Anyone else?"

"I've been looking into the ex-husbands of my former clients, the ones who seemed to have a lot of anger toward me over how their cases resolved. I can text you some names." She'll add Miles to that list, but not Kiersten for confidentiality reasons. Though Kiersten did just fire Esther so it's a bit murkier.

"What about your personal life? Any chance it could be Hugh Warshaw?"

Esther startles. Does Detective Zelnik already know about the breakup? Or does he know something else about Hugh?

"I don't see why Hugh would do something like that," she says carefully. Silence on the line. "Do you have a reason to believe that he would?"

"He's not always the most forthcoming, that's all. I don't know that I'd outright call him shifty, but the connection between him and Peter Tramboni—that was a curveball."

"Mm-hmm." Esther's noise is non-committal. She wants the detective to go on.

"You know that Hugh worked for Peter years back, right? He must have told you that story."

"No," Esther says. "Maybe you could tell me now."

The detective must be feeling magnanimous because he

does. "Hugh was Peter's attorney back when Peter was a coder working for a tech company. He sued his employer for stealing his intellectual property. He claimed his bosses had taken work he'd done in his off-hours from his private laptop and then used it to create a best-selling product for themselves while giving him no credit or financial compensation beyond his salary."

Esther shakes her head in disgust. So Peter knew exactly what it felt like to have his work appropriated and yet once he had his own company, he did the same to countless others. He truly was the lowest of the low.

"Did Hugh win the case?" she asks.

"Yep, Hugh and Peter won. But they never worked together again. Peter started his company and proceeded to hire the biggest hotshot attorneys in Silicon Valley."

Is Detective Zelnik suggesting that Hugh has been nursing a grudge all these years against Peter and then decided to commit murder? That seems pretty far-fetched. Hugh did seem jealous of Esther and Peter, though, didn't he?

Much as Esther would like to think that there's an ulterior motive behind Detective Zelnik revealing Hugh's prior association with Peter, that perhaps he's trying to get Hugh and Esther to turn on each other, that doesn't mean she can discount what she's hearing. She can't imagine he's lying about something that's a matter of public record. Esther could verify it as soon as they hang up.

Which means Hugh lied for months. He deliberately withheld this information from her, acting as if his knowledge of Peter was only from what he'd read.

Shifty indeed. It suddenly seems way too convenient that Hugh had bumped into her at the Berkeley Rose Garden tennis courts when he doesn't live anywhere near there.

Esther and Hugh share a profession that's nominally about the law but is ultimately a high-stakes poker game. It's all about human nature, and reading people. Seeing the worst in people.

At first, Esther had seen the worst in Hugh during the Stanton divorce and then she'd allowed herself to rethink that opinion. That might have been one of the biggest mistakes she's ever made.

Just like Esther, Hugh has an extensive network of private detectives to whom he refers his clients. He could have hired them at any time to investigate Esther. His wouldn't be on the same level as Peter Tramboni's, would they? Or maybe he used the very same ones. Or he didn't need to, if he and Peter had stayed in touch all these years and traded information. The fact that Hugh never represented Peter again doesn't mean that it wasn't still a mutually beneficial relationship.

How well does she really know Hugh Warshaw?

It's possible she's underestimated him since they met. Once they got involved, he was quick to agree that she's the better lawyer, and the more principled person. He told her outright that he was morally agnostic. And while she was beating him at tennis and at life and assuming an overall superiority, he could have been operating in the shadows, gathering intel and gaining the upper hand.

Last night, he really seemed like he loved her. It had torn her up to let him go.

But it's a new day, and she's going to need to take care of Hugh, once and for all. He's given her no choice.

FORTY

"You don't need to do that," Esther says. "I can make up my own bed."

Dot finishes smoothing the fitted sheet over the mattress of the pullout couch. "I just wish we had a guest room."

"You did the right thing, not moving to a bigger house. Saving that money."

Esther had done the right thing, too. If she hadn't taken action, Dale would have continued to drain the life force from everyone she loves. He was really just another villain, wasn't he? The proverbial wolf in sheep's clothing. The bad guy cloaked as the good guy, and Dot had never been able to see through his disguise. She still believes he was a good man who died too soon.

Esther wishes it could have been otherwise. She'd really wanted Dale to prove her wrong, had hoped fatherhood would change him for the better. But Tyson came along first, and then July, and Dale only got worse.

When she was pregnant, Dot had to be on bed rest but she'd done it with her laptop, making incredibly simple shopping lists with recipes even Dale could follow, placing orders and having groceries delivered (this was before the days of Instacart), and opening every jar herself from bed (with Dale claiming "substandard grip strength"). Esther had to bite her tongue because, ostensibly, Dot was happy with Dale. He was the antithesis of their father so Dot always felt safe and in control.

But as the years went by, Esther could see the toll that the marriage was taking. Dot had a full-time job, two kids, and a household to run. She did absolutely everything because Dale was always demonstrating his incompetence. Esther was sure that it was intentional, as no sentient being could be that inept, but Dot never faulted him. She picked up the slack to the point of extreme exhaustion. Still, she continued to defend him, saying, "He's the kindest man, E. He really is. He'll listen to me complain for hours." But the reason Dot had complaints, why her life felt so overwhelming, was because of Dale. On the rare occasions Esther pointed that out, though, Dot shook her head definitively.

No. Stop. Go no further.

Then there was the IBS. Irritable bowel syndrome. Most people who have it continue to go about their lives and meet the needs of their family but Dale was debilitated and wanted everyone to know it. He wanted pity. If Esther heard about that man's gastric tract one more time she thought she would scream. He had to manage his diet and his stress, which meant that Dot had to do even more for him and never make him feel bad about it in the slightest because that could trigger another episode. "Besides," Dot would say, "it's not like he wants to be this way."

Esther wasn't so sure about that. It was his get-out-of-jail-free card, a way to contribute even less to his home and family. He was nice enough to the kids but he wasn't very involved and Esther suspected that was just how he liked it.

Over time, it continued to eat at Esther, and it was hurting her relationship with Dot. Her blood boiled every time Dot complained, because Esther was starting to feel like her sister was choosing misery by choosing Dale. But there was clearly no getting through to her, and if Esther kept pushing, who knew what would happen?

Then Dale suddenly announced he wanted a divorce. Since the marriage had seemed to benefit him the most—far more than it benefited Dot or their kids—Dot had been confounded and stricken. But Esther knew she'd get over Dale soon. How long could someone mourn for a person who brought virtually nothing to the table?

Esther made sure the divorce was wrapped up immediately, strongly in Dot's favor. No one thought it strange that Dale had rolled over and given his family everything. He wanted it to look like a sign of how progressive he was, though it was also a sign of his general lack of an animating force. He'd never had any fight or ambition in him. But even Esther had been surprised that, after the divorce, he barely saw his children.

Less than two years later, he was dead.

Dot, July, and Tyson can never know Esther's role in all of it. But what Esther knows in her bones is that what she did was the most loving act of her life. It was her legacy. She'd been okay with keeping it secret. She only wishes Peter had never found out.

"There," Dot says, fluffing the pillow and adjusting the duvet. "Let me just grab you some pajamas."

"Thank you," Esther says, abashed, wishing she didn't have to lean on her sister. It's supposed to be the other way around.

"This is what family does. We take care of each other." Dot's tone is brusque, an indication of the distance that's been growing between them.

Has Dot been the one pulling away, or is this Esther's doing?

"I'm sorry about Small," Dot says. "I know I never met him but in a strange way, I was pulling for him."

"I guess I was, too," Esther says quietly. When she arrived tonight, she'd told Dot that she broke up with Small because he'd started drinking again, and that she didn't want to sleep in her bed without him. Really, she broke up with Hugh because she can't trust him but she truly doesn't want to be alone tonight. It feels like dark forces are amassing against her. But she isn't about to say that out loud.

Maybe that's the gulf between her and Dot, the growing collection of micro-lies. Not to mention the whopper about Dale.

An awkward silence descends. Esther is bracing herself for Dot asking more questions about Hugh but it doesn't happen. Instead, Dot walks away, returning a minute later with a pair of aged flannel pajamas.

"Try to get some sleep, okay?" she says. She gives Esther a quick hug. "Love you, see you in the morning."

Could Dot have beaten a hastier retreat? But then, she knows that Esther isn't one to talk about her feelings. This is probably just Dot respecting her sister's privacy. Still, Esther wouldn't have minded some company.

She puts on the pajamas. They smell like Dot's floral fabric softener, which is comforting. She turns the light off and climbs onto the sofa bed. It groans under her weight, and she groans at the metal bar that's pressuring her lumbar spine.

She rests her head on the pillow (also floral scented) and tries to think of nothing. Because it'll all still be there in the morning. Tomorrow, she'll come up with a solid plan of attack. She needs to do what she's always done: wait for the right high-probability shot so that, when she fires, she won't miss.

She's worried that she can't afford to wait long. Hugh might fire first.

He *brought a gun* on their vacation and still she kept him around for weeks, dithering and vacillating. She still doesn't understand her own motivations. Love? Fear? Ego? All three? Or had it been some other element of her unconscious?

She forces her eyes to close but she can't force her mind to shutter. She's besieged by images of the various suspects interspersed with her own victims—little Phil Tillman and Naomi Emerson and Dale—though she tells herself those kids weren't her victims; their parents are the ones who did this to them. Esther had done her best to mitigate the damage. And how had Dale gotten in there? He'd brought everything on himself.

Esther's doing battle with herself, trying to thrash her way to sleep, when July walks into the living room.

"Oh, hi, Aunt E," she says in surprise. "I didn't know you were here."

"What are you doing up?" Esther says. July is taking all those AP classes; she needs her rest.

"I got hungry."

"You didn't eat enough dinner?"

"I ate a lot. I just get hungry. Mom says I'm probably on the verge of another growth spurt." July comes over and sits down on the edge of the mattress. "Why are you here?"

It's even more embarrassing to say to July than it was to Dot. Fortunately, it's too dark for them to make out each other's features. "I had a breakup."

"I didn't even know you had a boyfriend. What was he like?"

"He was..." Esther can't bring herself to answer. "It was a complicated relationship. Doomed from the start."

"But you loved him?"

"I didn't say that."

"You didn't love him but you're so upset that you have to sleep on our shitty sofa bed?" July is just too damn smart, and always has been.

Time for a subject change. "It's felt a little off between your mom and me. Do you know why that is?"

"Maybe it's about Dad?"

"My dad?" Esther says.

"No, mine."

Now Esther's gone and stepped in it. She should probably say something about what July and Tyson overheard on speakerphone, soften her comments about Dale. She's not opposed to telling just one more lie to protect July's feelings, only she's not sure she'll be able to do it convincingly. July's awfully shrewd.

"I'm sorry for what I said when you were in the car with your mom the other day," she says finally. "That was really out of line."

"Wow! I didn't know you apologized." July sounds impressed.

"I do when I'm wrong."

"You don't think you're wrong much, do you?" July doesn't wait for an answer. "I don't think I'm wrong much either."

"It was an accident. If I'd known you and Tyson were in the car, I never would have badmouthed your father."

"But you never liked him. I mean, I could tell that when I was five."

"I should have hid it better." Esther pauses. "So you think your mom is mad at me for talking that way about your dad?"

"I don't think she's mad, exactly. She just... she thinks about him a lot more than she lets on to you. I do, too. And sometimes when we want to, like, grieve or mourn or whatever, we have to pull away from you."

Esther stares at July. "You don't have to."

"Sure, we do. Because we know how much you hated him."

"It wasn't hate," Esther protests. She tries to think of a diplomatic slant. "He just wasn't my kind of person." July laughs. "What? He wasn't."

"You thought he was garbage for not pulling his weight. But really, he was sick in bed—or sick in the bathroom—a lot of the time. I love you, Aunt E, but you're not always the most compassionate."

"Do you really feel like you need to keep it from me when you grieve?" Esther is hit hard with the image of Phil sitting coloring, how he waited until his mother left the room to scamper over to Esther and share the secret that he still loved his father.

"Mom and I both do. I don't know about Tyson. I don't think it affects him much."

"You still feel affected by your father's death?"

"Of course!" July sounds like she can't believe that Esther wouldn't know that. "I love him and I miss him, but for the longest time, I didn't want to tell you that."

"Why?"

"I didn't want you to think I was weak."

Tears prick Esther's eyes. Not only did she have a hand in taking July's father away from her, but all this time, July's been afraid to be honest. She didn't want to risk losing Esther, too, by admitting her feelings for her dead father. What a burden for a young girl to carry.

Has Dot felt that way, too? Has Esther made her family feel like her love depends on them agreeing with her?

Phil Tillman's "confession" about loving his father had given Esther pause, enough so that she sought out Wilfred von Holten. But she never wanted Wilfred's true assessment of her; she only wanted confirmation of her rectitude.

He tried to tell her that she's been destroying lives. She's hurt people deeply, including the ones she values most, because she hasn't recognized the impact of her own childhood. He'd challenged her binary view of the world, intimating that maybe she's not a good woman going after bad men but is instead a damaged woman trying to turn her scars into badges of honor.

And what did she do? She immediately and aggressively discounted him. *To his face.* Then she turned around and went after Miles with even greater ferocity, turning him (and Kiersten) into additional suspects for her list.

What kind of woman is Esther Kahn, really, and what has she wrought?

For perhaps the first time in her life, she hasn't the foggiest idea.

FORTY-ONE

"Good night, Esther!" her assistant calls from the reception area. It carries through Esther's locked door.

She startles, coming to as if she's been in a trance, and in a way, she has. The entire day has passed in a miasma and now it's five o'clock. She feels panicked, realizing that she doesn't want to be left there alone.

"Good night!" she yells back, scrambling to get her things together. She thinks for a second of asking her assistant to wait so they can go to the garage together but then remembers that her assistant takes the bus.

What she needs to do is hurry to the garage, get in her car, and drive home. Then she'll pack a bag quickly, head to downtown Oakland, and check into one of those massive hotels that span an entire city block. Sure, whoever's stalking her will be able to tail her somehow and know the location but they won't know which room she's in, not right away. Plus, there would be security personnel and surveillance cameras and other guests to contend with. The stalker couldn't avoid detection nearly as easily.

On her way out the door, she catches sight of herself in a

reflective surface and shudders. She's in yesterday's wrinkled clothes, having come directly from Dot's house this morning. She should have scheduled a blowout with Stylist but all day long, she hasn't been able to muster the energy. She couldn't think productively, couldn't work, couldn't plan. All she could do was ruminate on that shattering conversation with July, recognizing how neatly it dovetails with what she'd witnessed of Phil Tillman and with what Wilfred had told her about children of divorce.

How many times has her gut been wrong over the years? How many families could she have decimated as a result?

She gets in an elevator car alone and takes it down into the garage, which is peculiarly empty given that it's rush hour. Where is everyone? She finds herself moving faster and faster, perspiration dampening her hairline.

She's headed down the row toward her car when she hears the urgent clacking of footsteps behind her. She whirls around, mace in hand, to find that it's Avery and Bianca. Bianca's in a tight dress and heels (hence the footsteps), and Avery's in shapeless athleisure with a pair of high-top sneakers (silent as a ninja). They're an odd couple, like Hugh and Esther are. Used to be.

"I don't want to talk to you," Esther says, walking even more briskly. "Either of you."

Avery must break into a full-out sprint because she catches up to Esther in what feels like a nanosecond. "Oh, Esther." Avery's doing that disappointed thing again, which would be galling if Esther had the energy for gall. Because how dare Avery be disappointed? How dare she hold any expectation of Esther at all?

Avery runs around so that she's blocking the driver's side door. Esther starts to walk around the car, she'll get in the passenger side if needed, but now Bianca is there. She's surrounded.

"What are you, a couple of thugs?" she asks.

Now Avery's doing that delighted laugh of hers. That diabolical laugh.

Esther is standing by her trunk, in between the women, not sure what to do. Should she dash back into the building? It's not like they'd hurt her physically. Would they?

She glances around to locate the nearest security camera. Good, it's right there. But is it just recording, or is someone viewing this? Someone who could either come to Esther's aid, or at least provide corroboration or testimony later?

Esther can see that Bianca wants to cause bodily harm. There's pure hate on her face.

"I hated Peter, too, okay?" Esther says. "I wish I hadn't worked for him. There, I said it. Now can you both leave me alone?"

"No," Bianca says. "You need to say publicly that you lied about me."

"I didn't lie. I presented a case." Peter may have lied in his documentation, Esther has no way of knowing for sure, but she didn't lie. She spun. "I operated within the bounds of the law."

Neither woman budges. Are they going to kill her and stuff her in her own trunk? Did one—or both—of them murder Peter?

"There are cameras," she points, "all over this garage."

"Right. The cameras." Avery's expression is affable and amused. Then her eyes widen. "Do you think we're here to hurt you?"

"I don't know why you're here! I've told you repeatedly and in no uncertain terms that I'm not going to be a part of WAPT."

"What's WAPT?" Bianca asks Avery.

"Private joke," Avery answers. Then to Esther, "We just want justice, and you're an integral part of that. The fact that Peter was able to get a principled woman like you to do what you did to Bianca is further proof that he was evil incarnate."

"And why do you need to prove that now?" Esther says.

"I'm suing his estate for slander," Bianca says. "I'm entitled to way more than what was in that prenup and you know it."

"I thought you were suing me for slander. Didn't you visit Hugh Warshaw?" Or had that been another of his lies?

"I told her that was a dumb idea." Avery shoots Bianca a look. "You catch more flies with honey, right? I don't know why you've been dousing Esther in vinegar. She's a victim, too."

Bianca says, "This is about providing for my son. I want him to have a mother he can be proud of. I'm going to launch a comeback, starting my own fashion line." Her tone suggests that's akin to curing cancer.

"Is it a comeback, if you were an up-and-comer who never actually arrived?" Avery asks Esther conversationally, as if they're buddies sharing a covert laugh at Bianca.

This whole scene is surreal.

"I just want to go home," Esther nearly moans. She doesn't even care how she sounds. She's dispensed with pride. "Please, stop with the texts. Stop with the Sleight messages."

"Sleight messages?" Avery's curiosity seems to be piqued. "What do they say?" As in, they're not from her? Or is she only pretending they're not?

"Are they from you, then?" Esther stares at Bianca.

Bianca puts her hands up as if she's pure innocence. "I'd never use Sleight."

"Oh, fuck you, Bianca." But Avery sounds good-natured. "I'll never wear your clothes so I guess we're even." Bianca gives her an annoyed look.

Esther doesn't understand the relationship between those two, with all the barbs and the shards. But then, they do have a common enemy in Peter. And neither of them seem to realize that he's dead.

"I'm done fixating on Peter," Esther says. "I'm done talking about him and thinking about him."

"But he's not done with you," Avery says. "Isn't that one of his classic lines?" She lowers her voice in imitation. "'I go on and on.'"

Bianca nods seriously. "He did love that line."

"But it's not true," Esther says. "Don't you get it? He's dead! You're alive! Move on! Let me move on!"

Avery smiles. "It's good to finally see some life in you, Esther. Sometimes I thought I was dealing with an android." Then she stops smiling. "But you're wrong. Peter does go on and on. The trauma is still inside us and it has to be purged."

"Just because you feel that way doesn't mean all women do," Esther says. "You can't browbeat people into discussing their trauma."

"So you admit it!" Avery points at Esther triumphantly. "You are traumatized!"

Esther's not insane, right? Avery is. This entire interaction is.

"I'm not trying to help you," Bianca says. "I meant what I said. I think you should rot in hell, just like Peter. You made sure I got the bare minimum in my settlement, and now all Peter's ex-wives are contesting his will. My attorney says it could be years before my son and I see a dime, if we ever do. So this slander suit against the estate is all I have, and you're going to help me win it."

"I couldn't do that, even if I want to," Esther says. "Attorney-client privilege means I'd get disbarred."

Bianca takes a step toward Esther, her jaw working furiously. "You're going to do it, Esther. You owe me that much, and you know it."

"You don't have to break privilege," Avery says. "Just tell what he did to you. Tell your story, not his. Talk about the blackmail."

"How do you know about the blackmail?" Esther asks. Is there anyone who *doesn't* know?

"Ha! So it's true!" Avery turns to Bianca. "I knew it had to be blackmail. I mean, that's Peter's bread and butter, and Esther's not the type of woman who'd work for him otherwise."

Esther inhales deeply. She's just confirmed for Avery and Bianca that she has a secret big enough to have forced her into servitude to Peter Tramboni. Bianca might be strapped for cash at the moment but Avery's got deep pockets. If she wants to find out the secret badly enough, she'll be able to do it. After all, Peter had.

Esther feels faint.

Avery must be able to see the change in Esther because she says to Bianca, "Stop being so aggressive, okay? Esther's with us."

"No, she really isn't," Bianca says.

"What I mean is, Esther's a victim, too."

"Agree to disagree." When Bianca addresses Esther again, her tone is steel. "You're either with us or you're against us."

Avery looks regretful but then says, "She's right, unfortunately. What's it going to be, Esther?"

All Esther wants is to get away from them. She can't be part of some feminist movement right now, or whatever plot those two are hatching. She's not fit to be around anyone. She can't save anyone. She's coming apart at the seams.

She barrels into Avery, who goes flying out of the way, probably more from the surprise than the force. Esther leaps into the car.

"I'm against you," she shouts. "Now get out of my way!"

She starts the engine. If she has to, she'll run them over. It would be self-defense, wouldn't it? If she stays here another minute, she'll go mad.

Mad enough to kill?

She hopes not. But all bets are off.

FORTY-TWO

The next morning, the news is everywhere: Avery Brengle is dead.

Murdered, by a single shot through the back of her skull, just like Peter Tramboni. The same perpetrator, or a copycat? Is there a billionaire serial killer on the loose in Silicon Valley?

Esther doesn't even come close to the income requirement, but she's terrified, nonetheless.

It could be that whoever killed Peter and Avery will be after her next. Or is she being framed? Because Esther—along with Bianca—must have been one of the last people to see Avery alive.

Avery and Bianca had to jump out of the way when Esther put her car into reverse. Later that same night, Avery was gunned down.

Bianca might tell Detective Zelnik that Esther had intended to kill her and Avery, and then Esther went back to finish the job. But it's not true. Avery and Bianca had been the aggressors, not Esther. All Esther wanted—all she wants—is to be left alone so she can begin to reconcile what she's done. Maybe she does deserve to rot in hell alongside Peter. Who knows? She can't get a moment's peace to figure it out. They're all coming for her.

Could Bianca be the murderer? It's unlikely, since Avery seemed to be integral to Bianca's plan to clear her name and sully Peter's. But maybe something happened after Esther peeled out. There were quite a few points of tension between Bianca and Avery, and Bianca does have issues with impulse control.

If that's the case, Esther could really be in trouble. She outright said that she was against Bianca, who has a definite vindictive streak. Not as wide as Peter's but that's not saying much.

Esther debates whether to go to Detective Zelnik and tell the truth about the previous day: that Avery and Bianca had made strange bedfellows, with pretty apparent fault lines, and that they'd been trying to strongarm Esther. The parking lot cameras will show they were the ones accosting her.

But she has no idea what the detective is thinking about the case, or about her. He'd seemed sympathetic during their last conversation when he dropped that intel about Hugh but that could have been an act, a way to get her to spill. And spill she had. She told him Avery was stalking her, which could now look like a motive to kill.

Who's higher on his current suspect list, Bianca or Esther? He could easily be partial to Bianca, the young, pretty "widow" and single mother. While the court hadn't found Bianca to be more persuasive than Esther, Detective Zelnik might. For all Esther knows, Bianca's gotten to him first and told him her version of events, implicating Esther.

On the other hand, there might be other, more likely suspects. Like, say, Xander Tillman? Esther could be driving herself crazy for no reason. Maybe with Avery dead, her problems have all been solved.

FORTY-THREE

Esther had been wondering about her place on the suspect list and she gets her answer when Detective Zelnik shows up at her house that afternoon. She's in an oversized sweatshirt and joggers, her hair unbrushed.

"Home sick?" Detective Zelnik raises an eyebrow.

"If that's what my assistant told you." Esther steps aside to let him enter. She should have been ready for this, yet she'd found herself incapable of preparation. Incapable of strategy. Her whole life, she thought she was the hero; now it's looking like she might be the villain. She's ravaged, and she doesn't have the acting chops to hide it.

She sits down on one sofa; the detective takes the other. They're facing off but instead of the usual rush of adversarial adrenaline, she feels resignation. She just wants it all to stop, one way or another.

"You must realize how this looks," he says. "The day after Avery Brengle's murder, you skip work?"

Just because it has a question mark on the end doesn't make it a question. Esther says nothing.

He sighs, as if he wants to help but she's not making it easy.

"It's time to lay our cards on the table, Esther. You were intimately involved with both victims, Peter Tramboni and Avery Brengle. Peter blackmailed you, and Avery stalked you. Now they're both dead."

She doesn't speak.

"Where were you last night at ten p.m.?"

"Driving around. I drove around most of the night. I'd packed a bag and intended to go straight to a hotel but then I realized I felt safer when I was moving." She can't tell if he believes her or not.

"Did you stop for gas?" She shakes her head. "So there's no one to verify your whereabouts. What time did you check into a hotel?"

"About two or three a.m."

"I'll need the name." So he can ask questions of the front desk staff that were on duty, see how memorable she was, if she came in seeming like a woman who'd just committed murder.

"Oakland Marriott, downtown."

"Thank you." He's probably wondering about the change in demeanor, why she's so cooperative, whether it indicates innocence or guilt. Might as well cut to the chase.

"If you haven't talked to Bianca Tramboni yet today," Esther says, "you should. She and Avery accosted me at about five p.m. in the garage under my office building."

He looks surprised. That she's volunteering information, or that she was accosted?

"I told you I was being stalked. If you need proof, get the security footage."

Further surprise, tinged with... pity? "I've already been to your building and reviewed the footage." So he was a step ahead of her, arming himself so he could spot a lie.

But he won't be able to. Esther is being entirely truthful. She doesn't have the bandwidth for keeping stories straight. "If you already watched the footage, then you know what happened. They surrounded me. They were trying to force me to talk to them when I kept saying I didn't want to."

"There's no sound."

"But you can see their body language. You can tell I was just trying to get away."

"I saw the footage." He's speaking slowly, reluctantly, like he doesn't want to be the bearer of bad news. "You were walking to your car alone."

"Right. Until they came after me. They chased me down."

"No, Esther. It was just you talking to yourself. Almost like you were having an argument with someone in your head."

For a minute, she thinks maybe he's right, she has lost it. But then it dawns on her. "Avery's lipstick. And her vape." He tilts his head in confusion so she starts to explain. "Avery approached me at Peter's house and she had this technology that blocked sound waves. It might block camera waves, too."

"There's no such thing as camera waves."

"All I know is she must have done something because she and Bianca were in that parking garage last night but somehow they're not visible in the footage." Esther had mentioned the cameras to Avery and Avery had been entirely unfazed. "I'm not crazy."

"I never said you were."

"But I am haunted." She takes a deep breath. She hadn't even known she was looking forward to this moment, to finally letting it all out. "I'm haunted by my sister's dead husband, Dale. By what I did to him. I guess you could say I killed him. No, I did kill him."

The detective's eyes widen. He came here for one confession but he's going to get another.

Esther can't keep running from her past, and from her culpability. She tried to do something to help her family but that conversation with July showed her that it was dead wrong.

"All my life, I've appointed myself judge, jury, and executioner," she says. "My rulings are based on my gut, and my gut spoke up from the beginning about Dale, loudly. I thought he was a selfish leech. A parasite who sucked my sister Dot dry. An awful role model to two growing children. I stand by that assessment, actually. But that doesn't excuse what I did."

"Which is?"

"I took him away from the family that loved him. I didn't think they should love him but they did, and I didn't respect that. I thought I knew better. I thought I knew best." She stares down at her hands, feeling the enormity of what she's done and the overwhelming shame of it.

She tells the detective that she didn't start out wanting Dale to die, but she did want his role in her family's life significantly reduced. So she engineered a divorce. She paid a shady private security firm to download child pornography onto Dale's computer. Loads of it, slowly, over the course of a year (Esther knows how to play the long game) and then have it deleted all at once as if he feared discovery while ensuring that the traces couldn't be erased.

"Like it's written in invisible ink." That's what she told Dale. "If you try to take it somewhere to have it cleaned up, then you'll surely be reported to the police. At which point you'd be up on charges." Protective mother that Dot was (and is), he'd be kicked out of the house. He'd be humiliated and likely fired and no court would ever let him see his kids again.

Or he could just go quietly, without making trouble. He'd still get to see his kids; he could still maintain his dignity, what little he had.

He'd folded quickly. "I know I can't go up against you," he said. He told her she's too smart and too connected but between the lines what she heard was, "I'm a big lump of nothing, just as you always suspected, with no personal agency or self-respect. I have nothing to give my family; all I do is take."

"I felt vindicated," Esther says. "Can you imagine? I see this man in front of me sobbing and I don't have an ounce of sympathy. All I'm thinking is that this leech will no longer be feeding off Dot and the kids. I'm setting them free. I couldn't even see how much he loved them and what he was losing. Or what Dot and the kids might be losing."

Detective Zelnik hasn't said a word throughout her soliloquy. When she glances up, she can't read his expression. "You must think I'm a monster," she says.

"I don't think anything yet. I'm just listening."

Esther stares at him in amazement. Could he really be able to stay that open-minded? That's a skill Esther's never developed. Has she actually tried, though? Maybe it's not too late for her.

But it is too soon to even think about redemption. Her whole life she's believed that people need to pay for their crimes. That has to include her.

"Dale did as he was told," Esther continues. "He went to Dot and said he wanted a divorce. He gave her very little explanation, just said he'd realized he needed out, and she was..." It hurts to even remember it, how shattered Dot had been. "I never told him that he shouldn't see the kids afterward. I wrote up what I thought was a generous visitation schedule, given the circumstances, and submitted it to the court. He would have them for a weeknight and every other weekend. That was more influence than I wanted him to have, honestly, but I went with Dot's wishes." She glances at the detective again. "I know how that sounds."

"How does it sound?"

"Like I'm trying to pat myself on the back or excuse myself. But I get it. I understand what I've done."

"What have you done?"

So he's going to make her say it.

"I destroyed their family." It comes out not much above a whisper. She can barely breathe but she has to keep going. "He was supposed to still be in the kids' lives. But he wasn't. He never came around."

"Because he was too ashamed?"

"Too broken, I think. I don't really know. At the time, I thought it was more evidence against him. I'd been right all along; he really didn't care about anyone but himself."

"You don't think that anymore?"

"I think it doesn't matter what I think." She lets out a shuddering, juddering sigh. "I've always thought my opinion mattered the most. It's kind of a family motto: Esther knows best." Though she hasn't said that lately, has she? And neither has Dot. "Whether he was a good man or a bad man, he was a husband and a father. He was a person. I treated him as if he had no value at all. I even told him that he had to get a life insurance policy and keep Dot and the kids as beneficiaries because he was worth more dead than alive."

Detective Zelnik's eyebrows go up. He deals in murder every day and even he's appalled by that.

"I know. It was a disgusting thing to say. I thought I was being honest. And protective of my family, which he didn't deserve to be a part of. I didn't know about the cancer that was probably already growing inside him. He bought the life insurance policy and then he basically spent the next two years withering away. He died of colon cancer without ever getting treatment."

"So you didn't actually kill him?" She thinks she detects a note of disappointment.

"Haven't you been listening? I separated him from his family. I told him he was worthless. I sapped his will to live."

"But he made the decision not to see his kids, even though he had visitation rights. He also made the decision to ignore all his symptoms until it was too late."

"If he'd taken his own life, the policy wouldn't have been paid. In his way, he was truly selfless."

"No, he was selfish." Detective Zelnik shakes his head. "He robbed his kids of years they could have spent with him."

So much for non-judgmental. But somehow he's letting Esther off the hook, which isn't what she wants.

"You were selfish, too, don't get me wrong," he adds. "What you did was nine kinds of fucked up. But he should have pulled himself together for his kids. Made sure he stayed in their lives, and seen a doctor, for Christ's sake."

"Maybe. But I shouldn't have been preying on the weak. I can be a bully, in my way." Like with her clients' husbands. Some of those men are irredeemable, no question about it, but like Wilfred said, others should be treated. They could be healed.

"I can see that," Detective Zelnik allows. For some reason, she finds that comforting.

"Peter Tramboni had private investigators looking into me and somehow—I have no idea how—he pieced together what I did. He said that he'd see that I was brought up on charges, that he could get the firm who downloaded the porn to testify against me. If that happened, I'd be ruined, and my sister and her kids would know what I'd done. Or, he said, I could work for him."

"Sounds like an easy choice."

"Deceptively easy. It was a devil's bargain. Not to put too fine a point on it, but Peter was the devil. You must know that. By now, you've heard all the stories." She stares off into space. "Maybe what he did to me was a sort of cosmic payback. After all, I blackmailed Dale long before Peter blackmailed me."

"So why did you decide to kill Peter? Was he going to release your secret even though you held up your end of the bargain?"

"I didn't kill Peter."

"Come on, Esther." Detective Zelnik's expression is surprisingly soft. Fond, even. "You want to clear your conscience; I can feel that. You believe in justice."

"I do. But I didn't kill Peter."

"Next you're going to tell me you didn't kill Avery either. Even though she was stalking you and supposedly attacked you in the parking garage and you've got no alibi for the time of her murder?"

Esther shakes her head. "I'm sorry, but no. I didn't kill Peter or Avery."

"And you didn't actually kill your sister's husband either. Cancer did." He'd been almost smiling but now he looks nearly angry. "What do you think this is, the library story hour? I've got two murders to solve. I'm not your priest; I'm a homicide detective."

He's not wrong. On some level, she had been hoping that confession would clear her conscience. Deep down she'd known how unlikely it was that she'd be up on charges for what she did to Dale. The story is far too convoluted for any district attorney to want to present to a jury. They like to keep it simple. As simple as, "Esther was blackmailed by Peter Tramboni so she killed him. Esther was stalked by Avery Brengle so she killed her." The person Esther really needs to confess to is Dot, but that would likely kill her sister. So there can be no absolution. Esther's just going to have to live with what she's done.

Detective Zelnik is getting to his feet. Weirdly, she feels sorry for him. She can only imagine how eager he must be to close these cases and exit the seedy world of billionaires.

"I'm guilty of a lot," Esther says apologetically, "but I'm not guilty of killing Peter or Avery. I don't even own a gun." She does, however, know someone who does. Yet somehow, despite everything, she can't bring herself to say Hugh's name. It hurts too much, and besides, she can't trust the law to take care of him. It moves too slowly. She's the one who'll have to protect herself and her family. "Don't you have ballistic reports? Can't you trace the gun?"

"Gee, why didn't I think of that?" The detective doesn't attempt to disguise his annoyance, which feels like a form of intimacy. "Do you have any idea how many unregistered guns there are in this state? How many homemade guns there are? Some people are very, very smart about how they procure and dispose of weapons."

"Unfortunately for you, I'm not one of them."

"That is unfortunate." He gives a wry smile. "Now stop wasting my time. I have a serial killer to catch."

FORTY-FOUR

Esther's doing her civic duty, trying to help Detective Zelnik. If all goes according to plan, she can take out a stalker and a serial killer in the same go.

According to Instagram, Xander Tillman is back in town. On social media, he was mum on the subject of his former boss Peter Tramboni's murder, but he's ostentatiously grieving for Avery Brengle. All Sleight employees have been given the rest of the week off, and there's a flag atop the headquarters at half-mast (that's Xander's new profile pic).

She sends him a Sleight message:

I have information about Avery's murder.

Who is this?

Don't worry, you'll recognize me when we meet up.

Why would I meet up with you?

Because I know where you were last night, and it wasn't Ibiza or Corsica. Avery can't protect you anymore.

Esther holds her breath. She's borrowing from the stalker playbook, issuing a vague threat that can be interpreted in multiple ways. Will he take the bait?

Minutes pass. Then Xander messages:

How do I know I'm not going to get a gun in my back?

You choose the location. Then you can see me coming. But if anything happens to me, the police will be all over you. If they're not already.

Xander chooses the Sleight campus. She knows from the news that it's shut down, which seems to confirm what Julianne said about Xander's stature at the company.

Now Esther's in for another interminable gridlocked drive out to Menlo Park, into the belly of the beast, the heart of Silicon Valley. This reminds her of all the times she was unceremoniously summoned by Peter Tramboni. Is Xander another man on a power trip? Had Peter gotten in his way? Had Avery?

Esther has no clear idea what to expect. During the Tillman divorce, she'd been convinced that Xander was a ruthless psychopath. Then in meeting with Julianne a few weeks ago, it had sounded like he might just be a dad trying to do his best while co-parenting with a hateful ex. Of course, it could be that Julianne's become a cold, hard bitch as the result of dealing with a ruthless psychopath for all these years.

In other words, the jury's out.

Esther's also still trying to decide how she feels about Avery being gone from the world. Peter's evil had been undeniable. Avery is a far more complicated character. Like Peter, she wouldn't take no for an answer and didn't believe the rules applied to her. She repeatedly crossed Esther's boundaries, so she must have done it to others, too. When you're young, brilliant, and beautiful, your trespasses are forgiven far too easily.

The fact remains, Avery's death had been shockingly premature, and Sleight had only been her first venture. Had she lived, WAPT might have come to fruition, starting a cascade in Silicon Valley, its own belated #MeToo moment. Sure, her fortune came from an app that makes it easy to harass and terrorize but as she pointed out in what was to be her very last profile, Sleight's also an equalizer. "You can get to anyone," she said, "including those in power who assume they're untouchable." She claimed it had always been intended as a tool of accountability, a means for the disenfranchised to form whisper networks and organize movements, a way to anonymously call perpetrators out for their crimes. "It reminds predators that they're being watched," Avery said. "That they're being *seen*."

When Esther first read that, she thought it was self-serving bullshit and that Avery was trying to avoid her own accountability. After all, everyone knows that by a wide margin, the app is used for more harm than good. But now Esther realizes that in her own life, Sleight served the very function that Avery intended. Esther's finally having to see what she's done. She's having to face that she doesn't know everything.

In that same profile, Avery said she was working on something big, a game changer. A society changer. The last line? "I want to leave this world better than I found it."

Esther had assumed that was bullshit, too. Now she's not so sure. She feels a surge of regret. She wishes she hadn't tried so hard to shut Avery down. To keep her out. What might Esther have learned if she'd let Avery in?

Now Avery's dead but Sleight will live on for humanity to use as it sees fit, to its benefit and to its detriment. Esther wonders who's at the helm now and if they'll have access to whatever new technology Avery was developing. Could it wind up being Xander?

Esther is startled out of these musings by another Sleight poem. It emerges from her phone, read aloud. The disturbing content is rendered creepier by the AI voice, that uncanny valley, how it closely replicates humanity but can't quite pass.

People are wrong about you

your heart isn't entirely made of stone

you love few but you love fierce

those you love are set to suffer

and you'll know won't you

that it's all your fault

you did this to them

in the name of love

It has to be Hugh. None of her former clients would know how many she loves, or how she loves. The author of this poem has been on the inside. All along, she's continued to hope against hope that it wouldn't be him. That it would be anyone but Hugh.

She's officially out of hope. And if that message is to be believed—*those you love are set to suffer*—she's also running out of time.

It's hard to imagine Hugh is the murderer, though. He might have killed Peter, but why Avery?

Xander, however, has a few potential motives. He could

have murdered Avery for passion, revenge, or ambition, assuming he's next in line at Sleight.

Esther's going to find out the truth, once and for all. A plan is starting to come together in her mind. It's a little risky but it has the potential to kill two birds with one stone.

If she gets very lucky, she'll destroy both bad men tonight.

FORTY-FIVE

Hugh's house is a large and sprawling rancher, located in an unspectacular neighborhood. It's a behemoth, by far the largest on the block, and every Halloween, Hugh goes all out, turning it into a haunted mansion. He plays a vampire or assorted ghouls. Most recently, he was an evil henchman with a hunchback. How had Esther missed those clues?

She knocks on the door, more angry than nervous but nervous that she'll show her anger. She still can't believe he'd threaten her family. Did he really think he could get away with that?

He opens the door, looking haggard and shocked. "I never thought I'd see you again," he says. He's obviously drunk, and it's made him melodramatic. Hopefully, it'll also make him susceptible to manipulation. But she has to proceed with caution, because he could be more erratic.

"Could I come in?" she asks. "I was hoping we could talk."

"Of course." He steps to the side and ushers her in.

The house is a wreck; he's a wreck. Is he too intoxicated to even be embarrassed? Or is he too happy to see her? Insanely enough, that's the impression he's giving off. Maybe he doesn't even remember sending the Sleight poem. If he's in a blackout state, she needs to be even more careful. He'll have no inhibitions at all.

The living room looks like a rock star has been partying there, with several pieces of furniture upended and the coffee table covered in food wrappers and liquor bottles. He doesn't bother to tidy or conceal anything, which is ironic given all the things he's been hiding from her. He sits in that ridiculous high-backed armchair of his, the one that used to make her jokingly call him Louis XIV. She sits on the equally ridiculous olive-green baroque sofa.

"How are you?" she says, feigning concern. Well, it's not entirely an act. Some tiny part of her—a very stupid part—actually is concerned about him. He's clearly not in his right mind.

"Rotten. And yourself?"

"It's been rough." That, at least, is true. Because he's made sure of it.

"I thought maybe you were overjoyed to get rid of me." He's not actually slurring, but his consonants lack their usual crispness.

"No, it's actually the opposite." She takes a deep breath. Showtime. "I've been thinking I might have been too hasty, that maybe we could try again."

"You? Too hasty?"

"It's been known to happen." To her ears, it's a painfully wooden performance but he seems to be buying it completely. She should be overjoyed but instead she feels a little bit sick. Has it really come to this? "You think it over, okay? I'm going to use the restroom. Traffic was bad; it was a long drive." She's talking too much, overexplaining. He's going to see through her.

Except he doesn't want to. "I can give you my answer now," he says.

"In a minute." She stumbles to her feet and then does her

best to steady herself. She heads down the hall, hoping he won't follow her. Hoping that the gun is where it's supposed to be.

"I like your hair that way!" he calls after her. "All messy and sexy!"

She bypasses the guest bathroom and instead heads for his bedroom. He has an en suite bathroom and, if she gets caught, she can claim she wanted to use that one for privacy. It's easy to be stealthy since he has plush wall-to-wall carpeting. And no security system, thankfully. He thought his gun was all he needed.

She slips into the master and makes a beeline for his nightstand. It has a lock that he never uses. She remembers a conversation they had one time where she chastised him for his carelessness. "Don't you know how often intruders end up using the gun on the owner?" she asked.

He had a twinkle in his eye as he said, "No, do you?"

She's shaking a little as she pulls open the drawer and sees that it's still there. She lifts it up, feeling the familiar heft, remembering when she last held it while Hugh slept beside her. Remembering when she last held him. How did they get here?

This is no time for nostalgia.

She's done research since that first time she discovered it and she checks to make sure the safety is engaged. It is. She also learned how to disengage it, though that's currently theoretical knowledge. Later tonight, it might become actual.

She thinks she hears his steps in the hall and she shifts the gun in her hands so that it's pointed toward the door. Her heart is about to explode out of her chest as she waits.

But then... nothing. It must have been her imagination. More likely, he's passed out in his armchair.

She tries to calm herself as she slips the gun into her purse. Then she goes down the hall and into the guest bathroom. She flushes the toilet, turns on the water to feign washing her hands for the full thirty seconds that she always does, before heading back to the living room.

He's moved over to the couch. He smiles and gestures for her to sit beside him. "I've missed you so much, Esther," he says.

"I'm sorry." Tears fill her eyes and she's not even acting. "I don't think this is going to work."

"No, it'll work. You came back to me for a reason."

"You're drunk as a skunk, Hugh. You won't even remember this in the morning." She can't believe she feels guilty for tricking him after all he's done. She just needs to get out of here. Finish this. Finish him.

"It's the stress of losing you," he says desperately. "I can quit any time. If you give me another chance—"

"Get sober and we can talk again," she says. She turns away from his stricken face, hoping that he won't say anything more or come after her.

It's only when she reaches the pavement outside that she can finally exhale. Phase One has gone off without a hitch.

So why does she feel so awful?

She has to remember that if he lied to her for months about something as big as his prior association with Peter, he could lie about anything. If he could send her those Sleight poems, then he truly has no conscience. He's a threat to her and her family that has to be neutralized, no matter how pathetic and lovesick he looked just now. For all she knows, he's a murderer who's trying to frame her for the killings.

She has plenty to feel guilty about, but framing him right back won't make the list.

FORTY-SIX

Esther could be driving out to meet a murderer, in his own lair, on his terms. But she's not empty-handed. She comes bearing a gift.

It takes over two hours to get to the Sleight campus from Hugh's house, and dusk is falling as she pulls up to the large iron gate. Esther's never been here before and she's startled to find that it has a similar aesthetic to her house, that it's fortressed brick like a castle in a fairy tale. The compound inside is shaped like a tower. It must be Avery's sense of humor, that the princess isn't the one imprisoned inside it; she built it herself.

"Who goes there?" a voice booms through the intercom.

"Esther Kahn."

The gate creaks slowly open. Esther wonders if there's some other entrance because this seems like an extremely inefficient way for employees to arrive every day. Maybe it's just meant to impress visitors, or to amuse them. Avery did laugh a lot; Esther knows that from experience. The thought that someone deliberately silenced Avery with a bullet to the brain is almost too much to process.

And is Esther about to come face to face with that person?

She drives along the lane toward the tower. It's further than it appears, almost seems like it's receding into the distance. A Sleight message comes in. Xander's telling her to meet him on the grassy knoll. What the...?

Oh, there's a sign, with an arrow: The Grassy Knoll.

The name seems prophetic, given the way Avery was killed. It wasn't quite like JFK but it was assassination style. She could have called this large patch of grass something more beatific, like the Lovely Meadow, but that wasn't her style. Instead, she'd gone for a name associated with not only violence but conspiracy. The campus is an architectural manifestation of its contradictory founder.

Esther parks her car, gets out, and looks around. She sees one lone figure up ahead sitting on a bench. It's too dark to tell but she has to assume it's Xander. She's glad she has the gun. Just in case it's not him. Just in case it is him.

As she approaches, Xander takes her in, without expression. He's handsome as ever, a sloe-eyed matinee idol from the 1940s, as if all his features are edged in charcoal.

"You're not surprised to see me," she says.

"Avery's dead," he says dully. "There are no surprises anymore."

And she knows instantly. He was in love with Avery. He still is. Julianne had said that he was involved with someone he worked with; she must not have suspected it was the boss or that certainly would have merited its own rant.

"You have some information?" he asks, standing up. He and Esther are about six feet apart, facing each other.

"Do you know Bianca Tramboni?"

His face shifts into barely suppressed rage, and Esther feels a note of fear. "If she had something to do with this, I'll..." He trails off, probably realizing that it would be wise to keep the rest of that sentence to himself.

"I think Bianca hated Avery."

"I thought so, too. I told Avery that, but she just laughed. 'So what? That'll make it more exciting.'"

"Make what more exciting?"

He doesn't answer. Is that because he doesn't trust Esther—because why should he—or because he doesn't know what Avery was planning either?

"Bianca and Avery were threatening me," Esther says. "They wanted me to join them in exposing Peter."

"Why wouldn't you want to expose Peter? He abused everyone who ever worked for him, or ever loved him." From the way he says it, Esther has an intuition that Xander might have fallen into both those categories.

"You and Avery had both slept with Peter?"

"I'm attracted to powerful people." Xander shrugs. "And they're attracted to me. Julianne and I never made sense but we had an amazing little boy and she's ruining him. Thanks to you. Now she's in full control."

"I know." It comes out regretful.

Xander looks surprised. Then he's angry again. "So what are you going to do about it?"

"What do you mean?"

"You cruised into our lives, you got the court to hand Julianne the keys to the kingdom, and now that you can see it's a mistake, you just say, 'Oh, well'?"

"I can't wave a wand and undo what I've done. But if you take her back to court, I can promise I won't represent her again."

He studies her. "Why are you here? To tell me that Bianca's the killer?"

No, to see if you are. "I don't know if she's the killer, but she was with Avery the night of the murder. At five p.m., they were confronting me in a parking garage, only the security footage makes it look like I'm all alone."

He nods knowingly. So Avery did have some sort of magic tech.

"Why was Avery coming after me?"

"She thought you were some kind of kindred spirit. Or maybe a linchpin. I don't know, but she was obsessed with Peter and then, after he died, she was obsessed with you. I couldn't understand it. I told her about my divorce and what you'd done to me. I told her what a piece of shit you are but I guess she needed to find out for herself." See, this is what Esther remembers, what Julianne used to describe. The abrupt mood changes, the volatility, the way he could go from vulnerable to furious without any clear warning or trigger.

How dangerous he was.

Esther fingers the gun, which she'd transferred from her purse to her pocket. She's sure he wouldn't expect that from her.

But his eyes have gone to her pocket, and now they're back on her face, appraising.

"It was you," he says. "You killed her."

"No."

"Avery was sure that Peter was blackmailing you, and that you turned the tables on him. She knew you killed him. She admired you for it."

"She was wrong."

"When she confronted you in the parking garage, did she tell you that she knew? Is that why you killed her?" He's staring at Esther with a look that's both glazed and vicious. A look that Julianne had told Esther all about.

Then he pulls out his gun.

And Esther pulls out hers.

"Do you really want to do this?" she says. Her finger twitches, both from nerves and raw desire. Shot or be shot, and in that split second, she's not sure which she'd prefer. "You have a son."

"And when he's old enough to understand, he'll be proud of me. I'm taking a serial killer off the streets."

"Are you sure of that?"

She sees him tremble slightly. He doesn't actually want to kill an innocent woman, but he must also know that even if she's not a murderer, she's far from innocent.

He's her mirror image. She's accused him and so many others of being arrogant and devoid of empathy, of putting their own interests ahead of everyone else's, of hurting people without any true awareness, acknowledgment, or responsibility. They assumed what felt right to them was right by definition.

The difference is that often they were acting impulsively, whereas Esther acted with great calculation. She took her time when she meted out punishment. She savored. Yet she took precious little time to make sure her initial read was correct. She went at every one of them, guns blazing. Or rather, guns smoldering.

She knows for a fact that Xander behaved badly and rationalized it all away. She has no illusions about him. But really, he's only hurt one family. Esther's hurt many.

She lowers her gun. "If you're going to do it, do it."

"You killed Avery." She can see that his righteous indignation is fading fast. He's scared now, afraid to make the kind of mistake that can't be rectified.

"I've done terrible things, but I haven't done that."

"I've done terrible things, too." His arm sags, like the force of gravity has become too much. Esther knows just how he feels. "Can you please get the fuck out of here?"

If only she knew where to go to escape herself.

FORTY-SEVEN

"I have something that belongs to you," Esther says. She takes the gun from her purse. "Don't worry, the safety's on."

Hugh's eyes widen slightly and he extends his hand. She has the impression that he's sobered up since she was last here four hours ago. "Has it been fired?"

"No."

He appears to consider whether to ask her anything further. She considers whether to offer anything.

"Come in?" he says.

They enter the house, which has been transformed since the afternoon. She casts him an inquiring look.

"I realized I needed to clean up my act," he says.

You didn't think you'd gotten rid of me that easily.

She and Hugh both jump. It's coming from her purse, another Sleight message being read aloud. Shit, she'd forgotten to turn her phone off again. She fumbles for the off switch but she's not quick enough on the draw, and the voice continues.

Just what have you done now?

If Hugh had set the app to send those messages, would he have jumped a second ago, and would he look so disturbed now? Maybe Esther hasn't solved either mystery. Her stalker and the murderer are both still at large.

The plan might have been an abject failure but at least she hasn't killed anyone.

She and Hugh take the same positions from earlier: Hugh in the Louis XIV chair, her on the green sofa. He places the gun on the coffee table between them. She notices that it's pointing toward him, not her, but it's also slightly closer to him than it is to her. But he's not going to shoot her in his own home hours after he begged her to take him back.

Is he?

"I'd feel more comfortable if you put that away," she says.

His eyes widen like he can't believe she needs to ask but he does as requested, carrying it out of the room. When he returns, he says, "I even used the lock."

"Thank you."

"Why didn't you ask me for the gun?" Hugh says. "I would have given it to you. It's not only for my protection. It's for everyone I love."

She flushes. She can't tell him that she not only contemplated killing someone earlier but had also considered framing him for it. It already seems inconceivable that she'd ever thought of going that far. The confrontation with Xander has brought her back to her senses.

"I took it but I wasn't going to use it," she says.

"Of course you weren't."

Somehow that annoys her, his presumption that she's harmless. She would have run over Avery and Bianca if they hadn't gotten out of her way, and she pretty much engineered Dale's death by robbing him of his entire reason to live. She's dangerous, dammit.

He seems to sense her irritation. "You're morally questionable, I've always known that, but you're no killer."

"What do you mean, I've always been morally questionable?"

"I saw you in action on the Stanton case, remember?" He does a low whistle. "You were not to be trifled with. I thought you were the hottest woman I'd ever seen."

Really, Hugh? He's always had a peculiar sense of timing.

"I know you've kept secrets from me," he says. "I understand why you didn't trust me fully, seeing as I've been keeping secrets from you, too."

"Why?"

"What do you call it, impression management? I've always been a little afraid of you changing your mind about me. The other night was my worst fear realized. You looked at me and found me wanting."

"What have you been keeping from me?"

He hesitates. "For starters? That I knew Peter Tramboni years ago. That I was his attorney on an intellectual property case where he sued his former employer. I should have just told you from the beginning but you acted so strange on the subject of Peter and then once more time passed, I felt I'd missed my window. It would seem like a bigger deal than it was, like I was in cahoots with Peter or something. I was so worried you wouldn't trust me that it made me act in completely untrustworthy ways."

"Like bringing a gun on a romantic getaway?"

"You knew about that?"

"I found it in your suitcase when I was looking for aspirin."

Light's dawning on his face. "No wonder things changed between us after the island. I'm sorry. You seemed so scared that I thought maybe someone really was after you. I figured that if anything went down, I'd be able to look after you. I'd prove I was worth having around."

"Why didn't you just tell me you had the gun?"

"Why didn't you tell me that you found the gun?"

"Because I wouldn't have accepted your explanation. Not because you're you," she adds quickly. "My whole life, I've had walls up. While working with Peter Tramboni, I erected entire fortresses."

She's embarrassed by her paranoia. But even now, she sees it as a survival skill. She's not about to take everything Hugh's saying at face value, no matter how believable he seems. How much she wants to believe him.

"I get it," he says. "I could tell you were freaking out inside, and that you hated Peter. I did, too. He made me feel like such a peon when I worked for him that I vowed I would never do it again. He told me he was going to be a big shot. I said who gives a fuck, lose my number."

"Uh-oh." It feels good to share stories with Hugh. Is this what Avery had in mind when she came to Esther's office that time?

"You said it. I didn't realize I was waving a red cape in front of a bull. Over the years, he'd stop by to laugh at my digs and brag about all he'd accomplished. He talked about where I could have been if I'd stuck with him. I never knew why he wasted his time, but my guess is that he could never forget an insult and created a whole sadistic rotation. He probably did a circuit."

"I think you're right."

"The last time he visited me was about a month before he died. He was practically rubbing his hands together with glee, like he was going to get me good." Hugh meets Esther's eyes. "He knew you and I were dating. He told me you had a secret, and it was a doozy. He wouldn't go into details. He probably wanted me to beg, at which point he'd still deny me. He dropped breadcrumbs, though."

"Of course he did." Esther closes her eyes.

"He said he knew your sister's ex-husband. That they grew up together. What's his name?"

"Dale."

"Right. Dale. So yeah, Peter and Dale grew up together, and I'm not sure how close they stayed over the years but Peter acted like Dale had made some sort of deathbed confession to him."

Esther's eyes fly open. So the information Peter had used to blackmail her hadn't come from a security team at all; it had come straight from the horse's mouth.

"I don't know what you did, Peter didn't tell me, but he seemed to have some sort of twisted sense of justice when it came to you. He said you needed to be punished, that you deserved to be brought to your knees. And obviously he was the man to do it." Hugh's face is full of loathing.

Esther hopes it's for Peter and not for her, though once she tells the truth, she has no idea how he'll be looking at her. "I'm starting to realize," she says slowly, "that my entire personal and professional identity has been built on a misapprehension."

"What's that?"

"That I'm one of the good guys." She thinks of what just happened with Xander, how close she came to killing or being killed. "I've shredded families."

"But not on purpose." Wait, so this is no surprise to Hugh? How long ago did he figure her out?

"I like black and white. I've never been comfortable with gray. Just get rid of the asshole husbands and fathers, pull them out by the roots, toss them aside, and the rest of the family will thrive." Her whole career has been guided by a philosophy that sounds insane once it's spoken aloud. "I've stayed willfully ignorant for years; I didn't want to see the truth. I wanted to be right."

"We all want to be right."

She shakes her head. "But I needed it. Because of, I don't know, my childhood. Or something. I'm sick, Hugh." Peter didn't force her to do what she did to Dale. No one forced her to work her cases the way she has all these years. "Peter must have thought he was doing the right thing, too, that I needed to be stopped."

"No. Peter tortured people for fun. He ruined lives for fun. There's no comparison." Hugh meets her eyes. "So all right, you've overlooked some things. But now that you can see, you care. You care so much that you're damn near splintering apart. That means you're a good person, Esther."

"Is that what it takes?"

"Fuck if I know what it takes. But I love you, Esther, and I know that whatever you've done, you thought it was right at the time. Now you've found out new information and you wouldn't do those things again. I trust you to learn. I trust you."

"Then you're an idiot."

He sits back, stung.

"And a liar. Why didn't you tell me that you knew about Dale?" Anger surges through her. How much could have been avoided if he'd come to her sooner?

"I didn't know about Dale. Not really. I mean, Peter didn't tell me any specifics. I assumed maybe there'd been an affair—"

"Absolutely not. I would never betray my sister." Not like that, anyway. What Esther did turned out to be far worse.

"Well, whatever it was, it was your business. We've all got pasts. Peter was trying to plant this time bomb in our relationship and I wasn't going to let it detonate. I wasn't going to give him the satisfaction." Hugh is looking at her with a pure and defiant love. "I do know you, Esther. I never needed Peter to tell me that you had secrets. You've always been haunted."

That's news to her. "I never felt it, you know? I've never felt a lot of things."

Hugh's face clouds over. "I have to tell you something else. Once I do, you may walk out of here and never see me again."

"Is that what you want?" After everything they've talked about tonight, she could hardly blame him.

"I want there to be no more secrets. I want a clean slate and a fresh start and all the clichés." He averts his eyes. "I didn't send you all the Sleight messages, but I sent some. When I was drunk and angry."

"Which ones?"

"The ones about being on a crucifix and..." He stops, clearly overcome by shame.

"The ones that were like poems? That talked about people I love?"

He nods, still unable to look at her. "I was so hurt, which is no excuse. It was really self-sabotage since you probably guessed they were from me, given the timing. But I swear I didn't send the others. I didn't have anything to do with that drone or whatever else was happening to you."

She stares down at her hands, not sure if she should be upset or relieved that this makes them even. She and Hugh are both lowlifes. They deserve each other.

"I hope I didn't actually scare you, that you saw through those and realized they came from an immature fuckbrained heartbroken alcoholic." Now he's looking right at her, into her eyes. "I'd never hurt you. I love you, and I miss you like a phantom limb, and I'd give anything to have you back."

"You know," Esther says slowly, "I've encountered some bad men in my time. Ones who were unrepentantly violent, who sadistically abused their wives and children, who systematically tried to turn those same kids against their mothers. Those cases were black and white."

Hugh is watching her with bated breath, wondering how this will end. The truth is, she doesn't know either.

"But I've been thinking back, and those were rare. There were a lot more cases that I treated as black and white. I've poured gasoline on a thousand fires, amplifying my clients' negative emotions toward their spouses. I wanted them to think the worst of those men so that I could use every tool in my arsenal to destroy them. I told myself I was doing it for the kids but really, I was making broken children who are likely to become broken adults. I'm one of those adults, even though my parents stayed together."

Hugh is nodding, though she's not sure she's making any sense.

"I know I wasn't wrong about everyone, that sometimes I was fighting true evil. But I was seeing nails everywhere because I was always holding a hammer. And the way I wielded that hammer might have been part of why their behavior looked as pathological and extreme as it did. I'd goad them into being their worst selves and then present that to the court as if it was the whole picture."

"Don't beat yourself up so much," Hugh says. "That's the job. We're paid to slant."

"I always thought I was better than other attorneys because I was more principled. I wasn't doing it for the money, not really. But you know what? I was worse. I was a vigilante."

"You?" He looks bemused.

"Don't laugh. A vigilante can have a perfect blowout. The point is, over the years, I got more and more judgmental and less and less compassionate. Like how I've been about you. How I looked down on you, and how I acted about your drinking."

"It's all right. I look down on myself for my drinking, too."

"No, I was wrong." She grabs his hands. "I'm so sorry for how I've treated you throughout our relationship."

"You can't be the one to apologize! I sent you gory poems." It's true, he did. So where do they go now?

Hugh is a good man and a bad man. A gray man. But what kind of woman is she?

The kind who's going to finally face the music. She has one last stop to make tonight.

FORTY-EIGHT

Dot stares at Esther, rubbing the sleep from her eyes, and then says, "Let's go in the yard."

"Good idea," Esther says. "That way, we won't wake up Tyson and July." She's not taking any chances that they'll overhear this conversation.

Dot pulls on a pair of Crocs and comes out. She and Esther walk around the side and unhook the gate. "Loungers?" Dot asks, gesturing toward their usual recliners.

"No, let's sit at the table. Then we can look each other in the eye."

"That sounds foreboding." But Dot doesn't argue. After all, Esther knows best. Dot's going to need to find a new mantra after this.

They settle across from each other, and Esther launches into her opening statement. She explains to Dot all she's been realizing through the former client visits, and through the talks with Hugh and Wilfred and even Xander (leaving out the gun, of course), and the awful yet potentially liberating epiphany that all this time, she's been haunted by their childhood. She's been acting out their own family drama and trauma on unsuspecting clients and families.

It's a very long wind-up and soon Esther will have to throw the pitch. She'll have to tell Dot what she did to Dale, and why. She'll admit that she'd overruled Dot's life choices, robbing Dot of agency as well as a husband and the father to her children. She'll express copious remorse but really, how can a person ever apologize for something like that? How can they ever be forgiven? Once Esther says what she has to say, it's likely that she'll no longer have a sister, and neither will Dot.

Which is one of the reasons she's stalling.

"Maybe we should talk through our memories," she says. "Excavate what really happened during our childhoods. I've spent years seeing everything in such a limited way, in black and white, and maybe together we can see it in color."

Dot looks bewildered as well as exhausted. "It's the middle of the night."

"I shouldn't have punctured Dad's tires. He should have been at your recital, and he would have if it hadn't been for me."

"You came here to talk about that again?"

"I took your father away from you." What Esther is really saying is, *I took your husband away from you*. This is a way of preparing Dot, a small earthquake so that the big one won't be as jarring. "I'm sorry, Dot."

"You don't need to apologize for protecting me. Sure, he's a feeble old man now, he's barely got two brain cells to rub together, but that doesn't excuse what he did. The way he psychologically battered us, it's amazing we got out of there with any self-esteem. I mean, I still had my issues but you're the miracle, that you could—"

Esther shakes her head. "I've got huge issues that I've been trying to work out through my clients. That's what I've been trying to tell you. I'm a mess, Dot."

"I don't believe that." Dot's chin is set stubbornly. "All the recent stress has distorted your thinking." She stands up. "Why don't you stay here tonight? In the morning, I'll make us blueberry pancakes."

"No, no. I have to get through this tonight. You have to hear me."

"What I know is, you've helped hundreds of families over the years. You've saved women and children. I know you have."

"You know what I've told you." But that's not why Esther's here anyway. They need to talk about Dale.

"Dad has nothing to do with all the good you've done in the world. You did it all in spite of him." Dot glares at the hedge like it's their absent father.

"He went on tirades and he said nasty things. None of that was okay. It was abuse," says Esther. "But he wasn't always like that. He got worse and worse over the years. When he saw there was no changing our opinion, he stopped trying and just became angrier. It was a self-fulfilling prophecy. It was an *Esther*-fulfilling prophecy."

"No. You were right about him, and you did right by me."

"We need to try to remember everything. Dad wasn't just a monster and I wasn't just your protector. It's way more complicated than that."

"So what if it is?" Dot's face is unyielding.

"What do you mean, so what?"

"I mean, why do I care? Why do you care? He's going to die soon, and that's fine by me."

Esther has always been shocked by how cold Dot can be toward their father when she's normally such a warm and feeling person.

"Truth matters. Facts matter," Esther says.

"I have all the facts I need."

Dot's only been this recalcitrant a few times before, always about Dale. In those instances, Esther backed down, as her unstoppable force had met an immovable object. She wants to tell Dot all that she's discovered, not to excuse her own ignorance but to prove it. She should have known better than to do that to Dale, only she didn't. Esther had enormous influence over her clients and she misused it. Abused it. Because all this time, she's never recognized the enormous influence of her own childhood. She's been seeing all men as dispensable and disposable, trying to eradicate them from their families as a way to avenge hers.

She's spent her adult life calling her father weak but really, he hadn't seemed like that when she was a kid. She'd often felt powerless, and her home life was unpredictable, which she hated. To make it predictable, she'd set about ignoring all the times her father was loving, calling them false and dismissing him as worthless, focusing only on his anger outbursts, and getting Dot to do the same. There was a certain selfishness in appointing herself Dot's protector, as it gave Esther the control her life otherwise lacked. She prevented Dot from having any chance of a true relationship with their dad. She prevented herself, too.

Ever since, she's been strutting around, calling herself a strong and independent woman, when so many of her professional actions have been a way to master the past. She's been keeping her demons at bay by pretending to be some kind of superhero when really, she's been too afraid to face them. All these years, she's said that her father is irrelevant and she's completely free of him but she's set up her life in reaction to him. She's picked cases that reinforce her low opinion of men and allow her to think in binaries. Black and white, good versus evil.

Every human is subject to confirmation bias but Esther's taken it to extremes, never questioning herself, leading to devastating consequences for at least some of the families involved. She still hasn't reckoned with how many.

Esther knows she's done some good, that she's not all bad

either. But it's time for an honest assessment of the impact she's had on the world. The impact she's had on Dot.

"Dad wasn't a villain," Esther says. "He's no Peter Tramboni. He tried to show love for us. Sometimes he said sorry, do you remember that? I didn't. I blocked it out of my memories for a long time. It just came back to me the other day."

Dot's turned her head away, is again contemplating the hedge.

"Dad was mentally ill. He was deeply unhappy and he took it out on us, which he shouldn't have done. But his generation couldn't get help as easily as ours."

"Because he didn't believe in getting help."

He must have passed that along. Esther has never sought help, and come to think of it, neither has Dot. Despite all the pain of the divorce and Dale's death, Dot and the kids have never been in therapy.

"Dad was a bad guy," Dot says. "Peter was a bad guy. Who knows, Avery was probably a bad guy, too."

Esther looks at Dot strangely. How did Avery get in the mix?

"I just mean, not all bad guys are guys. Sometimes they're women."

"I know that. I mean, I had my problems with Avery. The detective knows that Avery was stalking me, which means I had a motive." Esther's pretty sure that Detective Zelnik believed her during their last conversation about her innocence but only time will tell. He's a lot more clever than he initially seemed.

"The detective thinks you had a motive to kill Avery?" Dot looks dumbfounded. "Did he say that?"

"He didn't have to."

"That's ridiculous! You weren't being stalked by Avery! She just wanted to take you to lunch, that's all." Dot seems more unhinged by the second. She's been strikingly unemotional this whole conversation but she's now making up for lost time. "You can't be a suspect!"

"The day after Avery's murder, Detective Zelnik was knocking on my door."

"No!" Dot bursts out, almost frenzied, as if it's not after midnight with her kids sleeping upstairs. What's going on here? "You were home the night she was killed. Your security footage will show that."

That was just one more white lie Esther had told Dot so that Dot wouldn't worry. Esther didn't want her sister to know that she was upset enough to be driving around for hours and then checked into a hotel.

Now Dot seems to be talking more to herself than to Esther. "Avery's death proves you couldn't have done it. It's a Silicon Valley serial killer, not an upstanding attorney. Your reputation is pristine, everyone knows that. The detective told you that!"

"I don't think—"

"This is outrageous! You have no reason to kill Avery. Avery's death exonerates you."

Except for the stalking. Except that earlier that day, Avery and Bianca Tramboni had showed up in Esther's parking garage to tell Esther she was either with them or against them. And Esther almost ran them over. But there's no way she's going to say any of that when Dot seems to be in an absolute panic.

She's gotten up from the table and is now walking in tight circles, repeating, "No, no, no." It's as if her circuits are overloaded.

With Dot this agitated, there's no way that Esther's going to be able to bring up Dale. Really, this entire conversation—this entire night—has not gone according to plan.

"The second murder should have cleared you of the first!" Dot says. "This is bullshit! This cannot happen!"

"You have to quiet down." Esther doesn't like the explanation that's forming in her mind as to why Dot could be acting this way. "You'll wake up the whole neighborhood."

Proving the veracity of this statement, July pushes open the sliding glass doors, bleary-eyed. "Hi, Aunt E." She looks at Dot. "What's going on, Mom?"

Dot shakes her head, seemingly incapable of speech.

It's all coming into focus, and Esther's plan is about to be rewritten. Her family needs her now more than ever.

FORTY-NINE

"This is unexpected," Detective Zelnik says, entering the interrogation room. Behind him is the two-way mirror, and Esther wonders if he's followed her instructions and is truly alone or if someone's back there, watching.

Well, she can't control everything. She's finally started to accept that.

Her heart is racing but not as much as she'd anticipated. In a way, she feels more like herself than she has in a while. She's full of conviction.

"I'm willing to confess," she says. "I'll give you everything you need wrapped up in a bow. But first, I have some terms."

"Terms," he repeats, sitting down heavily across the table from her.

"You have to talk to the D.A. Not the A.D.A. I want assurances from the top dog, in writing, that I'll be getting the minimum sentence with the possibility of parole. Because I can be rehabilitated, and I intend to demonstrate very good behavior."

"You want the minimum sentence for multiple murders?"

"It's two murders, total. There won't be any more."

He looks suspicious, and she can hardly blame him. The last time they met, she confessed about Dale while insisting she had nothing to do with Peter and Avery's deaths.

"There won't be any more," she repeats. "You can assure the D.A. that there were very specific circumstances, that I intend to reflect and grow during my time in prison, and that I'm extremely remorseful."

"You sure look it."

She ignores the sarcasm. Perhaps he's never liked her but then, likeability has never been her bailiwick.

"Here's the deal. I will cooperate fully. I'll answer all questions to the best of my ability and recollection. My confession will be iron-clad. And even though I'll surely be receiving interview requests from every journalist worth their salt, I'll turn them all down. I'll never do social media, or make any sort of public statement. You'll have free rein to present this however you want. You investigated tirelessly, you applied unrelenting pressure, you broke me down. You caught the killer, Detective. Congratulations."

He appraises her for a long minute. She doesn't mind. She can hold up to scrutiny when she knows she's doing what's right.

"What I'm saying is, I'll let you tell my story any way you want, however it benefits you. But I'd like a quid pro quo. We both know that's how the justice system really operates, one hand washing the other."

"This is unorthodox," he says slowly. "And I'm not sure I can trust you."

"In my way, I'm the most honorable person you'll ever meet. I make a deal, I stick to it. And this is a truly great deal, one where we both get what we want."

"Why do you want this? You know I don't have any hard evidence tying you to these crimes."

"You don't have any hard evidence yet, but I can see how

dogged you are." She can tell he doesn't believe her but is loath to deny the flattery. "Just bring it to the D.A."

"I don't have anything to bring. We need to get your confession on videotape first."

She shakes her head. "That's not how this is going to work. You go to the D.A. first and get the deal in writing and then I'll tell you everything you want to know."

"You're giving me a lot of credit. You think I have that kind of pull?"

"I think the D.A. has a lot of scared millionaires and billionaires breathing down her neck. She wants this case closed as soon as possible. She'll be willing to make some unorthodox moves."

"And if she's not?"

"Then you'll keep looking for hard evidence and if you ever get enough to arrest me, I'll hire the best criminal attorney money can buy. I'll drag this out as long as I can and drag your name through the mud. But I'd rather play nice, Detective, and let you play the hero." She smiles, almost kindly. "Go make your call. I can wait. I've got nowhere to be."

He shakes his head, like it's starting to hurt. "You're a real piece of work, Esther." She can't tell if he means it as an insult, a compliment, or both. "By the way, I know about your call to nine-one-one. About the perfume. They didn't believe you, but I do."

She stares at him, speechless.

"It turns out that Avery Brengle had technology like I've never seen before. She could make herself a ghost. Undetectable. She liked to haunt people." His eyes are bright on Esther's face, but she's doing her level best to reveal nothing. "And I know you were telling the truth about Avery and Bianca Tramboni coming after you in the parking garage. Bianca broke down and admitted it."

If she broke down and admitted that, what else did she

admit to? Judging from the detective's face, maybe enough to make her the prime suspect. But Esther knows who really killed Peter and Avery, and eventually, Detective Zelnik might get an inkling, too. So she can't take any chances.

"I'm your murderer," she tells him.

"Why are you doing this, Esther?" He sounds suspicious, yes, and a little bewildered, but also... worried. The detective is genuinely worried about her, and if she were allowing herself to feel, she might feel touched by that.

"Is this how you treat every suspect who's ready to make a confession?"

"No. Just you."

"How sweet."

"You're not as tough as you like to seem." He pauses. "You're tougher." Shit, now she actually is touched. "I'm not sure what's happening here, but I've never gotten an innocent person convicted before."

Not that he knows of. "So you still believe in truth, justice, and the American way."

"I believe in truth."

Someday, he'll learn. Or maybe he'll be luckier than she was. But right now, she's got a job to do, and he needs to get out of her way. "This is your golden ticket. Didn't your mother ever tell you that when someone gives you a gift, just say thank you?"

There's a long silence. She can practically see his conscience and his ambition engaged in a wrestling match.

Finally he says, "Thank you." As he stands up, he seems resigned more than pleased. Defeated, like she's beaten him. No, like he's beaten himself, like he's not who he thought he was.

She knows the feeling well. But she can't dwell in empathy. She has to focus on reviewing her statement so she can deliver it clean, with no obvious holes. She's not going to be able to provide every detail, but hopefully she's persuaded Detective

Zelnik that this is in both of their interests, and he'll help her out with some leading questions. At the moment, he's her biggest impediment, as she's sure the D.A. won't be inclined toward scrutiny.

For the past few days, she's been skimming through thrillers, learning forensic and ballistic details to make her statement more credible. She didn't want online searches that could then be retrieved and used as evidence that she hadn't actually committed the crime, that she was taking the fall for someone else.

She knows exactly what she'll say to the D.A.

"I killed Peter because he deserved to die."

"I killed Avery because she wouldn't stop coming for me."

And finally: "I'm here today to clear my conscience and do the right thing."

That last sentence is 100 percent true.

FIFTY

It's Esther's first visiting hour, and she knows Dot will be coming. But she's surprised to find another visitor. Two, actually.

Prison life isn't as bad as she expected. The orange jumpsuit has been washed to a velvety softness, and it's nice not to have to primp or choose outfits. Nice to let go of impression management. She doesn't even miss her blowouts.

She's been keeping to herself, reading a lot (the prison library is fairly well-stocked), trying not to think about what she's done or about her family or about anything at all, really. Not thinking is her new job, and she's applied herself to it diligently. But it can be hard work. There have been some dark hours, particularly late at night. Whenever her conscience eats at her, she tries to be grateful that she has one. It means that she's not beyond redemption.

Since she's a murderer, she's in a cell by herself. In the dining hall, as she barely eats, the chairs closest to her remain unoccupied. She doesn't exercise in the yard (after all, she didn't exercise outside this place; she sees no reason to start now). The others give her a wide berth. She keeps her head down and most days doesn't have cause to use her voice.

Only one woman has approached her. Tall, imposing, unsmiling. Hair wild because hygiene products cost a relative fortune. She said, "You're Esther Kahn. We seen you on TV."

Esther gave a slight nod, keeping her eyes downcast.

"We're almost all here for drugs. You, you're different. You kill billionaires." Something in her tone—something admiring—made Esther glance up. "Respect."

And that was it, the only real interaction she's had so far. Until now, when she takes a seat at the bolted-down white table in the visiting room across from Kay and Rex Emerson. They look like they couldn't be happier to see her. They're practically dancing in their chairs.

It clicks into place, how chummy those two have gotten, post-divorce. Esther thought it was just their daughter Naomi's drug addiction that had brought them together, or maybe making the joint decision to send Naomi to Utah for a Hail Mary treatment program. But shared hatred of Esther must have really cemented their connection. Nothing bonds like a vendetta.

Esther had confirmed that one of her stalkers was Hugh; she hadn't known who the other was until now. Honestly, she'd stopped worrying about it, thinking they couldn't get to her in here.

"Hello," she says, her tone subdued. As part of her penance, she'll let them gloat. They deserve a simple pleasure after what she's put their family through.

Kay turns to Rex. "That color really suits her, doesn't it?"

"It surely does." He looks jocular. They both do.

"I'll listen to whatever you have to say," Esther says. "Give it to me both barrels."

"Both barrels." Kay smiles, shaking her head. "That's not an idiom a murderer should throw around lightly. I always thought you were so careful with words, Esther, but prison's changed you."

"I love having a captive audience," Rex says. He looks over at Kay. "Don't you?" It's like they're starring in their own little variety show.

Esther finds she's looking forward to their performance. It means she'll get answers once and for all. Rex has always been a blabbermouth. It was one of the reasons she'd been able to beat him in court. She just had to get him talking and he'd dig his own grave, much to the chagrin of his attorney.

"We haven't been thinking about you all these years," Rex says. "We've been pretty busy with other matters, like trying to keep Naomi from overdosing."

"But then I happened to see an article about Peter Tramboni's divorce settlement," Kay continues, "and he had some disgusting party where you were quoted saying something like, 'I enjoy seeing justice served.' My blood started to boil, and afterward, Rex and I got to talking. We had a real heart-to-heart about the effect the legal system had on our family, the damage it's done, the damage we've done to each other and to Naomi. Despite how it may have seemed to you, Esther, I'm not actually someone who tends to blame other people. I like to take responsibility for my own actions."

"I know that, Kay," Esther says. "I've always thought very highly of you."

Kay looks at Rex. "You hear that, honey? A serial killer thinks highly of me!"

"It's like getting a congressional medal of honor," he answers. Then he eyeballs Esther. "Unlike Kay, I've never had trouble placing blame where it's due. You are a heinous person."

"Lower than low," Kay agrees. "Though it took me a lot longer to realize that. First there was that article, and then you showed back up with your smug face, and there was no mistaking it."

"At first, Kay couldn't believe you worked for that piece of filth Tramboni," Rex says. "She thought you were this principled person but I always knew that was just your shtick."

"I always thought you stood for something." Kay looks at Esther with naked disgust. Esther feels a fresh bout of shame. "I thought that even if the case hadn't worked out that well for me in the end, you meant well. But no, it turns out you're just some whore who follows the money. You don't actually care what happens to women and children."

Esther isn't going to argue with them; many of her actions have been indefensible.

"Then she turns around and kills him!" Kay lets out an astonished peal of laughter. "Who saw that coming?"

"It couldn't have been for the good of the country, or humanity," Rex says. "It must have been for her own gain."

"Oh, absolutely," Kay says.

Visiting hours are short, and hopefully Dot's on her way. So Esther decides it's time to speak and hurry this along. "You saw the article and then had a heart-to-heart and decided to start sending the Sleight texts?"

Kay nods. "It was very healing. And fun, too. Very *I Know What You Did Last Summer*."

"We figured everyone has secrets we could allude to but woo-wee! Yours take the cake!" Rex laughs.

"We had no idea we were tormenting a serial killer," Kay says. "Now it feels like we were doing a public service."

"We're just lucky she didn't turn around and kill us," Ray says. "But then, why would she bother? We're in the wrong tax bracket."

"Those texts were part of why I confessed," Esther cuts in. One more white lie can't hurt, and the Emersons deserve an ego stroke. Let them feel they helped catch a killer. "I really thought I was going crazy, being watched all the time."

Kay and Rex seem like they want to high five.

"The drone was a nice touch," Esther adds.

"Wasn't it, though?" Rex looks tickled.

"I wasn't on board with that one at first," Kay says. "It just seemed so childish. I mean, it was actually a child's toy; we don't have the money to buy something fancy. But Rex thought there needed to be something other than a bunch of Sleight messages, even though we were able to schedule and geotrack them for maximum effect. We wanted you looking over your shoulder."

"Well, it worked," Esther says.

"It was a great night." Rex turns to Kay. "Having a picnic on the hill and then flying that drone."

It occurs to Esther that this whole operation wasn't only about hatred, that it also could have been about romance. Rex was trying to get his wife back.

And maybe it's working. Kay laughs and pats his arm. "It was a very unique experience, I'll say that."

Esther's not about to give herself too much credit but she does like thinking that she could have a hand in restoring a family rather than the opposite.

"You were right about me," Esther says. "I thought I was helping families but I've realized that I hurt many of them. I'm very sorry for what I've done to you both, and to Naomi. I'm not asking for forgiveness but I'll pray that you can all heal."

There's a stunned silence. Contrition is clearly the last thing they thought she would be capable of.

Esther doesn't know what she's capable of anymore. When Dot arrives, she'll start to find out.

FIFTY-ONE

"Oh my God," Dot says, pressing her hand to her mouth, her eyes filling with tears as she approaches Esther. "You're in an orange jumpsuit."

They're permitted a brief hug, and so they do, Esther releasing quickly for fear of what the handbook calls "excessive contact." She's going to follow every rule to the letter and be a model prisoner. She intends to be out of here in as little time as possible. With two concurrent (minimum) sentences for murder and the earliest parole release, that would still equal twenty-five years.

"It's not so bad," Esther says, sitting down at the same white-topped table she recently occupied with the Emersons.

Dot lowers herself into the seat opposite, looking dazed and horrified. "It's not?"

"There's just so much time," Esther says. "You know? Before it felt like I never had enough time. And there's a certain freedom that comes from letting go of all ambition. With just existing instead of always needing to do."

Dot isn't hearing her. "We'll get you out of here. I've got calls in to all the best criminal defense attorneys in California."

"But they're not calling you back, are they?" Esther's smile is gentle. "Because none of them want to take this loser case. The plea deal is airtight, Dot. I made sure of that."

Dot's shaking her head vigorously, in her own world, and it reminds Esther of that night in the yard. The night Esther realized what Dot had done.

It was Esther's fault, really. Esther had spent months talking to Dot about how tormented she was by Peter. Dot must have assumed it would change once the custody battle concluded but that hadn't been the case. With Peter alive, it would never be over. Esther had even told Dot what Peter said: "I go on and on." So Dot took matters into her own hands.

After a lifetime of Esther protecting Dot, Dot had repaid the favor. Then she killed Avery for good measure, mistakenly thinking it would take the heat off Esther. Dot has never had the greatest strategic mind, but she does have a loving heart. Esther has to continue to believe that, because Dot is going to be raising Tyson and July. That's one of the biggest reasons for Esther's sacrifice. She can't let her niece and nephew lose their remaining parent.

"You've been railroaded," Dot tells Esther. "The system took advantage of you. That detective harassed you until you were basically losing your mind, and then put you in that confession room."

"It didn't happen like that. I called him. I went in willingly."

"You weren't yourself. Anyone could see that. I talked to Hugh Warshaw—who's actually a great guy, and he really loves you—and he said he would testify to how fragile you've been. He's making calls, too, trying to see if there's a way to get this overturned. You weren't of sound mind, E."

"I don't want it overturned." Esther wishes she could reach out and take Dot's hand. "You need to listen to me."

"First, can I just say how amazing Hugh's being? He completely believes in your innocence."

Has Hugh figured out Dot's guilt, though? Esther doesn't like what she's hearing at all.

"He's confident I won't have to spend my own money on lawyers, that we'll be able to get lots of donations for the legal defense fund that I'm setting up. Do you know about the Free Esther movement?"

Esther shakes her head.

"It's gaining traction on college campuses, especially the elite ones," Dot says, looking pleased. "The billionaires are the existential threats. You acted to save democracy. They think you're a hero!"

Seeing as Dot is the real killer, the crowing seems slightly obscene. Maybe she's using the Free Esther movement as a way to excuse what she's done. It's another indication of just how off-course Dot is, and that Esther's job as a big sister is not finished.

"I need you to hear me," Esther says. "When Hugh comes to visit I'm going to tell him the same thing: I belong here. I don't want to leave."

"This isn't you. To be so calm in a place like this?" Dot's eyes dart left and right, looking at all the other orange-jump-suited inmates meeting with their family members. "That's proof of insanity right there."

"I confessed of my own free will, and I'd do it again."

"See? Crazy."

"It's not crazy to protect someone you love, is it?" Dot must have thought that was what she was doing for Esther in killing Peter and then Avery.

Dot won't look at Esther.

"Dot," Esther says, "I know." She can't say anything outright because of the surveillance. There's a guard by the exit and also guards in the control booth looking down. Who knows what they can hear? What they're recording? Esther can't take any chances.

"You don't know!" Dot says plaintively. "You don't know what it's like being out there knowing you're locked up in here."

"This is where I want to be. It's where I need to be. I killed two people."

"No, you didn't."

"I'm telling you, I did." Esther's eyes bear down on Dot's. "Because if I didn't, then the investigation would resume."

Dot drops her gaze to the table.

"I'm here because if I wasn't, then Detective Zelnik might try to take down innocent people like you."

Dot's tears are dripping onto the table.

"I know the score, Dot. No one's doing this to me. I've made my choice, and I'm happy with it."

"I don't see how that's possible," Dot finally whispers.

"I'm not angry at anyone. I'm at peace." Esther has given it a lot of thought, and it's finally time. Dot deserves to know the whole truth about Dale. It'll actually set her free because instead of feeling guilty about Esther taking the fall, Dot will realize that prison is exactly where Esther should be. "There's something you need to hear."

Dot reaches into her purse and takes out a tissue, dabbing at her eyes. "Do you need a tissue?"

"I'm not crying."

"No, you're not." Dot sniffles. "You're so strong, E."

Esther takes a deep breath. "I have to tell you something I should have told you a long time ago. It's about—"

"Do you want anything from the vending machines?" Dot indicates the machines lining one wall. "The food here must be terrible. Not that the food from the vending machines will be much—"

"Dot, please listen. It's about Dale."

"I know."

"I don't think you do."

"How stupid do you think I am?" Dot's eyes are suddenly full of fire. "You think I didn't figure it out?"

"Figure what out?"

"E, come on. Dale left me without any warning or explanation. Of course it was you."

Esther does a double take. "How long have you known?"

"I'll admit, it took me a while to suspect. I mean, I didn't want to think you'd go behind my back. Then I started to get really mad at Dale. Why hadn't he come to me and told me what you said? Why did he just roll over? He really was the weakling you always thought he was. You basically proved it, the same as you prove it with all your clients' husbands."

Esther is speechless.

"I understand, and I forgive you."

"How can you be okay with what I did? You loved Dale, and I took him away from you. From you and the kids."

"You were right, E, as always." Dot is now the one comforting Esther. "I had to come to terms with the fact that the kids and I were better off without him. Sometimes I still get sad, and I miss him. July does, too. Tyson, not so much."

"But... but... you loved him."

"I did, but he was weak. And I was strong. You made me strong, in your image."

Esther's heart plummets. She doesn't want credit for this.

"I'm not saying I didn't have a few moments of weakness. Like one time after the divorce, Dale and I got drunk and slept together. That's when he told me the whole story. Maybe he thought I'd turn against you and take him back. But what I felt was disgusted. He was blaming you but he was the one who hadn't fought for our family. He didn't deserve us."

"But you loved him! Didn't you think about trying again?"

Dot shakes her head. "What would you have thought of me then? You would have lost all respect for me."

Esther begins to cry.

"No, no, it's not your fault," Dot says. "It was his. So I told him to stop coming around. To leave us alone." So Dot is the reason that Dale didn't visit with his kids anymore? "Then once he got cancer, I didn't exactly say not to get treatment, but I told him it was a moment where he could show his character. Where he could make sure he really took care of July and Tyson."

Wait, is Dot saying she convinced Dale not to treat his cancer? Dot wanted him to die so she could have the insurance money? Esther is crying harder. She doesn't recognize the woman sitting across from her and yet, she might have created her.

Esther doesn't know how much of this is her fault, if she's the one who so profoundly disrupted Dot's moral development that it's landed them both here. Did Esther lead her impressionable sister to believe it was okay to kill three people, or all this time, has Esther been unable to see who Dot truly is?

"I'm sorry, Esther. I didn't mean to upset you." Dot glances toward her watch and then back at Esther with regret. "We're almost out of time. I'll be back next week, though. Do you think I should bring Tyson and July? Tyson can handle anything but July—you know how sensitive she can be even though she doesn't like to admit it."

"You and I should probably talk more before we bring the kids into this." Esther grabs one of Dot's tissues. She needs to pull herself together and talk some sense into Dot, for July and Tyson's sake. Their mother's all they have now.

"July is pretty torn up. About Avery, especially."

"You don't want to say too much," Esther says. "You realize they're monitoring."

"Did you know that you really can text anyone on Sleight? And that anyone will meet *you* anywhere?" Dot smiles. It's like she's trying to tell Esther in code how she did it. How she committed the murders. Is she a little bit proud at her ingenuity?

Esther gets Dot's meaning. It's as she suspected: Dot had messaged Peter and Avery on Sleight, and asked them to meet Esther at the site of their future murders. But how could Dot have known for sure that they would show up alone? Or that even if they were alone, they hadn't told anyone where they were going and who they were meeting? It was so risky it's nearly hare-brained. But then, Dot's never been a mastermind. Only somehow, she's gotten away with everything.

"Come back next week," Esther says. "Alone. But tell the kids that I'm thinking of them, and that I miss them. Aunt E loves them—and their mother—very, very much."

"They already know that," Dot says. "And we all love you something awful."

Yes, it is awful. Esther just needs to know one last thing, one tiny detail that would be helpful if there are ever any follow-up questions or concerns about her confession. It's about the gun.

"July must like that you've taken such an interest in the 3D printer," Esther says. "The two of you can make all sorts of things together now."

"You know me and technology." Dot waves a hand. "I couldn't begin to comprehend the 3D printer. I wouldn't even try."

Esther's final remaining shred of denial slips away. Of course July had made the gun and the bullets for her mother.

Dot leans forward, placing her hand on Esther's arm despite the rule against touching. She makes her voice low and soothing. "You know what July said to me? She said, 'Avery's not my hero. My hero—my inspiration—is Aunt E.'" Dot beams, her hand pulsing on Esther's arm.

Esther stares down at it, like it belongs to an alien force and yet it's all too familiar.

"July's just like you. There's nothing she won't do to protect the people she loves."

As if from far, far away, Esther hears a security guard shout, "No touching!" and Dot's hand is withdrawn from Esther's arm.

"I'm going to get you out," Dot says, "even if I have to sell my house and spend every penny of the life insurance money. You don't deserve to be here."

But you do. Only Dot can't see that. She thinks no one should pay since justice has been served. She's even convinced July that murder was a moral act. If there are no limits on what you can do to the people who threaten those you love, then maybe there are no limits to what you can do to people who get in your way. Where does it end?

Like Peter, it goes on and on.

All Esther can think about is Tyson and July. Who they're going to become. Who they might already be.

She drops her head to her chest and sobs.

FIFTY-TWO

Esther is alone.

She feels bolted to the chair that's bolted to the floor. For minutes now—or is it eons?—she's been trying and failing to pull herself together. Soon a guard will come and hustle her along, back to her cell. She can't stay here forever. But it's like time has been suspended. She's silent and shattered, trying to process what she's heard. It feels like an impossible task. She can't metabolize this.

Dot's responsible for the deaths of three people, and she made her child her accomplice in two of them. What if July had something to do with the death of her father, too?

Esther hears the guard calling out that it's the end of visiting hours.

Only her eyes are capable of movement. They're roaming the room and she's not actually looking for anything or anyone but suddenly there she is. Another woman whose eyes are doing the exact same thing. Someone who seems equally lost and bereft and uncomprehending.

It's the first significant eye contact Esther has made since she arrived, and it feels electric somehow. It feels... clarifying.

There's work to be done here. How had Esther not seen that sooner?

Peter's finished. He said he would go on and on, but he didn't. He couldn't. Esther still can, and she has to, because she has so much to atone for. What she's done to her clients. What she's done to Dot. And by extension what she's done to July.

Esther's not a lawyer anymore; she'll never have a license again. That's for the best. She shouldn't wield even that amount of authority and power. But a lot of the women now exiting this room could probably use a consultant. There's always been more than enough injustice to go around, and there always will be. That's additionally true in a place like this.

Yes, there is definitely work to be done here.

That knowledge is not comforting exactly but it's enough to propel Esther to her feet. All her limbs feel heavy, and she adopts a shuffling gait like she's aged thirty years in one visiting hour.

She approaches the woman who met her eyes. Short and broad with a homemade tattoo snaking its way up her neck, her expression is wary, her face tear-stained.

Esther is part of a different sisterhood now.

"Hello," she says, her voice soft and cracking and so full of trepidation that it could almost belong to someone else. "I'm Esther Kahn."

A LETTER FROM ELLIE

Dear reader,

I want to say a huge thank you for choosing to read *The Divorce Lawyer*. To keep up to date with all my latest releases, just sign up at the following link. Your email address will never be shared and you can unsubscribe at any time.

www.bookouture.com/ellie-monago

I hope you enjoyed *The Divorce Lawyer*. If you did I would be very grateful if you could write a review. It makes such a difference helping new readers to discover one of my books for the first time.

I love hearing from my readers. Please get in touch with me through Goodreads.

Thanks,

Ellie Monago

goodreads.com/elliemonago

PUBLISHING TEAM

Turning a manuscript into a book requires the efforts of many people. The publishing team at Bookouture would like to acknowledge everyone who contributed to this publication.

Audio
Alba Proko
Sinead O'Connor
Melissa Tran

Commercial
Lauren Morrissette
Jil Thielen
Imogen Allport

Cover design
Head Design Ltd.

Data and analysis
Mark Alder
Mohamed Bussuri

Editorial
Natalie Edwards
Sinead O'Connor

Copyeditor
Donna Hillyer

Proofreader
Becca Allen

Marketing
Alex Crow
Melanie Price
Occy Carr
Cíara Rosney

Operations and distribution
Marina Valles
Stephanie Straub

Production
Hannah Snetsinger
Mandy Kullar
Jen Shannon

Publicity
Kim Nash
Noelle Holten
Myrto Kalavrezou
Jess Readett
Sarah Hardy

Rights and contracts
Peta Nightingale
Richard King
Saidah Graham

Printed in Great Britain
by Amazon

47968934R00189